IBID: ᴬ ᴸᴵᶠᴱ
a novel in footnotes by
Mark Dunn

MacAdam/Cage
155 Sansome Street, Suite 550
San Francisco, CA 94104
www.macadamcage.com

Library of Congress Cataloging-in-Publication Data

Dunn, Mark, 1956–
    Ibid : a life / by Mark Dunn.
      p. cm.
    ISBN 1-931561-65-6 (hardcover : alk. paper)
      1. Biography as a literary form–Fiction.
2. Abnormalities, Human—Fiction. 3. Cosmetics industry
–Fiction. 4. Philanthropists–Fiction. 5. Carnivals–Fiction.
I.Title.

    PS3604.U56I25 2004
    813'.6–dc22
                                                    2003028137
Manufactured in the United States of America.
10 9 8 7 6 5 4 3 2 1

Book and jacket design by Dorothy Carico Smith.

IBID: A LIFE
a novel in footnotes by
Mark Dunn

For my wife Mary
who rocks my world

Thanks for all the years of love and support,
and for rescuing me from the Young Republicans

"Footnotes let us hear the missteps of biases,
and hear pathos,
subtle decisions, scandal and anger."
—Chuck Zerby
The Devil's Details

"The author may, therefore,
include in the notes such things
as lists, poems, and discursive adjuncts to the text."
—*The Chicago Manual of Style*

"I just love footnotes, don't you?"
—Diana Gabaldon
The Outlandish Companion

February 18, 2003

Pat Walsh
Editor
MacAdam/Cage Publishing
155 Sansome Street
San Francisco, CA 94104

Dear Pat,

Greetings to you and all my other friends in the City by the Bay. I have just completed my latest book project, a biography of Jonathan Blashette, the child circus sideshow performer who later made his fortune in male deodorants before engaging in philanthropy and other high profile hobbies. Blashette, for all his accomplishments, is best remembered for having three legs.

Please find the manuscript enclosed. I am in the process of completing the book's extensive endnotes and will send these along shortly. If you choose to consider the manuscript for publication, I ask only one favor: please take care not to lose it, as it is my only copy. I had a second copy, but it was accidentally shredded along with other typescripts given to my friend Ellen Zeisler. I was curious to see how her new shredding machine worked.

I look forward to hearing if another one of my offerings might find its way into the venerable MacAdam/Cage catalogue.

With all best wishes,

Mark Dunn

February 26, 2003

Mark Dunn
P.O. Box 40
Old Chelsea Station
New York, NY 10011

Dear Mark,

Please brace yourself. Perhaps you should even sit down. I have some bad news.

Your manuscript has been accidentally—and tragically—destroyed.

Remembering that it was your only copy, I thought that I should make a Xerox before leaving work yesterday evening, but I did not. I was simply too excited to get home and get into it, a decision I shall rue forever.

As you, and a precious few others know, I do all my editing in my bathtub. I find the fragrant bath-powdered waters conducive to exploring story arc, character development, correcting noun-verb disagreement, and discouraging the overuse of the passive voice. I had set your manuscript carefully upon the rounded edge of my ancient claw-foot, and went into the other room to find CDs for setting an appropriate editorial mood. (To accompany your book, I selected Vivaldi's *The Four Seasons*, Blue Oyster Cult's "Agents of Fortune," and the soundtrack to *Streets of Fire*.)

While I was poking about in my music library and letting the tub run, my three-year-old son, Jack, who only moments earlier had been quietly contenting himself with seeing how far he could stick his finger into a ripe pear, decided to venture into the master bath in search, I like to think, of his father. Not finding me there, he turned his attention to your manuscript, and promptly deposited the loose pages into the rapidly filling tub.

I returned mere seconds later, but too late—sad to say—to rescue the manuscript. The agitation of the water pouring into the tub had quickly turned your paper to soggy pulp and the ink to purple broth.

I am completely at fault, something I am loath to admit (ask my wife). I trust that you will find it somewhere in your heart to forgive me. In the meantime, may I know if there is any chance you can re-create the book from notes or memory? We'll happily send out one of our many hard-working interns to assist (perhaps the one who keeps leaving his lattes on my slush pile; I don't like him anyway). Failing that, may I at least see the endnotes?

Call me. I know you never use the phone, fearing electrical shock. Perhaps you could make an exception, considering the circumstances.

Your editor, still…I think,

Pat Walsh

March 3, 2003

Pat Walsh
Editor
MacAdam/Cage Publishing
155 Sansome Street
San Francisco, CA 94104

Dear Pat,

I am still reeling. It is hard for me to write, let alone pick up the phone and form coherent sentences. I forgive you, I do. But this is a blow.

I do not see myself rewriting the book. The original task took two years.

Per your request, I have enclosed the completed endnotes. Knock yourself out. I'm going into retirement.

Best wishes,

Mark Dunn

March 11, 2003

Clay Dunn
c/o InSouth Bank
6141 Walnut Grove Rd.
Memphis, TN 38120

Dear brother Clay,

My editor, Pat Walsh, has just made an offer to publish the endnotes that accompanied my now tragically water-pulped biography of businessman Jonathan Blashette.

By themselves.

I am quite torn over what to do. These notes, while extensive, are still, by definition, subordinate to the lost text—a text which I do not wish to invest another two years of my life attempting to reconstruct. While the notes illuminate the dusty, crepuscular corners of this man's life, they tell its story only through sidebar and discursion. The book, therefore, becomes a biography by inference.

I should confess that over the last two years I've grown fond of both Blashette and the odd cast of characters that formed the retinue of his colorful existence. I wished that I had given more attention in the text to each of his girlfriends— the high-spirited childhood sweetheart Mildred; the former prostitute and Blashette's odd soulmate Great Jane; home-front heartthrob Lucile; the spitfire bohemienne Winny; and Clara, his wife and mother to his only child; as well as to Blashette's bumbling right-hand man Davison, and life mentor Andrew Bloor. Publishing these notes by themselves allows me the opportunity to examine the role that each played in the man's life, in ways that I could not in the original text. There is a certain freedom here—stitching as I am upon the fringes of that life the kind of colorful piping that usually defines the whole garment.

On the other hand, can the cloth of a man's life truly be defined by its embroidery?

What do you think? What would you do? How are things with you? How's the ol' back?

Your brother,

Mark

March 14, 2003

Mark Dunn
P.O. Box 40
Old Chelsea Station
New York, NY 10011

Dear twin brother Mark,

My back is better. Thank you for asking. I think you should
do it. Why not?

Good luck.

Your brother,

Clay

PS. I don't know what the word *crepuscular* means.

Epigraph Grover Bramblett, *The Quotable Sanford and Son* (New York: Ebony and Ebony Press, 1984), 215.

1

LITTLE JONNY SPARE LEG

1. **"'Turned out that womb of his mother's wasn't barren at all. A right healthy little fellow grew inside her, grew big and strong and popped right out on March 17, 1888.** Interview with Jonathan's first cousin Odger Blashette.

2. **Barnum's Dead; at least write to Pulitzer and Hearst.** Nowhere could I find documented proof that William Randolph Hearst ever accepted Addicus's invitation to come to Pettiville, Arkansas, to see the "amazing quintuple-limbed child," but there is ample evidence of Joseph Pulitzer's visit, followed by a series of sensationalist articles in the *New York World* somewhat bizarrely illustrated by Richard F. Outcault, who gave Jonathan both the oversized ears and gap-toothed smile that would later characterize his "Yellow Kid." Pulitzer never got to see the illustrations, however. A. Candell Moseley in his biography of the publisher, *Pulitzer's World* (Chicago, Prather Press, 1968) notes that at this point in his life the publisher was almost totally blind. He also possessed a debilitating hypersensitivity to sound. His first words upon arriving at the Blashette house were, "Bring the baby to me. I want to feel that third leg. Spread sawdust upon the lane while I am here. I require almost total silence. And a cup of hot tea. With lemon. And a little nutmeg. Strange request, yes, but that's me. Ah, there's the leg. Fully formed. With all his toes. He shall have music wherever he goes. Waltzes. Teach the boy to waltz. He should be a natural."

3. **Doctors were baffled.** The third doctor to attend the child in his first weeks, Able Stanton, agreed with the other physicians that the extra appendage should pose few physiological difficulties for the boy. However, he differed

---

with his colleagues on another point, writing in his unpublished memoir *Three-legged Boys and Birdbeaked Spinsters: Fifty Years of Doctoring Freaks:*

> *It was my early estimation that young Jonathan would probably be walking much sooner than other children his age because the third leg would have a helpful stabilizing effect on the young man, much as a three-legged stool stands better than a two-legged one.*

4. **Challenges presented themselves.** Jonathan Blashette writes in his *Early Memories* of an argument between his mother and a local cobbler over the cost of making three shoes, Emmaline contending that she should only have to pay half again more than what she would pay for a pair. The cobbler, however, deemed the request a "special order" and tacked on a surcharge. Jonathan continues:

> *Mother threatened to take her business elsewhere, only to discover that all the cobblers in town were related by blood and had somewhat of a rudimentary price-setting system in place, one which put her at a decided negotiatory disadvantage. In the end, Mother and the shoemaker reached a compromise. She bought me a pair of handsome boy's lace shoes and the cobbler threw in, at only a nominal additional charge, an orphaned remnant from the previous year's Thanksgiving pageant—a shiny black-buckled Pilgrim's shoe which didn't match the others by any stretch of the imagination but nonetheless had a certain historically evocative charm about it.*

5. **And yet on the whole, Jonathan was generally well-regarded and with the help of friends and family adjusted easily to his unique anatomical circumstances.** Several years were to pass before Thaddeus Grund arrived with his invitation for Jonathan to join his Traveling Circus and Wild West Show. This relatively quiet interstitial period in the

boy's life was disrupted only on those rare occasions in which a visitor to town might gasp or emit an unguarded, "Dear me! *Three!*" The only concrete exception to this "era of good feeling" for the boy came when Emmaline and Addicus were asked by indelicate roustabouts, many of whom Addicus would bring home for Sunday dinner, "If that's where the third leg goes, where the hell's the pup's little willy?" Upon such occasions Emmaline would usually sweep Jonathan up in her arms and fly indignantly from the room while Addicus was left to explain to his uncouth guests that his son's third leg branched off the left leg like the limb of a tree, "the willy hanging free like wisteria."

6. **Jonathan did not even seem to mind his "only child" status.** According to Blashette's cousin Odger, the boy made friendships quite easily. He was an outgoing child and had a healthy curiosity about the world unveiling itself all around him. By the age of three Jonathan was cantering eagerly behind Pettiville's one-eyed blacksmith, Cletus Meeker, who took an instant liking to the boy who he felt had "all the stuff, a spiffin' smithy to make." Odger recalls the story of the one exceptional morning in which Cletus showed Jonathan an uncharacteristic lack of respect: the blacksmith arrived for work in a bilious humor following a long night of binging after catching his wife sandwiched in bed between the Bellamy twins, bright-witted Henry and doltish Benry. That day he found fault with everything Jonathan did, and eventually hung an oat bag around the boy's neck and deposited him beneath an active rainspout. As Odger tells it, Jonathan responded by looking up at the irritable blacksmith and inquiring in a tiny, tearful voice, "You don't *really* mean to be doing this, do you, Mr. Horsy-shoe Man?" Meeker, stabbed by sudden shame and contrition, gently pulled the boy from the miniature cataract. Embracing him tightly, he blubbered, "Never again the oat bag! Never again the rainspout! Oh Jonathan, this foolish momentary lapse,

please forgive!"

And Jonathan apparently did.

Later, a four- or five-year-old Jonathan joined milkman Roddy Chalmers on his early morning rounds. In an interview with Roddy's great granddaughter, former exotic dancer Trixie Twirl, I learned that Roddy quickly developed a paternal fondness for Jonathan and sought to hire him even at this young age as milkman's apprentice to spare the boy a life of exploitation at the hands of unscrupulous carnival sideshow proprietors "just waiting in the wings for the lad to reach an age at which he might be put on permanent tour and display." Following my interview with Ms. Twirl, she sent me several pages of additional material on her great-grandfather who she claimed invented low-fat chocolate milk. Her thoughts are excerpted below:

> *I know that the story of my great grandfather will constitute only the slightest of footnotes in your book, but I do want the record to show that there was someone early in the young child's life who demonstrated a genuine and selfless concern for his well being. The fact that he did not succeed in preventing little Jonny from being swept into the demoralizing carnival life is no reflection upon the efforts my great-grandfather made on the boy's behalf. I have met few men in my life who have demonstrated such concern and compassion for a fellow human being. With only two exceptions, I believe that most men are snorting, rooting swine. The exceptions would be the following: my dentist who treats my mouth as a temple, and Harvey Spools, the man to whom I bore five beautiful babies before I boarded up my womb and moved to the convent.*

7. **He sat on eggs like young Thomas Edison.** Matthias Huber, *Jonny of the Circus*, Great Americans Every Child Should Know, vol. 32 (Chicago: Pete the Patriot

Publications, 1968), 14. Huber reports that a full dozen eggs were crushed. Odger believes the figure to be closer to a dozen and a half. In any event, young Jonathan carried a mash of yolk and feathers on the seat of his trousers for the entire afternoon.

8. **"Father let me place our order."** Jonathan Blashette, *Early Memories*, JBP. This particular trip to Claiborne's General Groceries and Sundry Dry Goods must have, indeed, held special meaning for Jonathan. I found, carefully preserved among his childhood possessions, the very piece of recycled butcher paper upon which Emmaline had hastily scribbled shopping instructions to her husband. The letter sheds light on his parents' close but no-nonsense relationship.

Addicus,

Jonathan has been looking forward to being a little man and placing the order for our weekly supplies for some time now. He takes the responsibility very seriously. So please do not let any of Claiborne's mischievous spawn poke fun at him or, Heaven forbid, make light of his little extra leg. If he does a good job, or even if he doesn't but shows conscientiousness in the task, please allow him to have some stick candy.

Here is the list. I have made a second copy for Jonny with pictures. Step back and do not interfere unless he makes a mistake that we cannot afford. You may exercise your good judgment here.

This week's home needs:

1 lb. fatback

2 lbs. sausage

2 cans peaches in syrup

5 lbs. lard

10 lbs. flour

5 lbs. sugar

1 box Uneeda Biscuits

Small bag of ginger snaps (make sure they are not stale)

3 oz. nutmeg

3 oz. cinnamon (Xmas will be upon us soon and I need to be well stocked!)

Bowel-stopper (paregoric)

Laudanum (If Mrs. Claiborne waits on you, she will make a jest, I predict it: "Lawdy!, Lawdy! Why would a tyke need laudanum?" I have asked Jonny not to respond with, "Because you are a pain in the bottom, Mrs. C!")

Don't forget your carpenter's nails—I don't remember which penny you are out of.

Can you do without chewing tobacco FOREVER?

Also, I need two yards of gingham and one yard of unbleached muslin, and two spools of white thread. I still need some nice lace for my collar, but I would prefer not to leave its purchase to my two men. I will get it next week when I am feeling better.

That's all. And don't forget about the stick candy. And don't get into a game of dominoes and have the boy waiting around or wandering off.

Or checkers.

Emmaline

DUSTING OFF THE FAMILY ALBUM

1. **Jonathan's maternal grandfather Lutherfurd Plint was a quiet man.** Unlike his wife (Jonathan's grandmother) Daisy Day whose stentorian voice has been likened to the trumpet of a female elephant during full rut. Nancy Nesmith, *Arkansas Fellow Travelers* (El Dorado, Arkansas: Ouachita Publishing, 1993).

2. **The only tailor in a village of seamstresses, the dexterous Plint found it difficult at first to earn respect.** Ibid., 172

3. **"I do not appreciate the ribbing. My oven mitts, hand puppets and omnibus conductor uniforms are finely crafted; no seamstress could do better."** Ibid., 173.

4. **"Please stop calling my husband 'Itchy Stitchy Puppetman.' It affronts him."** Ibid. Other sources, notably Arkansas historians Lina Gilford and Jake Elliot (interviews with author), contend that the source of the nickname was Letty Humbree, a jilted lover from Lutherfurd's youth, who was perhaps otherwise motivated by the fact that avid fruiter Lutherfurd, while usually generous with his figs, never saw fit to share them with her.

5. **"Everybody gets figs but me."** Letty was often heard to grumble her displeasure within convenient earshot of her neighbors. "First Itchy Stitchy stands me up at the altar, then he goes and marries that human foghorn and if that isn't enough, he continues the abuse by denying me tasty, juicy figs." Gilford and Elliot interviews.

6. **Daisy Plint's death came unexpectedly, like a fizzy-water**

nose belch. Nesmith, *Arkansas Fellow Travelers,* 189.

7. **Lutherfurd, however, lingered for days, his ultimate expiration well attended.** No one among the cluster of friends and relatives who attended Lutherfurd at his deathbed seems to be in agreement as to just what constituted the old man's last words. I have listed some of the more colorful contentions, gathered by Ms. Nesmith, apparently for her own amusement. She reports with unusual candor that she takes them out and reads them for an "emotional lift" when her daughter Octavia comes home at dawn looking disheveled and reeking of "man-stench and cheap hooch." Ibid., 189-191.

According to Strother Bump: I suppose, my dear children, that these comprise my last words on this beautiful planet....No. Perhaps not....These then....No. Wrong again....Maybe I should just lie here and be quiet. Breathing is difficult as it is....And yet you're all looking at me as if you want me to say something profound....Oh hello, Oveta. I didn't see you there. Is that a new hat? It's very.

According to Annabelle Goodman: "Yes, doctor, the discomfort beneath the navel does radiate ventrally, with a slight shift from left to right away from the gastric obstru—"

According to Benjamina Tasslewhite: "The light. It shimmers so beautifully. Look! Look! The arms of my Redeemer are open and beck—!"

According to Rev. George M. Plint: "Satan, I come to you now, the bargain fulfilled."

According to Cloris Plint: You are all so precious to me. Every last one of you. Not her, though. Or him. Sorry. I thought you were someone else. Nearly everyone. So precious. Such a treasure to a dying—"

According to Travis Gourd: "I had no movement today or the day before. Or even the day before that. No, wait, I had a movement on Wednesday. Yes, I do recall it, although it wasn't a totally successful evac—"

According to Corley Madison: "Don't talk to me. Talk to the puppet."

According to Richard Threadweaver: "And as to my burial clothes, I should like to be interred in an omnibus conductor's uniform of my own stitching."

According to Letta Hinkle, née Humbree: "Don't push. There are figs enough for everyone."

8. **The deaths of her parents within only three months of one another left Emmaline in a protracted state of depression.** Emmaline Blashette to Laurel Malloy, 7 August, 1879, Jonathan Blashette Papers, Pettiville Library and Interpretive Center, Pettiville, Arkansas (hereafter abbreviated JBP).

9. **"My life is draped in black crepe. Addicus has to understand; I am not the girl I once was."** Ibid. I submit that the lengthy period of mourning was cause for the postponement of the nuptials proposed by suitor Addicus Blashette around the time of the death of Emmaline's mother, Daisy. Indeed, rebuff from Emmaline may have been the reason that Addicus left for a lengthy sojourn through Utah which ultimately found the young man and his older brother, Chimp, working in silver mines until late in 1884.

Addicus and Chimp's months out West are sadly under-documented. Nonetheless, there is a wonderful picaresque quality to the few stories about the brothers that have come down to us orally. Jonathan's first cousin Odger Blashette in one of my many interviews with him before his death at 102 (of a coital heart attack!) related one particularly colorful story in which Addicus and Chimp were given up for dead following a mine collapse which claimed a number of human lives in addition to the lives of seven mules, three caged canaries and one pet chicken named Pebbles. The two brothers dug themselves out from beneath a pile of rubble but were then forced to feel their way like moles through the blackness, eventually discovering the tiny beam of light that would represent their deliverance. The light, which turned out to be the deposit hole of one of the mining camp's latrines, came and went depending on the timing of buttocks placement over the opening.

The brothers stumbled toward the light, nonetheless, and finally found themselves standing in the reeking muck and calling up to the one man who could not have heard them, Deaf Jones, who, in the throes of amoebic distress, proceeded to make their lot slightly more miserable. Nor did a visit to the outhouse by slow-witted Simpy Mathune guarantee expeditious rescue. His report that Deaf Jones had just shat out two full-grown men was angrily dismissed by the grieving villagers as "that same ol' Simpy Lunacy."

I don't know whether to believe Odger or not (thus, the reason for the story's relegation to these endnotes). Even though he seemed earnest, Odger had previously claimed— just as earnestly—that he had written the pop hit "Volaré" and was sole inventor of the adjustable spud wrench.

10. **The Plints and the Blashettes had been residents of Wilkinson County for fifty years.** According to Mary Jane Pucci in her *An Encapsulated History of Wilkinson County, Arkansas* (pamphlet, n.p., n.d.), Wilkinson County, Arkansas (like its sister counties in Georgia and Mississippi)

was named for the cowardly, venal and historically discredited General James Wilkinson (1757-1825) who first conspired with Aaron Burr in his acts of treason, then persecuted Burr to save his own neck. In 1979, the county, under pressure from local historians who likened their lot to that of one living in, say, Borgia, Hitler, or Judas County, Arkansas, held a referendum to choose a new name. The highest vote-getter was Tubman, for abolitionist and former slave Harriet Tubman. Some white residents bristled at the idea of having their county named for a black woman, no matter how historically significant. In reaction they created one Billy Tubman, a "local farmer, beloved by all who knew him." Legend has it that Billy was popular with the local gentry, friendly to a fault, and had a pet pig, also named Billy, who could smoke a pipe. Billy (the man) was fluent in seven languages and once grew a squash that resembled either a boot or the nation of Italy depending on one's familiarity with footwear and European geography.

11. **Nobody came.** Jewel Romine in her richly detailed, self-published family history *The Blashettes and the Plints: A War of the Roses, Arkansas Style* (Pettiville Library Local History Collection) departs from the accepted notion that the lack of attendance at the wedding was due to the family feud that had divided the Blashettes and the Plints for decades (but which had dipped to its nadir the year of Emmaline and Addicus's nuptials), insisting, instead, that attendees had been directed to the wrong church. She admits, however, that as the families awaited the arrival of the bride and bridegroom at the second chapel, a feud-fueled melee did, in fact, ensue. Ms. Romine describes it in her breathless style:

The Blashettes fell back against the north wall of the chapel, and the Plints regrouped against the south wall and the minister, a Reverend Aloysius Green, best described as a little man attached to a very large goiter, played the role of conciliator until he was silenced by a hobnail boot to the head, and both parties commenced to flinging hymnals and psalters at one another with the exception of three young female Blashette cousins who sat behind the chancel fence guiltily eating book paste.

12. **The chivaree lasted until dawn.** The serenaders also sang, "A Ribbon in Her Hair; A Smile Upon Her Lips," "Sing me a Berceuse, Berenice," Come Down to the Bandstand, Malinda," "Roll the Hoop to My Heart." "Gazebo Gazibo, This Boy's in Love, Oh," "I Have Posies; Kiss m' Nosey!" "How Do I Know? A Little Birdy Told Me So!" "Spoonin' 'Neath the Willows," and "Pretty as a Picture (without the Corset Frame)" and, as the night wore on and the singers exhausted their honeymoon repertoire, "Dixie," "Nearer, My God, to Thee," and "Cry-baby, Cry (Wipe Your Little Eye; Go Tell Mammy to Give You Some Pie)." Odger Blashette, interview.

13. **While Emmaline took in knitting, Addicus became a jack-of-all-trades.** Seeking to contribute to the nearly empty family coffer, Emmaline also took in wash, baked rhubarb biscuits, scoured out post-office spittoons, sold her own line of shirtwaists, provided lemonade at local temperance meetings, raised rabbits for ladies' muffs, led calisthenics at the Pettiville School for Orphaned Indian Girls, sold home-boiled lye soap, hired herself out to 450-pound Opal Jamfry to "scratch the unreachable places," picked apples and pecans, chopped cotton, raced a crippled nag on a bet with the horse's owner, and read law to young law student Stanley Crew who, although illiterate, entertained dreams of being a Lincolnesque litigator. Jonathan Blashette, *Early Memories* (unpublished manuscript), JBP.

3

GROWING, GROWING…THEN GONE

1. **The fire started in the barn.** All sources agree on this fact. They differ, however, on how the fire reached the house. Brett Benningfield in his excellent *One Hundred Years of Fires in Wilkinson County, Arkansas; a Pyrogenealogical Guide* (Little Rock: Cottontail Press, 1977) writes that cinders from the flaming barn must have been blown to the flammable wooden roof of the farmhouse. Odger insists, however, that the overalls of Blashette's farmhand Slow Jimjoe McKessick caught fire at about the same time that the hay was ignited by an ill-placed cigarette, and instead of dropping and rolling upon the ground, flaming Jimjoe actually ventured into the kitchen looking for baking soda and immediately ignited a pile of wood-stove-desiccated newspapers stacked by the door, kicked over a bottle of turpentine, its lid left carelessly underscrewed, and knocked off a leaking camp lantern teetering precariously on the edge of the kitchen counter. Miraculously, according to Odger, the dimwitted farmhand not only recovered from his burns, but went on to implication in the *Arkansas Queen* steamboat wreck of 1895 that claimed the life of Hector Hamlen, the doily magnate.

2. **Aunt Renata was not a happy hostess.** Renata Goldpaw pulls no punches in her own assessment of those months in which she boarded her temporarily homeless brother and sister-in-law and their three-legged son. In her diary, Renata calls the time spent in the company of her brother's family "hell, pure unadorned, unadulterated hell." One entry offers a particularly insightful look at her harsh feelings for young Jonathan in particular.

Everyone thinks Jonathan's such an angel. Ye Gods and Little Fishes, ain't that a rip-snorter! Ask my little Timmy. He reports that when no one is looking, Cousin Jonny kicks him—not once, not twice, but three times! Each with a different leg. Good God and Jesus Pudding, this unbearable situation had better end soon or Timmy will become a nerve-frayed little quiver-boy whom no one will want to look upon and may even throw stones at. I could not bear that! I volunteered to go with Addicus to that farm and help him rebuild the house to speed up their departure, but he declined. This morning Timmy came to me and said that Jonathan had hidden his toy soldiers and had stolen the little sweet I had tucked beneath his pillow for helping Mommy roll the dough for the lattice pie we had last night. This is while everyone else is singing the demon child's praises. I cannot wait until the evil is removed from this house!

Apparently Renata never confronted her brother Addicus with these charges. I am certain they were baseless. Little Timmy's tendency toward mendacity and self-bruising was widely known, even at the time of the Blashette's stay.

3. **A fresh coat of paint was all that was needed now.** Odger Blashette, interview.

4. **Memories of a merry Christmas, however, were marred by an unfortunate accident.** According to family historian, Candida Isbell Loring, it is unlikely that the story is true. Given the personality profile she has pieced together of Jonathan's Great Aunt Harriet, it is doubtful that the old woman would have simply lain without complaint beneath the fallen Christmas tree and waited patiently for her presence there to be detected. She would, in all likelihood, have bellowed without recess until rescue became assured. One can only subscribe to the truth of the prevailing account by accepting the theory that the ornament lodged

in her mouth made the broadcasting of her whereabouts a futile endeavor.

Incidentally, Jonathan was blessed with eleven aunts and twenty-one great-aunts from both sides of the family, almost all still alive at this point in his life. I have made no effort to catalog them or to gauge the degree to which he was close to each. Some, Harriet Blashette being a good representative, were nearly daily fixtures. Others he hardly had the chance to meet. For example, Jonathan did not see his mother's sister Nydia for nearly thirty years, the result of her banishment to the wilds of Alaska for bearing a child out of wedlock and for attempting to assign paternity to successful local confectioner Henry Bellamy when it was clearly his deficient twin brother Benry whom the baby favored.

5. **"Your pomade has soiled my antimacassar."** Jonathan was fond of Aunt Lindy in spite of her eccentricities. However, this particular trait—the tendency to assail houseguests upon their leave-taking with charges of having done damage to her furniture and other household items— even Jonathan found a little irritating. Jonathan Blashette, *Early Memories*, JBP.

6. **"You put sticky wicky on my stereopticon."** Jonathan had been eating jam and bread but his hands had been tidily wiped, so the accusation was unfounded. Ibid.

7. **"That smelly stethoscope has been up someone's ass."** Even Aunt Lindy's last days were colored by baseless allegations against her doctor and the hospital nursing staff. Ibid.

8. **Spring brought a number of visitors.** Others who visited the boy during his sixth spring were Opton Van der Schoop, an itinerant "purveyor of wares exotic," who taught Jonathan

to play the spoons; Lucy Smythe, a suffragist with whom Emmaline had been corresponding for many months and who angered Addicus in one particular heated dinner table exchange by insisting that women not only had the God-given right to vote but should do so wearing men's work clothes and theatrical beards; and Anne Maye Powell, a beautiful teacher of the blind and deaf whom Emmaline had offered to put up for the night when the young woman missed her connecting train. Anne Maye, convinced that Jonathan was not only deformed but a blind and deaf mute when he knocked a glass of water from the dinner table and didn't respond quickly enough to a request by his mother to help her clean it up, snatched the boy from the table, delivered him to the farmyard well pump and began spelling the word "water" in his hand. As Jonathan stared blankly at her, uncomprehending, his brain slightly fuzzed from having sneaked several potent swallows of Addicus's stash of corn liquor thirty minutes earlier, Anne Maye tired of teaching the boy the word for water and instead delivered into his hand all five verses of Sidney Lanier's "Song of the Chattahoochee." Odger Blashette, interview.

9. **Jonathan spent part of his summer at the home of his Aunt Gracelyn in Clume.** The towns of Clume and Pettiville were as different as two communities could be. I wanted to find out more about the former, which is located fifteen miles north of the town of Jonathan's birth. Early attempts were unfruitful. The official town website is composed of a single unlinked page offering a picture of a little pigtailed girl with two missing front teeth who tells us to "come to Clume. There's lots of room!" I wrote to the town historian and chief librarian of the Clume Library and Discovery Center, Ada Demion, and received the following letter—a disturbing whitewash of the town's dark and controversial past.

Dear Mr. Dunn,

Thank you so much for your kind letter. Historical information on Clume is rather hard to come by, you are right. There has been no town history written (although I am in the process of gathering material for one). Generally, genealogists come here and proceed to pull their hair out.

I will give you a thumbnail sketch of Clume. First I should say that Jonathan Blashette was one of our most illustrious residents even though we have been obligated to share him with Pettiville. It has been said that he got his idea for male deodorants while living with his Aunt Gracelyn Boosier whose third husband Cully was a real stinker! Ha ha!

Clume was founded in 1837 by retired beggars. During the *War of Northern Aggression*, some of our slaves did not want to be free. They were happy right where they were and made up a little song that schoolchildren sing to this day: "Lincoln Sminken. Rinky Dinken. Fudgin' Mudgin'. We Ain't Budgin'!" Meaning they had no desire to join the ranks of their northern cousins who were "free" but hungry and destitute as you know most Negroes are.

Some say that during the *Years of Carpetbagging Pillage* which followed the *War of Northern Aggression*, we held the world record for lynchings. Now, this simply is not true. There were only a handful of lynchings and the rest were trick lynchings in which the rope would break in just the nick of time and everybody would go home chuckling at the cleverness of it all. The real lynchings were not funny, of course, and I am not defending them, but remember also that the intendees weren't always Negroes, to be sure. There were two Chinamen, an Italian who was mistaken for a Negro, a parrot who wouldn't stop saying the dirty words no matter what anyone did, and a Romanist (which is different from an Italian in that Romanists display Catholic arrogance), and then after a while we started to lynch the ones who had done all the lynching because we began to feel that the whole thing was wrong and the wrongdoers needed to be appropriately punished. And in so doing, the town of Clume demonstrated that it had a conscience after all and this truly warms me as you can imagine. So that there would not be an endless spiral of lynching, the sheriff decided that the guilty parties should lynch each other and this pretty much cleared up the problem. By 1891 when a law was passed by the Arkansas Legislature outlawing lynching except in exceptional cases, we had already put an end to it in this town, even though people still said our record was a formidable one to beat.

In the 1930s, Mr. Ripley wanted to put us in his newspaper feature, but the townspeople squeezed their eyes into little slits and said, "*You better not.*"

The Twentieth Century was generally uneventful except that Main Street burned down in 1918 caused by an incident of self-combustion that was recently featured on the television program, "Fire From Within." In 1924, Babe Ruth came to town and played some sandlot baseball with some of our boys until he found out that the uncle of one of his Yankee teammates had been lynched here when some of the townspeople thought that he was an anarchist. There isn't a lot of evidence that he was an anarchist, but he did look like one of those Italian Negroes who had always given us so much trouble.

When the hostages were taken in Iran, we held a young Iranian man against his will in the basement of the hardware store to show him what it was like. It was a lesson he would never forget!

I hope this information has been of some use to you. Let me know if you ever decide to spend some time in Clume. There's lot's of room!

Yours sincerely,

Ada Demion

10. **Jonathan had his heroes. Buffalo Bill was not one of them.** The following letter speaks for itself.

April 4, 1899

Dear Buffalo Bill,

What do you do each day? I can guess. I'll bet you get up in the morning and stretch and yawn and then reach for your rifle and point it out the window and kill a grazing buffalo that has come a little too close to your cabin for his own good. And then you make yourself a big breakfast of scrambled eggs and hot cakes and sausage and while you are chowing down, you look up and there is another buffalo all tangled up in your clothesline and you shoot him in the head because, why, he's all tangled up the clothesline, will you lookit! And you go down the lane to visit with your friends Wild Bill Hickok and Calamity Jane and 'Ol Doc Grubbs and along the way you just happen to kill a buffalo or two, because they were getting just a little too close, if you want the truth of it. And when you finally reach your friends you all go prancing about together in fancy plumey hats and you decide to have a picnic—a buffalo-killing picnic. And you eat a devil egg and blam! blam! Did you see him topple? Tasty egg, Jane. Blam! Blam! And then later you play some baseball and you slide into home plate and everybody is still cheering while you get up and run over with your baseball bat and beat a nearby buffalo into a motionless fur mound. And that night you go to the theatre to see a hootchie kootchie show and a buffalo comes out on stage. And you jump to your feet. "What's that buffalo doing up on that stage!" you say. "This is no buffalo show! This is a hootchie kootchie show!" And you shoot the buffalo right between the eyes. And it falls over dead and you sit back down and say, "Somebody get that dead buffalo off the stage! On with the show!" And on the way home that night, you guessed it. A buffalo comes out of nowhere. And then another and another. It is a whole herd that is crossing the road and you wish that you had more ammunition because you can't kill as many of them as you'd like, and you are gnashing your teeth and saying to your friends, "Why it's too danged dark! I'm only crippling them, Gawd-darnit! Oh well. A crippled buffalo is better than a happy, healthy frisky one." And when you get home and go to sleep, I think I know what you dream of. Do I have to say?

When they are all gone, Mr. Bill, what will you do? What will you do then, I wonder?

Your friend,

Jonathan Blashette.

(PS. I am eleven and I have three legs. And I wish that you would go to Florida and kill alligators for a change.) JBP.

11. Jonathan knew the moment he met Mr. Grund that his life was about to change forever. In Cordell Glover's monumentally flawed, indolently under-researched, and offensively over-embroidered biography of Blashette, *Three*

Legs, One Heart: The Story of Jonathan Blashette, (Fairhope, Alabama: Hollon House, 1989)—from which I have drawn sparingly and only when other sources are in full corroboration—the biographeraster provides us with a ludicrously contrived, yet too deliciously accoutered description of the arrival of Thaddeus Grund to the town of Pettiville that pivotal autumn afternoon of 1900 for me not to include at least a paragraph or two for your amusement:

> *The train was late. Oh it was late all right, and everybody knew it. The crowd that had gathered at the station shifted from leg to leg, in one great concerted sway of impatience, like an enormous beast with many heads and twice as many legs hungry—hungry for what?—the beast only knew this: that a banquet awaited one of their number. The young twelve-year-old, the one they called "Jonathan" or "Triple Threat" or "Spare Shoe." And the beast sniffed. Sniffed and snorted loud and without apology. They could all smell it; the pungent odor of fate, of a destiny materializing. Grund was Pettiville-bound and bearing a wheelbarrow full of cash. And they smelled the cash, the people did, with nostrils opened and stretched clean and wide by the sweet perfume of fame and fortune. The boy was brought to the edge of the platform, held aloft, as a distant whistle announced the iron horse's arrival. As the steam folded back like a great wet curtain and the locomotive pushed through, chug-a-chugging into the Pettiville station, the crowd itself whistled and tooted and tossed the boy high into the air, ready to deliver him to a future of assured acclaim. The tracks sang out and the men and the women and the little ones with two legs, each sang out as well. The train slowed and stopped, and the man who would mold young Jonathan's future like a potter of brash fate, with muscular, knowing hands, stepped down from the train and smiled and tousled the boy's dusty brown hair. And a cheer went up. And tears*

flowed down the excitement-rubied cheeks of Addicus and Emmaline Blashette. Tears of loss, for, yes, the child would be taken from them within hours, but tears, yes, also of joy for what the future might hold for this most special child. And the crowd parted and made way for Addicus and Emmaline and Jonathan and their evening guest, the spangled showman Thaddeus Grund, to climb into the festooned barouche that would transport the foursome to the Blashette farm. To talk of a future bright, of a destiny held in the hand and grasped firmly and kissed and sniffed and stroked with tender anticipation.

It was a night the boy would always remember.

The train, in fact, wasn't late. It was on time. And no one had gathered on the platform but Addicus and his farmhand Bill Boils. Jonathan was off picking apples for a "last meal" lattice pie. To be sure, Addicus was aware that Thaddeus Grund's Traveling Circus and Wild West Show was popular and successful, and might provide ample income for the struggling Blashettes, but Emmaline's resistance had diminished the ebullience of the welcome. The three men rode back to the Blashette farm in a rickety buckboard, in funereal silence. Emmaline wasn't even around when her husband and his showman guest arrived. She had ventured off to Inspiration Creek where she wept in protected solitude for the future of her special child.

4

UNDER THE BIG TOP

1. **"Hello Mr. Diary."** Biographers of Jonathan Blashette are indebted to their subject for a couple of reasons. From the first week of his employment with the Grund Circus, Jonathan put down his thoughts and impressions and a detailed listing of each day's activities in a diary—a habit to which he would hold for the rest of his life. We are indebted to Jonathan, as well, for carefully maintaining this collection of diaries, and for entrusting them to the perpetual custody of the Pettiville Library and Interpretive Center to which he also bequeathed the rest of his voluminous papers and many of his personal effects. This institution offers researchers unrestricted access and extensive assistance, including, even, a daily refreshment hour of tea and "biscuits," and the occasional neck massage.

In a bizarre sense, it is almost as if Jonathan anticipated me in particular. It was as if he knew of my special affinity for Mint Milanos and Malawi tea, and the fact that I can always do with a good neck rub.

In a codicil to his will Jonathan writes:

> *I have few secrets. Most who know me know this. I should be flattered if some future researcher or biographer found this life important enough to write about. I know that it was an odd one, to be sure. But then isn't each life unique in its own way? Delve if you wish into the eclectica of my existence on this planet and marvel at the incongruities, as I myself have marveled over them. That a country boy with three legs would grow up to hobnob with nabobs alongside "jest plain bobs" and girls who bob their hair,*

---

and guys named Harry and hairy French guys named Guy, and I better stop here before my heirs begin to question the compos of my mentis!

Welcome all comers! Friend and enemy alike. Turn my pages all you wish, for I am and have always been an open book.

Life has treated me well—a life which I have always shared with others, and which I now share with you, bob and nabob alike.

These words were obviously penned prior to Jonathan's descent into the depths of gut-wrenching late-life reassessment. All tellers of the story of Jonathan Blashette are grateful that their subject postponed this intense self-examination until after his papers were donated to the Pettiville Library and Interpretive Center. Had he waited, it is entirely possible that he might have burned them all. (Final additions were made by Jonathan's son Addicus Andrew after his father's death.)

Incidentally, we are blessed with a nearly complete run of Jonathan's diaries with the exception of the years 1917 and 1918, both of these volumes having been lost in France during Blashette's tour of duty with the American Expeditionary Force. (This lacuna is bridged by correspondence and the journals of Jonathan's contemporaries.) Seldom has a subject left such a rich reservoir of source material from which to draw.

2. **"The train whistle lulled me to sleep."** Jonathan's Diary, 6 September 1900, JBP.

3. **"I have yet to make any friends."** Ibid., 8 September 1900.

4. **"I am sorely homesick."** Ibid., 9 September 1900.

5. **"I am alone in my trailer but tomorrow another boy will join me."** Ibid., 10 September 1900.

6. **"I have met a boy who wishes to be my friend. My spirits have risen."** Ibid., 11 September 1900. Thaddeus Grund in his celebrated autobiography, *Ringleader: A Life in Circus Management, with a Foreword by the Bastard Ringling Brother "Skippy"* (Sarasota: Three Ring Press, 1921), notes that young Jonathan "took some time to warm to carnival life" but agrees that meeting Toby-the-Monkey-Boy Brancato was a positive development. This early difficult period of adjustment was due in no small part to the cold reception Jonathan received from the other sideshow performers who were often slow in welcoming newcomers into the fold.

So enamored was Jonathan of the jocular and gregarious Toby, Grund notes, that the circus impresario would often find Jonathan even during those first budding days of friendship with Toby, happily combing the adolescent's furry arms and shoulders, or clandestinely munching bunches of pilfered bananas with Toby under the bleachers during big top performances. According to Grund, the two boys quickly became inseparable.

It speaks to the durability of this friendship that many years later Jonathan would bear the cost of maintaining Toby in a private room at the sanitarium where he was to spend his final declining years. Having advanced in hirsute florescence from monkey fur to a full body coat of hoary-white shag, Toby convinced himself that if he wasn't the Abominable Snowman, he must at least be a very close relative.

7. **"I think she likes me."** Young Jonathan misinterpreted the wink. Little "Annette of the Skies" was victim to periodic blepharospasm, or spasmodic winking. Jonathan later suspected his error after catching the prepubescent trapeze

wonder winking at a draft horse. Joseph Alksnis-Lochrie, "Childhood Under the Big Top," *Calliope: The Magazine of the Circus* 12 (fall 1957): 37-38.

8. **One by one the sideshow performers came around.** No one seems to agree on who next extended hand (hoof or flipper) in friendship to Jonathan. Alksnis-Lochrie insists that it was Needleman, the Human Pin Cushion, who reportedly showed up at Jonathan and Toby's trailer door one night with a freshly baked chess pie and a set of darning needles for "postprandial amusement." Jacques Le Pelletier in his book on the history of the side show *Hawking and Gawking* (Philadelphia: Moyamensing Books, 1972) believes that Penny Pullman first broke the ice, much to the displeasure of her less sociable conjoined sister Patsy who was in the midst of a sponge bath when Penny dragged her off to Jonathan's trailer for a "hey and a howdy." According to Le Pelletier, Patsy never forgave her sister for this indignity and extended her grudge to Jonathan, nursing it for the duration of his tenure with the circus. Intending to boycott his farewell dinner, she arrived under obvious physical duress (the sisters were united at the hip) and protested this act of effrontery by spending the entire evening hidden from view beneath a saddle blanket, except for a brief moment when she poked her head out, turtle-like, to join in a toast to the health of President McKinley.

9. **Mickey and Benny and Doob represented Grund's very own "Lollypop Guild."** Doob Maxfield enjoyed a few moments of fame several years later when he volunteered, along with other Grund Circus dwarfs, to participate in Dr. Harvey Cushing's ground-breaking pituitary gland research project. His poem, "To Good Doctor Cushing," was published in *Tiny Writings by Tiny People* (Boston: Really Little, Brown and Company) and was well received:

Will you, doctor, make me tall?
I so tire of being small.
That is all.

10. **His schedule was grueling.** Jonathan's Diary, 2 October 1900, JBP.

11. **"I am forever called upon to display myself."** Ibid., 4 October 1900. Among the more bizarre requests Jonathan received from sideshow audiences dubious of the true corporal nature of his third leg, are the following.

Take off that shoe. Now wriggle the toes. Take off the other shoes. Now wriggle all the toes at the same time.

Hop around the room like a bunny. Like a three-legged funny bunny.

My little Margaret wants to sit on your knee. Don't be a wisenheimer; you know which knee.

That ain't a real leg. I'm bored with this humbug. Bring out the girl who eats things on a dare.

12. **"I am demoralized."** Ibid., 7 October 1900.

13. **"I have decided to escape."** Ibid., 8 October 1900.

14. **"My escape has been foiled. I was snared and returned to my captors."** Ibid., 10 October 1900.

15. **Jonathan was placed under lock and key.** As ghoulish as it may sound, there does seem to be substantial evidence that Jonathan was kept chained outside his trailer between performances for a period of several days following his return. This story is corroborated by a number of sources. However, one wildly erroneous contemporaneous account in the *De Leaux Falls Courier* would lead one to believe that Jonathan suffered a great deal more than credible sources indicate.

ESCAPED, POTENTIALLY HYDROPHOBIC CIRCUS FREAK BOY
CAPTURED, CHAINED, AND DENIED SWEETS
SOME CHILDREN DREAM OF RUNNING AWAY TO THE CIRCUS;
THIS CHILD DREAMED OF RUNNING AWAY *FROM* THE CIRCUS.

"THEY TOSSED HIM ONTO THE WAGON LIKE
A SACK OF FLOUR," REPORTS EYEWITNESS VITULA HART
WHO WATCHED THE CAPTURE FROM THE WINDOW
OF HER DENTIST'S OFFICE.

"THE BOY SHOULD NEVER HAVE BEEN SO
ROUGHLY HANDLED BUT IT IS ALWAYS PRUDENT TO DENY
CHILDREN SWEETS," OPINED THE DENTIST.

De Leaux, Louisiana October 10, 1900 Today this newspaper learned of the unfortunate condition of one twelve-year-old Jonathan Blahshit [sic] who, following escape from the circus that had been both a home and a prison to him for much of his young, brutish life, was captured and rudely delivered into the hands of his eager top-hatted wardens. As punishment for the escape, Jonathan was tethered to an elephant stake and left to dodge the ponderous shuffle of the restless pachyderms that encircled him. The boy received little sustenance during this three-day period including few, if any, sweets. He was whipped and denied access by local clergymen. A nearsighted elephant, one Baraboo, mistook young Jonathan's head for an oversized peanut and sucked his scalp. The young man is considering the filing of criminal charges against the Grund Traveling Circus and Wild West Show for reckless endangerment. He also seeks to have his contract with his present employers fully nullified. It is not clear if the boy has rabies. More than likely he does not. Illustrations on page 7.

The illustrations on page 7 included one in which Baraboo

was being fitted with very large glasses. The caption read, "She's got the memory of an elephant but the eyesight of Teddy Roosevelt!"

16. **"You are compelled to appear."** The full text of Athol Twainy Esq.'s letter of legal notification (October 17, 1900) follows.

To Mr. Thaddeus Grund

And to all other members of the Board

Of the Grund Traveling Circus and Wild West Show:

I have been retained by Jonathan Blashette to act as counsel on his behalf in the matter of Jonathan Blashette v. Thaddeus Grund et al. in which the party of the first part hereafter prays nullification of the contract binding said youth to the aforementioned circus entity. I set forth herewith the following reasons for termination of his contract:

1. The Grund Circus has violated the aforementioned contractual agreement through base negligence, careless wardship and rampant malicious cruelty, including but not limited to the showcasing of the boy's anatomical defects in a manner outside the boundaries of proper decorum and respect for the human condition. The boy was additionally chained among elephants, urinated upon (not by the elephants, but by a mischievous passing monkey), belittled, maligned and forced to endure an egregious assault upon his dignity by the owners and management of the Grund Circus.

2. The Grund Traveling Circus and Wild West Show, is, further, a fraud. While it resembles to some degree, a circus, its wild west show component has not been fully operational for some twelve years, and is, at present,

made up of two bronzed Irishmen in frayed Indian headbonnets, a three-legged buffalo with some form of bison mange, one Annie Oakey (make note: *Oakey*, not *Oakley*) whose markswoman skills generally leave so much to be desired that audience members are forced to duck for cover when she fires at targets and skeets, one Wild Bill Hiccup (a purveyor of patent medicines), and Buffalo Bill Coby who contributes little more to the evening's entertainment than stumbling about in a drunken stupor, wantonly spewing invective, and scratching his delicates.

The Plaintiff therefore prays release from said contract and swift return of the boy to his parents.

In their answer, Grund's attorneys made much of the fact that Mr. Twainy was not an attorney, did not possess a law degree, and had never, in fact, even studied the law beyond a passing glance at his cousin Claude's case books (such contact often involving little more than the lazy tracing of his index finger around the embossed lettering on their spines) and was obviously preying on the meager financial resources of Jonathan's mother and father. The attorneys cited the fact that Twainy had only once actually consulted with Jonathan after being retained to represent him, this conversation taking place over the telegraph wires and unfortunately truncated by a misapprehension of the word "Stop." Furthermore, the attorneys for Grund called Twainy's own sanity and credibility into question by reminding the court that Twainy had once vouched for the sound mental faculties of Mary Todd Lincoln even as she was discovered wading in a Washington, D.C., duck pond wearing a crown of Christmas garland and telling off-color jokes about Secretary Seward; instigated an ill-founded lawsuit against songstress Jenny Lind for shattering and collapsing the north wing of London's Crystal Palace; and posited in a recent Chatauquan lecture that the likes of the Tilden/Hayes presidential debacle wasn't anomalous at all, but would, no doubt, occur again, perhaps early in the twenty-first century, with the Republicans again besting the Democrats through wantonly political, extra-constitutional judicial intervention. JBP.

17. **For Jonathan, it was a Christmas without much cheer.** In the midst of all the legal wrangling, Jonathan received news that his favorite cousin Tibalt Fluck, a chaplain serving with American soldiers fighting the Philippine insurrection, had been wounded in the throat (and following a laryngectomy would only be able to communicate through compelled belches). Jonathan's worries didn't stop here. At a time when most boys his age were welcoming puberty with good-natured youthful insouciance, Jonathan was forced to endure bouts with ptomaine poisoning and ringworm, and fallout from the nearly fatal practical joke he and several members of the Clown Corps played on High Wire Harriet. By the time of Emmaline's visit, Jonathan was dejected and emotionally frayed.

Emmaline writes home to husband Addicus:

Dear Addicus,

Our son is dejected and emotionally frayed. It is both sad and ironic to see him this way. Sad because he has always been such a happy boy, ironic because he is generally surrounded by clowns.

I will be so relieved when this lawsuit is behind us and we have won the boy's release.

In the meantime I will try to cheer him as best as I can.

Do not forget to repair that hole in the roof of the chicken coop. And don't eat up all my preserves. And don't forget to snuff out the candles on the Christmas tree when you retire each evening. We have lost our home once to fire, and I will not have it happen again!

Your wife,

Emmaline

JBL.

18. **The fire was quickly contained.** Emmaline pretended not to notice the smell upon her return. Addicus, had, after all, patched the hole in the roof to the chicken coop and left all of her preserves untouched.

19. **It was Twainy who first introduced Jonathan to the doctor.** Dr. Meemo's claim that he had surgically detached a third leg very similar to Jonathan's is hard to confirm in the medical literature of the day. *The Journal of American Amputation* (February, 1892) does report an operation in which Meemo successfully removed an extraneous nipple from equestrian Kip Von Arnsburg in 1897, and another performed apparently with equal success in which Meemo skillfully excised a full tuft of superfluous eyebrow from the wife of an unnamed United States senator. Neither Twainy nor young Jonathan had any reason not to believe that Meemo could remove the extra leg with equal aplomb, and while they waited for the resolution of the lawsuit, Toby launched a fundraising campaign among circus employees to pay for his friend's surgery.

20. **Winter quarters were anything but accommodating.** Oronwaggee was originally a shipbuilding center. It flourished for approximately six months in 1877. Situated nearly 150 miles from the nearest navigable waterway, the town's location quickly became problematic for its numerous ship construction outfits, lured to the area by

cheap labor and a surfeit of whores. Upon the completion of each new ship, attempts would be made to transport the vessel overland, each craft ultimately left to die a slow, weather-assaulted death in one of the area's corn and wheat fields, except for those few upon which salvage rights by local farmers were successfully exercised. One such former "land" ship, the *Persian She-Ghost*, became home to Jonathan and Toby when their circus trailer was overrun by field mice. Oronwaggee Public Library Historical Clipping File.

21. **It was a long winter.** 1900 Farmers' Almanac.

22. **The raffle put Jonathan a few dollars closer.** Some sources say the raffle raised a little over $60. Other sources put the figure closer to $70. A third source inexplicably converts this amount to yen.

23. **The circus troop was never at a loss for entertainment.** Performers all, Jonathan's circus family found imaginative ways to entertain one another during the long, dark nights of their Midwestern winter encampment. (Grund discouraged his performers and roustabouts from venturing into town for their diversions due to the risk of altercations with local rubes.) For many of Jonathan's colleagues these vaudeville-like romps offered the opportunity to exercise talents that weren't being tapped by Grund who preferred to pigeonhole his performers by their physical defects and/or bigtop performance skills. A sample "programme," which I discovered among Jonathan's papers, follows. Apparently, the boy played the role of mere audience member that night.

The Programme

Flora Dora Galora Our very own Gibsonian delights will entertain you with a high-kicking, toe-tapping musical medley of madcap merriment. This will be followed by a heart-stopping bottle-washing competition.

Lee and Lipner Move aside Weber and Fields! Lee and Lipner are rip-roaringly funny and gay. They throw barbs while folding newspaper into Oriental origami, then engage in a madcap bottle-washing competition.

The Man of 1000 Responses Jinks Nyberg will offer bare-tongued rebuttal and rejoinder to all comers. Then he will do some long division.

Our Pint-sized Sarah Bernhardt Wee Clarissa McGill will play Lady Macbeth as we have never seen her before—only 27 inches tall! Miss McGill will then weave a small bath mat.

Husky Henry Holton delights and confounds with his perorations on the excesses of capitalism while whittling wooden fruit.

The Norwegian Songbird Who needs Jenny Lind when our very own Jean Norvist will stand before you and sing your tear ducts dry with her heart-wrenching ballads of love and loss and incontinence. She will then circulate through the audience, sniffing proffered objects and telling where they have been.

The Goony Goofballs will pound your funny bones with verbal ballpeen hammers, they are *that* funny. A madcap diversion that will have you howling, but then weeping your tear ducts dry over tales of personal loss through government-sanctioned deprivation.

The evening will close with a Sousa march in a high-flying patriotic tribute to our fallen American heroes in the War to Suppress Arrogant Philippine Self-determination.

Afterwards Mr. & Mrs. Grund will offer punch and pastry in the foyer.

24. **Jinks Nyberg's career was long and varied.** Among the many stops made by Jinks in his peripatetic performing career was a brief stint on the vaudeville stage as half of the comic duo of Jinks & Skinks. The two comedians were best known for their send-up of one of the first transcontinental telephone conversations—a party line involving Alexander Graham Bell from the New York City offices of the American Telephone and Telegraph Company, his assistant Thomas A. Watson from San Francisco, and others, held on January 25, 1915. One of the more sanitized versions of the sketch survives. Nyberg Collection, Mid South Community College Theatre Archives.

BELL: Mr. Watson, come here, I want you.

WATSON: I cannot do that, Professor Graham Bell.

BELL: And why is that, Mr. Watson?

WATSON: Because you are in New York City and I am in San Francisco. We are 2,572 miles apart.

BELL: And yet we are talking to one another by way of this miracle of science and industry at this very moment, and with no delay whatsoever.

WATSON: Yes! Yes! It is a wonder <u>and</u> a miracle!

(At this point the conversation is joined by Theodore Vail, president of American Telephone and Telegraph, speaking

via a spur line to Jekyll Island, Georgia.)

VAIL: Hello! Hello!

BELL: Mr. Watson, your voice has changed.

VAIL: It is not Mr. Watson. It is I, Theodore Vail, speaking to you from the Goober State.

BELL: And what has happened to Mr. Watson?

WATSON: I am still here. I understand there is someone else who wishes to join the conversation.

BELL: Ahoy! Who is there?

O. W. HOLMES: It is I, Oliver Wendell Holmes. Junior. In our nation's capital. I have President Woodrow Wilson seated next to me. He is eager to speak to all of you.

BELL: By all means, ask him to join us.

O. W. HOLMES: *(muffled)* Take the mouthpiece from your ear, Mr. President. You have reversed the apparatus in a comical manner.

WILSON: *(muffled)* Dear me. Yes, I see.

O. W. HOLMES: One moment, gentlemen. It appears that the president is having another little stroke.

(Momentarily, President Woodrow Wilson joins the conversation.)

PRESIDENT WILSON: Good afternoon, good afternoon. What a miracle of science to be having a conversation from points far flung!

BELL: Ahoy, Mr. President! It is indeed an honor and a

privilege to be speaking to you across such a distance.

PRESIDENT WILSON: May I say it?

BELL: Say what, Mr. President?

PRESIDENT WILSON: Tee hee. Come here, Watson, I need you.

BELL: Not <u>need</u> you, Mr. President. I <u>want</u> you.

PRESIDENT WILSON: Well, I want you too, sugar. Tee hee. Oh dear, I just made a monkey of myself there, didn't I?

WATSON: It's all the same to me.

VAIL: Mr. Watson! Come here! I want you! Ho ho!

PRESIDENT WILSON: Yes, come here this instant, you servile little man. Tee hee.

WATSON: I'm hanging up.

(A silence)

BELL: I believe we have offended Mr. Watson. *(Another moment of silence.)* This, gentlemen, concludes our demonstration of long distance communication. Please help yourselves to tea and cucumber sandwiches. What a day. What a day.

25. Jonathan's legal fees were paid by a mysterious benefactor. There is a difference of opinion as to the identity of this benefactor. Some say that it was Pettiville merchant J. P. Morgen. Morgen was occasionally confused with millionaire financier J. P. Morgan. The two did resemble one another, even down to their bulbous noses and rosaceous complexions. However, Morgen rarely left

Pettiville, and Morgan rarely came to Arkansas. Additionally, Morgen hailed from the rural Ozarks and took no pains to change his accent or retire his overalls or fix his teeth or divorce his sister.

26. **The lawsuit was finally settled.** Box 17, Legal Documents, JBP.

27. **The ether had already been administered.** The heroics as described by Nurse Monette (New England Medical Union Oral History Collection) were only slightly exaggerated in the yellow press. Jonathan's "rescue" by a motley band of side show performers and irate Blashette family members was the stuff of the "mellerdrama" or some heart-stopping Kinetoscopic short. What we know to be true is that the rescue party did indeed storm the operating room just as Dr. Meemo was positioning the amputation saw, not, in fact, over the tertiary leg—nor any leg, for that matter—but over Blashette's right arm. Numerous eyewitness accounts attest to Meemo's advanced state of inebriation at the time and the subsequent Keystone Cops-like arrest of both Meemo (for public intoxication and potential malpractice) and several of the more anatomically intriguing members of the sideshow brigade who mistakenly entered the children's ward and frightened the youngsters into eating not only everything on their dinner plates but their paper napkins as well.

28. **"I, Jonathan Blashette, make these solemn vows."** JBP. In addition to vowing never again to seek removal of the extraneous leg, Jonathan made a number of other promises to his thirteen-year-old self. Below is the full text of Jonathan's "Promissory Note to Myself."

On this day, February 12, 1901, I, Jonathan Blashette, vow the following:

1. Given the grave risk of accidental removal of a non-

designated appendage, I will never again seek to dispatch any part of my body with which I have been either blessed or inconvenienced by the good Lord, nor will I ever again complain of my lot on this earth.

2. I will apply myself to diligent study and mold myself into a man to make my mother and father exceedingly proud.

3. I will marry a woman with large and exciting breasts, like those on Batanya Batavia, the hatchetman's assistant.

4. I will seek a career in either the ministry or as a fitter in women's foundation furnishings.

5. I will serve my country and my fellow man through whatever means are offered to me but will never—regardless of financial incentive—dress up like a clown because some people find clowns scary or at the very least comically unengaging.

6. I will buy my mother an emerald choker, one size too large as a margin of safety.

7. I will transport myself thirty years into the future as did the gentleman in Mr. Wells's novel The Time Machine and I will find out where my future self will be stationed at that particular moment, and I will hide behind a hedge with the intention of jumping out and startling him but because my intended victim will remember being the me of thirty years previous, he will be prepared for this prank and will not be in the least bit frightened but will wag a finger at me, and say, "I've been waiting for you, rascal!" and invite me to sup with him and he will let me drink beer because he will know how much he wanted to but was prevented from doing so when he was thirteen, and it will be a very droll evening indeed.

8. I will become one of Governor Theodore Roosevelt's Rough Riders and serve with him on his next military campaign, especially if it is in some exotic place such as Hawaii or Tahiti where island girls wink at you as they feed you coconut meat with their supple island fingers.

5

HOME AGAIN, HOME AGAIN, JIGGITY JIG

1. **The homecoming was bliss.** Jonathan's Diary, JBP.

2. **The next morning he entered Pettiville High School.**
Some say through the north door, others the south door;
there is also a small camp that believes that Jonathan
entered the school through the kitchen and nipped a egg
cream cup as he passed. Obviously, this is inconsequential.
(It is also becoming obvious that this book has been
seriously over-researched.) The most salient fact here is that
Jonathan was home safe and sound, and back in school. His
circus days were over. Life for young Jonathan Blashette had
finally taken a promising turn.

3. **Even at this early age, Jonathan had become a crusader.**
Always a compassionate child, Jonathan's concern for others
less fortunate than himself and especially for the maltreated
and oppressed of society only grew stronger as he matured
into late adolescence. Living with side show performers
whose physical defects had left them open to abuse and
societal marginalizing only strengthened the boy's resolve to
fight for the rights of all those who were similarly relegated.
This group included Native Americans as well. I discovered
among Jonathan's papers a very telling letter from author L.
Frank Baum, dated January 27, 1904. It was apparently
written in response to one that Jonathan had sent him.
(Jonathan's letter no longer exists. According to Baum, the
drawing that accompanied it was immediately destroyed;
one suspects that the letter itself quickly met the same end.)
Nonetheless, the beacon of Jonathan's courage shines
through by inference.

Dear Master Blashette,

Thank you for your letter of January 22. For a young man of fifteen you express yourself quite well. If you were to choose a career as a writer you would be well served by your talent.

While I commend your command of the language, the content and thrust of your missive was most unwelcome. Your anger is curiously misdirected, or shall I say, microscopically directed. Is my position not one shared by hundreds of thousands of other white Americans? Will you write vituperative letters to all of these good people as well? You will be a busy lad. I suggest you get to work without delay!

I have not altered the opinion I held in the *Aberdeen Saturday Pioneer* editorials to which you refer, and that is that our safety even in this relatively new century continues to depend upon the total extermination of the Indians. I will agree with you that we have wronged the savage Red Man for centuries. But while you suggest that we make amends in whatever way possible for those decades of subjugation, I strongly argue the opposite course of action. The red-skinned barbarian will never submit to our civilizing influence. He will insist on retaining claim to land to which by his innate primitivism he has lost clear title. Anger-fueled violence toward our government will never subside. Without hope of reconciliation or redress, it is most efficacious for us to simply finish the job we started: wipe these untamed and untamable creatures from the face of the earth and be done with it. Unless we take swift action along these lines, our great nation will remain under-civilized, its enormous potential unrealized. We have no choice: the Red Man must be eliminated.

My secretary tells me that your letter was accompanied by a picture which you had drawn that was of such a distressing nature that she was forced to place it directly into the hearth fire to ensure that none of the many children who wander into my office would find it and be harmed by the exposure.

Young man, I think it should be possible for you to disagree with me on this matter without making a shamefully obscene mockery of my work. My secretary tells me that your drawing depicted a full scale Indian assault on the characters in my children's book *The Wonderful Wizard of Oz*. In the picture the savages have eviscerated the Scarecrow, chopped the Tin Man into a pile of scrap metal, and skinned the Lion and hung him upon a spit, his face twisted in agonizing death throes. Young Dorothy lay writhing upon the blood-streaked Yellow Road, her scalp peeled horrifically from her skull.

In addition to which, young man, your facts are erroneous. There **are no** Indians in the land of Oz. They were exterminated many years ago by the Munchkins. Oz is a far better (and safer) place for their absence. Perhaps some day you will see that our great country would fare even better (we have no witches here) should we follow the same course of action.

Perhaps it is good that I did not see the picture you drew. I am not sure that I would find it in my heart to forgive you for the violence you did to them.

Yours truly,

L. Frank Baum

4. **A high point of the year was the tug-of-war.** Griselda Duderstadt, *Halcyon Days in Wilkinson County* (El Dorado,

---

Arkansas: Ouachita Publishing, 1974), 178-79. The Wilkinson County tug-of-war had been an annual event going back to 1870. Traditionally, male citizens of Pettiville would gather on the south bank of Gobles Creek as male citizens of neighboring Ambless gathered on the north bank with the exception of 1889 when Pettivillians, finding the south bank rain-soaked and mud-laden—a disadvantage they would not accept—requested of their north county rivals a switch, or at the very least, the drawing of lots to determine bank assignment. Amblessites, staunchly adhering to tradition, rejected both proposals. Rather than canceling the bout, the two teams agreed to join forces for this one year, the men of both towns gathering *en masse* on the north bank to pull down a roped oak tree across the creek. Failing miserably at this task ("We removed some bark") the men were mocked by their female kin, and the *Pettiville Press* published a demoralizing story under the headline, "Wilkinson County Hangs its Head. Oak Tree wins Annual Tug-of-war" (24 July1889). The emasculated men of the county did, however, get the last laugh; the next week they chopped down the deeply rooted oak, milled its timber and turned the boards into backsplashes for a number of Pettiville and Ambless outhouses. "This way," explained Pettiville mayor Herman Sills, "whoever wanted to, could piss right on that damned uppity tree."

5. **Jonathan was caught playing craps behind the main tent of the Billy Wonder Traveling Revival.** Interview with Odger Blashette.

6. **Later Jonathan found Jesus at the Billy Wonder Traveling Revival.** Jonathan's chief duties as "silent deacon" during his summer on the tent show circuit after his conversion by Billy Wonder included standing as sentry to prevent "bedeviled" teenaged hooligans from pulling out the stakes and toppling the canvas tenting, collecting love

offerings from those in attendance, and lending a hand to those spiritually and physically "infirm" who might wish to approach the altar to obtain soul-cleansing and chiropractic adjustments. Sixteen-year-old Jonathan wrestled throughout the summer with a faith that seemed by turns impertinent and nonexistent. "Is it possible to be a Christian and not believe in God?" Jonathan posed in his diary. He put this question to Billy Wonder, as well. "That's a new one on me," Billy responded, and then added somewhat cryptically, "I suppose you can drink the milk without dancing with the cow." "And what milk would that be?" Jonathan inquired of the man who, in spite of his skillful religious legerdemain, did possess faith of a sort. "Why, the milk of human kindness!" Billy chirped, his bright, sun-glinted eyes reflecting thoughtful consideration of the concept. An interesting concept, Jonathan noted in his journal, from the wonder-working Billy Wonder. Jonathan's Diary, 30 June 1904, JBP.

7. **Jonathan was removed from the Epworth League for making a joke about the Holy Ghost.** Reverend Devon Stoddard to Eugenia Sellers, 20 September 1904, Sellers Family Papers.

8. **Jonathan was voted president of the Pettiville High School Debate Society.** Jonathan's Diary, 12 October 1904.

9. **Jonathan lost the presidency of the debate society when a rival challenged his legitimacy and he responded with, "Oh, really...must we debate this?"** Ibid., 13 October 1904.

10. **Jonathan considered quitting school and becoming a patent medicine salesman.** Interview with Odger Blashette.

11. **Jonathan decided not to quit school and become a patent medicine salesman.** Ibid.

12. **"I'm so glad that you decided not to quit school and become a patent medicine salesman. Your mother is too."** Ibid.

13. **"He's right. I am. Come give Mother a hug."** Ibid.

14. **Love finds Jonathan Blashette.** Mildred Boyers' family was relatively new to Pettiville. Her father sold Divine Bain sea sponges throughout a territory that included eastern Arkansas, northern Mississippi, and western Tennessee as well as, curiously, Atlantic City, New Jersey, where, it was said, he had a mistress named Sheila who either (sources disagree) ate lye and died, or ate dye and lied about it, bragging that blue tongues ran in her family. Mildred wasn't close to her father, but found comfort and solace at the rectory of St. Bartholomew Catholic Church of Ambless where she performed light housekeeping chores and posed as famous Greek statuary for the amusement of Father Dwayne and his toothless assistant, Toot. Maise Boyers Gabridge, interview by author, 16 May 2000.

No picture of Jonathan's first girlfriend, Mildred, exists (see Note 16). However, we have been left with several photographic likenesses of "Sheila," discovered among the Boyers family effects in an old Atlantic City taffy box. In one snapshot she wears a Gibson Girl bathing dress and a big grin. This particular picture was given to me by Sheila's great-granddaughter and it is now affixed to my refrigerator right next to the Michigan snowshoe magnet that secures my coupons for Mint Milanos.

15. **"Mildred's my gal."** As happy as Jonathan and Mildred were, they must have known that they were not destined to spend the rest of their lives together. Perhaps this note, slipped into Jonathan's hand at the Pettiville High School Homecoming bonfire, offers a few clues. JBP.

November 2, 1904

Dear Jonny,

You CANNOT, CANNOT, CANNOT think that I would go on the hayride with you. I simply will not do it. You will horse around as you always do when you get with Bub and Charlie and the Vox, and will pay no attention to me, you may be sure of it. I will sit in a corner of that wagon ALONE and watch the four of you make UTTER fools of one another and wonder why I ever FOR ONE MINUTE thought we'd be cuddling in the moonlight when that is probably THE LAST THING ON YOUR MIND! So you go on without me and I will stay behind and help Miss Britten dust her erasers unless you can absolutely positively assure me that you will pay attention to ME and only ME on the hayride and not act the fool with those ruffian characters you call your pals.

I made you a lattice pie last night and it is waiting for you in the home sciences room and you may have it for the price of a little KINDNESS for HEAVEN'S SAKE!

Love,

Mildred

PS. Daddy is off in Atlantic City again. He will no doubt try to make me feel better about his absence by bringing home TAFFY.

16. **Another favorite pastime was "kodaking" in Donlee Hills.** Each of these photographs of Jonathan and his friends (JBP and Maise Boyers Gabridge, Private Collection of Family Ephemera) was taken with Mildred's new Brownie camera, probably by Jonathan's high school chum Will "The Vox" Crispen. The oversize thumb-intrusions in the bottom right corner of each are identical.

Though camera-shy herself, Mildred loved her little Brownie and was careful to preserve all of her own efforts, including a photographic essay she entitled "Work, the Curse of the Drinking Class." Jonathan played one of the roles in this pictorial commentary on Upper Class indolence, dressing up as a moneyed swell, berating (in frozen pantomime) the hired help, and drinking himself into a nightly stupor. The photographic tableau assigned to "nightly stupor" shows Jonathan comically body-hugging a lamppost. I have discovered a number of variations of the lamppost clench. My chief researcher Billy Vivian was quick to demonstrate to me that by placing the photographs in a certain order and flipping them, one may animate the scene, thus producing a peep show of Jonathan dry-humping the post.

17. **Both a curse and a blessing was this second sight.** Jonathan's mother didn't always possess the gift of prophecy, but for a period of ten years it seemed that almost all of her predictions came true. In early 1912, however, Emmaline's second sight began to fail her and her back-porch prognostications started to miss their mark by wide margins. For example, she predicted that the Titanic would be drydocked after forty years of dutiful service to the White Star Line and then be turned into a home for old sailors, and that anarchist Emma Goldman would become a Republican senator from New Jersey. Later she predicted that Al Jolson would lose his voice and become a whispering Southern Baptist. Addicus Andrew Blashette, interview with author, 5 October, 1999.

18. **"Graduation comes none too soon! Hip Hip Hoorah! Tah Rah Rah Boom Dee-A! [sic]"** Jonathan's Diary, 25 May 1905.

19. **"I am leaving to spend my summer as a counselor at a fishing camp."** Jonathan Blashette to Mildred Boyers, 29

May 1905, Private Family Correspondence Collection of Maise Boyers Gabridge. Mildred was, incidentally, in Atlantic City looking for her mother who, according to Gabridge, had learned of her husband's extramarital dalliances and went to either "drag the man by the short-hairs all the way home" or "feed that sorry excuse for a husband and father to the fishes."

20. **"This was my welcome to the Fritz Fighting Camp."** The word "fighting" was a misprint. Jonathan spent his graduation summer paying—along with other members of the camp's staff—for this glaring promotional brochure typographical error. Given the misleading advertising, few arrived at the Minnesota camp expecting to fish and those who made the attempt usually, in the words of the camp's beleaguered administrator Trent Littlefeather, "had no sooner dropped their lines in the cool, placid lake water than their boatmate hauls off and knocks the dog crap out of them when they're not looking." It was the summer Jonathan learned fisticuffs, a little about lures, and the importance of accuracy in promotional circulars. Jonathan's Diary, 3 June 1905.

21. **It was the second tornado to hit Wilkinson County in as many months.** According to Blashette's step-granddaughter Vicka Lovett (interview), Jonathan was in the barn as the twister lifted the roof off the farmhouse. Emmaline was in the kitchen and Addicus was out in the field. Jonathan's diary disputes this. He places himself in the field, his father in the barn and his mother visiting with Pastor Stoddard's myopic wife, Margaret, at the parsonage. By Addicus's account (letter from Addicus to Lindy Blashette), Emmaline was in the barn, he was in the kitchen and Jonathan was off fishing with his friend Raymond Beams. Raymond (letter to his birth father soliciting funds) said that he was in the kitchen with Margaret Stoddard

looking for Emmaline's canning lids. Pastor Stoddard was in the Blashette barn looking for Margaret's eyeglasses. Addicus and Emmaline were at Claiborne's General Groceries and Sundry Dry Goods Store. Pastor Stoddard (church newsletter) said that everyone was seated at the Blashette kitchen table playing Uncle Wiggly. Margaret Stoddard (Bible Methodist Church Missionary Circle Circular) remembers that when the tornado touched down, Raymond Beams was in a barn located somewhere in the tri-county area helping her husband look for her eyeglasses. County historian Ida Sheridan (interview) insists that Pastor Stoddard was at Claiborne's store buying an Uncle Wiggly game and a comical monocle fob. Everyone else was at the Pettiville ice cream social discussing crop rotation and bungled Montgomery Ward mail orders.

·

6

HALLS OF IVY, CORRIDORS OF PROMISE

1. The first day at Devanter went smoothly. Devanter College and Seminary was founded in 1866 by three Confederate veterans who implemented an early Dixie version of the G.I. bill, offering free tuition, room and board to any veteran of Jefferson Davis's army whose application for its eclectic program was accepted. The school was financed by a wealthy British eccentric, Lord Hallowell who owned vast acreage in England's Lake District and whose large family fortune (acquired over a century of trade with southern planters) also financed full-scholarships at an art school in Leeds for students willing to paint only portraits of his estranged wife, Tildy, whose oft-reproduced image clutters the walls of that city's "Museum of Tildy" to this day. Alwin Chambers, *The Little Brown College in the Wildwood* (Pittsburgh: Academe Press, 1992), 222-25.

Devanter offered courses in the sciences, business management, and the "Biblical arts." Since Jonathan's interests included both of the latter two disciplines, the small Tennessee college seemed the ideal choice.

2. Jonathan was assigned to Orville House. Ibid., 225-26, 301, 321-23. Lord Hallowell's endowment carried several stipulations. First and foremost, Devanter College would be a place of study and fellowship for men of all races. Over the years, the college's charter had been altered to allow only half-white mulattos, then quadroons, and finally octoroons. It was because Jonathan was admitted to the school one week late that he was placed in Orville House (regarded by most as the "dormitory of last resort"), which bunked the college's twenty-two octoroons and its only Chinese student, Wing Lu, who, though there to study the recently developed quantum theory of German physicist Max Planck, found himself spending most of his non-classroom hours running the college laundry and grousing heavily over his lot.

A second stipulation: That students were to be of strong moral character. Smoking and drinking were strictly prohibited, although the young men were permitted a glass of watered sherry from time to time at the home of President and Mrs. Greaney when "some of the boys would be invited over for social and intellectual intercourse with the faculty." Most importantly, the men were to visit nearby Chucking with "only the most extreme caution." A wild and wooly railroad town, Chucking had twice as many saloons as churches. Any student found to be frequenting saloon, brothel, or dental parlor (where, it was understood, nitrous oxide parties sometimes degenerated into giggly orgies of lust and "just plain undignified tomfoolery") would risk expulsion.

Ironically, it was here in Chucking that Jonathan met one of the enduring loves of his life, a pocked syphilitic former prostitute named Great Jane.

3. **"She is the earth, the moon and the stars."** Though never allowing Jonathan to consummate their relationship, there is no doubt that Great Jane did permit him to hand her his heart. Nor is there any doubt that she felt the same. Such a love many have found inexplicable. Lucianne Flom in her study of love, romance and venereal disease, *A Canker of the Heart* (New York: Koppelman Publishers, 1990), offers the following stab: that Jonathan, being somewhat the social misfit himself, given his disability, identified with others who viewed the world through a slightly skewed lens, and it is entirely plausible that such empathy might in a special circumstance extend itself to romantic attachment. I believe

that Jonathan's feelings for Great Jane went much deeper than simple romantic attachment. To call the two soul mates would not be a far-reaching assessment.

4. **"Jonny, give me paradise!"** Ibid., 125. Great Jane was misheard. What she actually said was, "Jonny, give me a pair of dice!" The diseased ex-hooker loved craps almost as much as she loved Jonathan.

5. **Two months passed before Jonathan found the courage to mention Great Jane to his mother.** The reference was strategically buried within the letter Jonathan sent home on November 2, 1905, an excerpt of which follows. JBP.

> I am quite the diligent one when it comes to my studies, and my marks have been very good. Yet, I am not at all the proverbial dull boy and do spend some time in recreation with my mates. I have been learning to swing the tennis racquet upon the grassy patch that serves as makeshift tennis court here. Football is too rough-and-tumble for me, but I have a good arm for playing third base and I am happy that autumn has made a delayed appearance this year. We have a chef who once served a British earl in India and his offerings are quite exotic and flavorful. I am not a glutton but I do so enjoy the food here, as well as the company of a girl named Jane, backgammon, reading Owen Wister novels and lively conversation.
>
> I hope all is well with you and Father. Has his elbow healed?

6. **Jonathan displayed a knack for making easy friendships with some of the other students.** Jonathan befriended even the terminally friendless among the residents of Orville House. This group included Jiminy Crutch, a mestizo who lived in fear of squirrels, and thus found himself constantly

confronted by them in his bed, wardrobe, and dresser—placed there by the more mischievous among his dormitory mates. Young Jiminy won abundant sympathy and support from Jonathan, who encouraged the quaking, stuttering young man, to shake hands with his fear and turn it to positive use. Following Jonathan's advice, Jiminy went on to become the nation's foremost expert on squirrel aggression, and in 1941 was awarded the prestigious Van Weems Small Mammal Research Prize for his paper on the infamous 1826 Hamilton County, Indiana, squirrel migration—an aberration of nature that residents of Noblesville still speak of today. Contemporary accounts note that thousands of squirrels one morning decided to move *en masse* across the county. Swimming like otters across the picturesque White River, and foraging voraciously along the way, the squirrels were met by angry club-wielding farmers at every turn. The devastation wreaked by the two-week rampage took months to repair. Cordell Glover, *Three Legs, One Heart*, 45-48; Belva Curry, "On the Move" *Sciuridae; Journal of the American Squirrel,* 1952, No. 4, 366-75.

7. **Jonathan sold ads for the little literary journal; his friend Finley Sanders offered illustrations.** A passionate antiwar socialist, Jonathan's artistic college chum Finley Sanders was to gain some notoriety in later years through his opposition to what he referred to with great disdain as "The War to Trump All Wars," "The Industrialists' Carnage Party," and "The International Killing Machine Wilson Lubricates with His War-lusting Salivations." A political cartoon in *The Worker's Brow* in which Sanders depicted President Woodrow Wilson gleefully dining on a goulash of roasted miniature American soldiers while Lady Liberty tearfully serves him heaping seconds, resulted in a lengthy stay for Sanders in a federal penitentiary. He passed the time by forming a barbershop quartet with fellow antiwar advocate Eugene Debs; Philadelphia bond forger Gordon

Roman; and Dubuque serial ax murderer Eldred Jorguess, whom the others nervously allowed to carry the melody even when he seemed to be making it up as he went along.

Incidentally, Sanders' equally rebellious brother David was a stowaway on the ill-fated "Peace Ship," a Scandinavian cruise liner that had been enlisted to transport a disparate group of American pacifists to Europe in November 1916 with the ambitious goal of convincing the warring armies that human bloodshed was an expensive price to pay for national hegemony. Though bankrolled by Henry Ford, the most recognizable member of the delegation, the effort was doomed to early failure. Pope Benedict XV, the ubiquitous Helen Keller, and Ford's lifelong friend Thomas Edison all expressed early interest in joining the international diplomatic venture, but backed out long before the ship left port. Helen allegedly confessed that she had always been a poor shuffleboard player and, besides, Edison generally got on her nerves: "His lips never stop flapping; my fingers get so tired." (*Helen Keller, At Ease* [Indianapolis: Three Senses Publications, 1988] 238). Ford himself bailed out of the endeavor as soon as the ship reached Norway. In his uncharitable, self-published biography of the automobile titan, *Henry Ford, Jew Hater*, Garner Qualms surmises that Ford hadn't realized until he was already at sea how many of his fellow neutralists were Hebrew deniers of the divinity of Jesus Christ, and this discovery left him irritable and unmotivated. David, for his part, spent the trip rolling matzo dough in the ship's galley while happily debating the merits of the Zionist movement with the many shipboard followers of Theodor Herzl.

8. **"I promise to stop being so sesquipedalian."** Jonathan's Diary, 4 April 1906. A difficult task, it would seem, since the word itself means "given to use of long polysyllabic words." The irony was, nonetheless, lost on companion Crutch,

whose attention had been diverted by the sudden unsettling appearance of a tree squirrel upon the open-window sill.

9. **By Jonathan's second year, correspondence with his mother had become comfortably routine.** The following is typical of the many letters Jonathan received from his mother during his years at Devanter—brimming with chat and reportorially framed gossip. JBP.

October 3, 1906

Dear Jonny,

I am so proud of you I can hardly express it. You are now a college sophomore! No one in our family has ever been to college before except for your Great Uncle Phineas and it still isn't clear whether he was actually enrolled or merely pretended to be—a situation similar to that in which he pretended to be an assistant of Mathew Brady's—the one in charge of photographic portraiture of the "unencumbered female physique." While he was in prison I do believe he even pretended to be a guard at one point, but only in an odd exchange with a brain-addled sentry who on occasion liked to pretend to be an inmate to break the daily monotony. This is why your great uncle was able to walk out the front gate of that place to attend the Centennial Exposition in Philadelphia.

Your father is doing well, and the farm is on a slightly better footing. That new heifer had a beautiful twinkle-eyed calf we have named after Pastor Stoddard's daughter Igraine. (Remember the way the reverend would rub his temples and say, "That troublesome Igraine! She gives me such a migraine!") We may even make a nice profit at the end of the year.

Aunt Lindy sends her love. She had a nasty altercation

with the butcher. She accused him of placing his hand on a part of her body men generally should not touch without a marriage license. If she had been the one holding the cleaver, I don't know that he would be here right now. I think that your Aunt Lindy needs a doctor's care and some strong medication. Lydia E. Pinkham's Vegetable Compound is not doing the job.

I have seen little Mildred and she wishes to let you know that she is "doing quite well, thank you." There was an edge to her voice that belied the sentiment. She must have heard about your friend Jane.

With all my love,

Your Mother

10. **Jonathan's experiences at Devanter shaped his politics for years to come.** One individual, in particular, made the strongest impression of all. His name was Andrew Bloor and he was a young history professor who had taken an instant liking to this intellectually curious three-legged student. Ostracized by most of the Devanter faculty and subsequently sacked by the school's administration for his liberal views on race and gender, Bloor obviously recognized Jonathan's nascent early progressive tendencies and sought to encourage and nurture them.

His employment terminated only a week before Jonathan's graduation, Bloor wrote the following letter to his favorite student from a rooming house in Oberlin, Ohio, where he was in the process of applying for a faculty position with the famed liberal arts college there, a paradigm of progressive pedagogy. The letter has been preserved in Jonathan's papers.

May 27, 1909

My dear Mr. Blashette,

Congratulations on arriving at this special juncture in your promising young life. I am confident that you will take what you have learned from your matriculation at Ol' Devanter and make of yourself a man most exemplary among men. The loam of your character possesses sprouts of greatness, to be sure, but a species of greatness born of humanitarian compassion. You understand as do I the frailty of man and the ever-present need to repair human inadequacy with the sutures and dressing of tender respect. Man is a flawed creature, to be sure, yet has the potential for great healing, aided by the ministrations of the know-ledgeable and well-tooled physician of the soul. I hope that I have taught and supplied you well.

I have observed your thoughtful intercourse with the other students, the friendship you have formed with the pocked erstwhile prostitute they call Great Jane. I have watched you spend one particularly long evening pulling our alcohol-intemperate janitor Charlie Royce from the puddle of his own vomit, cleaning him up, and secreting him within your very own dormitory room to prevent his discovery and removal for serial intoxication. I have watched you rescue the mestizo Jiminy Crutch when he was pursued across the quadrangle by mischievous students holding squirrel puppets with exaggerated teeth. And when the prank caused young Jiminy to lose his breakfast, you cleaned up the resultant puddle of vomit knowing that Charlie Royce was unavailable, as he was himself sleeping off yet another night of heavy binge-drinking, curled upon the rag rug in your room.

And surely you must also recall the night that you extended your hand of kindness to me—the night that I spoke at the faculty-student forum on the need to protect the right of Negro men to cast their Constitution-given vote in a climate of strong disenfranchisement sentiment among members of the local community. You'll remember that I was silenced by a tomato which struck the left side of my face and proceeded to adhere—for the most part—drippingly to my spectacles. And then the second tomato which brushed my chin and left its rotted juices oozing down my neck. And then another and yet another while a sincere effort was launched by my fellow faculty members to do absolutely nothing to stop the assault. You will remember that they sat—each of them—quietly, with arms folded, not willing to move an inch, except for professors Rabdau and Gilbert who shifted and squirmed in most animated fashion as they debated whether the tomato was a vegetable or a fruit. Such a night of debasement and abashment it was to become for me. But such a night of heroism it became for you, as you sprang from your seat and took a tomato or two yourself (to the rump, I do believe) in the course of helping me from the red-plastered podium and off that slippery stage. I shall never forget your concern for me at that moment.

You are poised for great things, my dear young friend. I will stand in the wings and prompt if needed, but will mostly, I daresay, commend your time upon this world stage. It was a joy to have you as student and it will be a joy to have you as lifelong friend.

With sincere affection,

Andrew Bloor

11. **Jonathan unfortunately missed his graduation.** There are several theories as to why Jonathan was unable to attend graduation ceremonies at Devanter. His diary is strangely silent, stating only "I did not go." Some, including Glover and Cyril Furman in his unfinished biographical manuscript *The Story of Jonathan Blashe*—, believe that Great Jane was so distraught over the fact that Jonathan would soon be returning home and thus out of her life that she made a clumsy attempt at suicide which Jonathan had to foil. Lucianne Flom theorizes that Jane probably chose the then popular arsenic-incremental method—a painful and ultimately harebrained way to kill oneself—which involved taking larger and larger doses of the poison over a period of several hours. Flom imagines that Jonathan's heroic efforts involved intermittent dashes to the kitchen to restrain Great Jane from stirring arsenic into her freshened tea, followed by an ebb of casual conversation, and then another mad dash for the kitchen, upon Great Jane's sudden announcement, "I believe I'll have another spot of tea." Flom and Furman surmise that this pattern played out for hours and did not end until Jonathan thought to toss the vial of arsenic out the window.

Another theory, this one posited by Odger, is that Jonathan got his third foot caught in a loose floorboard and it took several hours to pry it out.

I find both theories ludicrous. My guess is that Jonathan was making a statement of protest regarding Bloor's dismissal.

7

SO BEWARE, SAY A PRAYER

1. **For Jonathan it was a summer of disappointment.** Cyril Furman, *The Story of Jonathan Blash—[ette]*. With the family farm back on uncertain financial footing due, in part, to Addicus's latest accident and Emmaline's not infrequent participation in a local quilting circle in which morphine was freely dispensed by the wife of local physician R. J. Blanton, it is no wonder that Jonathan sought emotional solace through reconciliation with Mildred. It came as a severe blow, then, for him to learn that his high school sweetheart had been secretly married to her alcoholic cousin Clyde for two years.

The threads of the rich tapestry of personalities and events that draped Jonathan's early years were tightly interwoven during this period. Within six years, Dr. Blanton would earn national notoriety as perpetrator of a scandalously unsuccessful experimental trans-species organ transplant—one that involved none other than Mildred's cousin/ husband Clyde. Clyde Haywood became, for three days, the proud owner of the liver of a chimpanzee, introduced by the morphine-careless Dr. Blanton for purposes of reversing many years of alcohol abuse.

In 1919, two years after the death of her husband from massive organ rejection, Mildred, hearing of Jonathan's own tragic personal loss (see Chapter 8, note 5), wrote her former beloved to express her condolences, as well as her desire to see him again and perhaps renew the ties that bound the two in their youth. There is no evidence that Jonathan ever replied, although Mildred's letter is preserved in Jonathan's papers, a hint of the fragrance she atomized upon it still lingering upon the page.

7

January 24, 1919

Dear Jonny,

Once we were young and gay and life held such wonderful promise for us both. Then you went away to college to learn Latin and history and commerce, and I pined miserably until Clyde rescued me from my pit of self-pity and asked for my hand. Oh, Jonny, HAD I ONLY WAITED FOR YOUR RETURN! But where was the assurance that we would pick up where we left off when you, with diploma in hand and a bit more tuft upon your chest, finally strode back into Pettiville and back into MY LIFE? Especially after you took up with that prostitute and had all the tongues in town wagging from the SCANDAL of it, and it seemed that your reputation would be forever PUSTULED AND SCROF-ULOUS itself from the association. Do you blame me, Jonny? Had I a choice? With Clyde's arms opened wide, his warm smile inviting me to share my life with one so kind and gay and morally unimpeachable?

For, yes, Clyde did treat me well. He gave me a beautiful little girl, Clydette. He gave me a spinet piano and a new living room suite with beautiful appointments. He never found need for the arms of other women.

He did, however, drink. Too much. He drank so much that his liver SHRIVELED UP AND DIED and he was forced to submit to an operation that would end his life after three short days, because the odds were too great that his body would ever accept a transplant from a monkey, much less a liver lifted from the body of a chimpanzee named BOPPO which Dr. Blanton confessed after the deed was done and the brown hepatic slab securely fixed in its new home, was a heavy drinker himself! Yes, my Clyde traded his cirrhotic human liver for an EQUALLY CIRRHOTIC PRIMATE ONE! Or perhaps one even more diseased than his own, for Boppo had a thirst for Brandy Melange that was nearly UNQUENCHABLE!

All this leaving me with a dead monkey-livered husband and murdered hope.

That is, until I read that you too had suffered tragedy and now lay sprawled single upon the marital bed. Until I came to know the hard facts about this bumpy road we call life. Facts acknowledged by us both. Fate has dealt each of us a losing hand, Jonny. But the game doesn't have to be OVER. We are permitted another deal, count on it. Yet we must move quickly. That quicksilver dealer of second chances will clear the table and depart if we tarry.

Shall we play that other hand? Shall I see you again, you successful entrepreneur, you! I have heard of your grand business plan. You will wave your magic wand in the marketplace and men will be wiped clean of the noisome odors of hard labor and sporadic ablutions, and I desire that a wand be waved over me as well. By your hand. Bringing me back THE LIFE I ONCE LIVED. When we were both young and you made me laugh and feel beautiful and much loved.

Am I wrong to write to you in this way? If so, please forgive my effrontery.

Yours,

Mildred

I have no way of knowing if Jonathan ever responded to her offer, even with only a polite decline. Mildred moved to Boston in the mid-twenties and lived there until her death in 1975 when she was struck by a school bus. Ironically, the fatal accident took place at the height of the citywide donnybrook over court-ordered bussing.

2. **Izzy and Moe shot straight with their new employee; he was hired because they thought the extra leg would bring in a few extra customers.** Several years later the Pettiville haberdashers would be famously confused with federal agents Izzy Einstein and Moe Smith who became celebrated during Prohibition for donning elaborate disguises to infiltrate speakeasies and bootlegging operations. As a result, Izzy Feldbaum received a bullet in the spleen courtesy of a Capone caporegime who had mixed up his Izzies. Unaware at the time that the attempt on his life had been a case of mistaken identity, Feldbaum told a reporter from his hospital bed, "If he wanted the suit, he should take the suit. What I need less is a hole in the kishke! " *Pettiville Press*, 22 July 1927.

3. **"I feel as if I have stepped into a deep furrow from which I cannot remove myself."** Working at the haberdashery for twelve hours a day in a struggling attempt to infuse operating capital into his parent's floundering farm left Jonathan fatigued, depressed, and more estranged than ever from the life that he had hoped to build for himself in the world outside of Pettiville. This low point in Jonathan's young life is articulated by the following entry from his diary.

August 15, 1909

Hee haw. Hee haw. I'm a work mule. A plow pony. A damned beast of burden, that's what I am. Mildred is married and Great Jane is a connubial impossibility and I see nothing on the horizon but nose-to-the-grindstone bachelorhood for me.

The silver lining: I am getting very good at selling. Suits and ties and shoes and spats. These days I can pretty much sell any fellow who walks into the store. In fact, there's only one person I can't sell: Father. And I'm not talking about clothes here. When it comes right down to it, Father's getting far too old to run that farm with so little help and with that fractured pelvis and I am just barely able to keep all of our heads above water, but will he listen to my pitch? If only I could make Mother and Father see that the best thing they should do now is liquidate the acreage and get themselves a nice little place in town. I'll be happy to help out as needed. Because I'll have no family of my own to place a drag on my income. Nose-to-the-grindstone bachelorhood for me. If that's my fate, I will reconcile myself to it.

Dr. Bloor would be sorely disappointed to hear what has become of me.

4. **"Izzie and Moe still won't give me a raise. I am going to look for work elsewhere."** Ibid., 15 October 1909.

5. **"Are you a hairy man?"** Jonathan noted in his diary (19 October 1909) that the interview for assembly line relief man at Pettiville's Sure-Fry Lard Works was one of the strangest encounters he'd ever had. He took pains to transcribe to the best of his recollection nearly the whole exchange.

JENKINS: Have a seat. Fritter biscuit?

JONATHAN: No thank you.

JENKINS: Crunkle cake, fresh from the vat?

JONATHAN: Thanks, but I'm not all that hungry.

JENKINS: Deep fried crackle crisp?

JONATHAN: I'm not sure I know what that is.

JENKINS: Shall we get down to business?

JONATHAN: Yes.

JENKINS: I don't beat around the proverbial bush. When I want to know something, I simply ask it.

JONATHAN: Go right ahead.

JENKINS: Are you a hairy man?

JONATHAN: Am I what?

JENKINS: A hairy man.

JONATHAN: Well, I—

JENKINS: I note a minimum of carpeting on your forearms. Does this indicate a lack of same upon other regions of your epidermis?

JONATHAN: I would suppose so.

JENKINS: That is unfortunate.

JONATHAN: I beg your pardon?

JENKINS: The fact that you are effeminately hairless.

JONATHAN: Perhaps I will grow more hair as I age. I am, after all, only twenty-one.

JENKINS: Yes. Hmm. There is that possibility. Though I must tell you, Mr. Blashette, that my preference is for the men who join this operation to have sufficient, well-established body hair.

JONATHAN: My father is somewhat hairy. Perhaps in time—

JENKINS: I'm afraid I need this position filled next week. (*A pause.*) There are, of course, ways for one to stimulate the growth of hair.

JONATHAN: Yes?

JENKINS: One proven method comes to mind. But there is a downside. On occasion, the hair growth is limited to the palms of the hands. And in some exceptional cases, one goes blind.

JONATHAN: I wouldn't want that, no.

JENKINS: Tripping and bumping into things. I'd have to keep you far away from the rendering room.

JONATHAN: I do think I would make a good employee, Mr. Jenkins, if only you could see your way to dismissing the fact that I am not an overly hairy man.

JENKINS: I'm sorry, Mr. Blashette, but that would be difficult. This is a factory of hirsute men and one Mrs. Beebe who joined us following a failed Rutgers pituitary experiment. You would not be happy among these people. You would inevitably be teased, taunted, perhaps even roughed up. And here I'm speaking only of Mrs. Beebe. It simply wouldn't be safe for you here.

JONATHAN: Could you not simply forbid your employees to go after me?

JENKINS: Lard men, Mr. Blashette, are hard men.

JONATHAN: Then, I assume this interview is over.

JENKINS: You assume correctly. By the way, would you know of someone with the requisite qualifications who might wish to apply for the position?

Jonathan's friend Toby "the Monkey Boy" Brancato was hired the very next day.

6. **Halley's hysteria was widespread.** Jonathan's exasperation over the paranoia that gripped Wilkinson County residents in the weeks leading up to the May, 1910, flyover by Halley's Comet is evident in this letter which Jonathan wrote to Great Jane on "the eve of the Great Apocalypse, May 17." (JBP.) I include it here in its entirety. It reflects Jonathan's growing impatience with "those trammeled by their own timidity" but also indicates Jonathan's growing bitterness and dissatisfaction with his own life.

May 17, 1910

Hawthorne Way
Pettiville

Dear Great Jane,

The citizens of this jerkwater Mongolian hamlet have decided that the world is about to end. It is the most ridiculous thing I have ever seen. In the face of all reason, they gather to make all right with God, to tearfully kiss their babies and hug their grannies good-bye, to sing their favorite hymns and eat up the best preserves from the fruit cellar, and I can't get anyone to wait on me at the five and dime because selling a tin of shoe polish means nothing compared to the destruction of this planet by poisonous cometic gases—sufficient reason, it would seem, to try to drink as many ice cream sodas as the human digestive tract can hold while customers in need of shoe polish who *don't* happen to believe that God is arriving tomorrow morning on the 6:07 must fend totally for themselves like I don't have better things to do with my time than walk through a store and claim items for myself without clerical assistance! I would be fired for treating my customers at Izzie and Moe's the way these apocalypse-obsessed imbecilic sales clerks treated me.

My parents are, thankfully, keeping their wits, although I can detect the occasional anxious thought percolating now and then, understandable when you consider that they are surrounded by men and women totally deficient in intelligence and possessed of not even the notochord of an embryonic mouse.

Yesterday I had the displeasure of talking seven men and women out of nailing themselves to crosses in a cotton field just north of town to wait Christ-like for what they believed would be the Second Coming, due to arrive in a cloud of comet dust. My exchange with these people went something like this:

ME: Hello there! What's with the crosses?

A LARGE, FURRY AGRICULTURAL SORT WHOM THEY CALL TUB: Where you been, son? The end is near!

ME: Right. But what's the reason for the crosses?

A TOOTHLESS AGRICULTURAL SORT WHOM THEY CALL LESTER: We will await our Lord and Savior in the manner in which He Himself was spirited to the arms of His Father.

ME: You're going to nail yourselves to these things?

AN EARNEST APRON-BEDECKED WOMAN WHOM THEY CALL EITHER BESS OR BETH (SEVERAL HAD CONFUSING LISPS): Yes. That is the plan.

ME: What about these little crosses?

TUB: They are for the children.

ME: Where are the children?

TUB: They require a bit more coaxing.

ME: And the tiny cross there?

BESS: I have a cat named Mr. Pink.

ME: So who goes first?

A GRIZZLED OLD MAN WITH A HUMP WHO I LATER LEARN IS NAMED PAPPY: We've drawn straws to decide.

TUB: Unfortunately, we can't tell which is the shortest of these two.

ME: Let me see. That was easy. *Here's* your winner.

TUB: Lester, this three-legged gentleman says you got the shortest straw. Pappy, we best get the hammer and commence to crucifyin'.

ME: What happens if the comet comes and goes and Jesus doesn't show up?

LESTER: If we're still alive and kickin', then I reckon we'd need someone to come get us all down. I also reckon the doctor would have to do himself some patchin' about our hands and feet.

DOC: Yup, I reckon I would.

ME: Here's a thought: maybe Jesus would prefer to find you all sitting quietly and without physical anguish in your parlors when He arrives.

BESS (nodding her head eagerly): That *is* a thought. Why, you know what? I could make Him lemonade. I couldn't make Jesus lemonade if I'm hangin' on that there cross, Lester.

LESTER: That's a right good point. Maybe we could study on it a spell.

In the end, even the cat was spared.

Your friend,

Jonathan

7. Lucile Moritz entered Jonathan's life through the peeled-back tarpaulin flap of a Chautauqua lecture tent. The lecture which brought Jonathan and Lucile together was delivered by a Professor Wilbert Wollensagen on the topic "Agronomy and Animal Husbandry in the Age of Industrial Encroachment" and included "a magic lantern slide show for illustration, and musical interludes provided by Judith Crevecoeur and her dwarf-harp." So instantly enamored of each other were Lucile and Jonathan that neither recalled much of the event beyond projected images of fruit flies and botflies and a gagging farm child who had apparently put one of the insects into his mouth. Jonathan's Diary, 4 June 1914.

Traveling tent Chautauquas were popular vehicles in the early 20th century for exposing nonurban communities to culture, intellectual thought, and the more refined performing arts. They also provided—as Jonathan and his new girlfriend, Lucile, were probably well aware—the opportunity for young men and women in such communities to meet and mingle outside the auspices of church and the socially regimented workplace. Indeed, for many of Jonathan's generation the word Chautauqua served as acronym for "*Clever, handsome and unambiguously tantalizing adults under-canvas quietly uniting anatomies.*" John B. Paperwhite, "Courting and Cavorting in Rural America," *Rustic Review* 17 (1975): 12-17, 72-79.

8. **"We spend long hours together working jigsaw puzzles...and doing other things."** Jonathan took an instant liking to the recently invented jigsaw puzzle and shared this interest with the new love of his life. Jigsaws would remain a favorite form of entertainment for him. He even carried a box in his "ol' kit bag" when he began his tour of duty for Uncle Sam in 1917. On those occasions during which things got quiet on the Western Front, Jonathan would pull out the box and try to scout a flat, clean surface upon which to reinstate the disassembled picture of a smiling Dutch school girl holding a bouquet of colorful tulips. He was rarely rewarded for his efforts; the pieces quickly became soiled and blood-blotted, a trench rat chewed a large hole in the box, and fellow doughboys made fun of him, calling him "Jigsaw Jugglehead." "It was a stupid idea," Jonathan later wrote to Lucile from the front, "but I did somehow finish those tulips." Ibid., 17 June 1914.

9. **"I will not rest until I am sent to the front."** This letter is typical of the more than forty earnest yet politely couched appeals Jonathan sent to various public officials and Army personnel in an attempt to overturn his disqualification from active duty in the First World War. The following, however, is a letter of a different sort, an unusual exception to the rule, submitted to demonstrate the degree of frustration Jonathan felt over not being able to pass muster for the muster. He later apologized for the harangue by sending its recipient a basket of fresh figs, following in the family tradition. JBP (carbon copy).

July 7, 1917

To Captain Reuben Milone
Draft Board

I beg you to reverse your decision regarding my suitability for service in the expeditionary force being assembled to fight in Europe. I was afforded not so much as an interview, receiving, as you must recall, the most cursory of visual inspections and a dismissal so preemptive that I was left brain-dazed from its celerity. In all my twenty-nine years I have never met a man so quick to prejudge another and so contemptuous of those who don't fit neatly into one's narrow concept of soldiering competency.

That very same day on which I was removed from any further consideration of my potential as infantryman, I learned that you had enthusiastically approved for active duty an obscenely obese baker with a maddening eye tic, three men wearing rouge and sequined pantlings, and a German-American youth who had just moments before his interview loudly professed his love for the Kaiser and his desire to sabotage whenever possible the efforts of the Allied armies to achieve victory and make the world safe for democracy. This was followed by a ditty that made my patriotic blood boil: "In my marrow I'm a Hun. Gonna have myself some fun. Shoot me a Yank, with a big ol' tank. Turn a doughboy into a hot crossed bun!"

You had no difficulty approving any of the afore-mentioned candidates for service. Why you would not afford me the same consideration I do not know, although I am tempted to attribute the fact to simple stupidity, your mother being a simian creature far down the evolutionary ladder, perhaps a rung very near the bottom just above the introduction of opposable thumbs.

With all sincerity,

Jonathan Blashette

10. **"Will somebody please enlist that courageous three-legged man before Colliers picks up the story and Pershing shits a brick?"** Newton Baker to Tasker Bliss, 17 July, 1917U.S. Defense Department Archives.

11. **"Now what do you want to go to that silly ol' war for?"** Lucile Moritz to Jonathan Blashette, 4 September 1917, JBP.

12. **"If you must go, I will be resigned, but I will miss you so."** Lucile Moritz to Jonathan Blashette, 15 September 1917, JBP.

13. **Each soldier was also provided a book of helpful French phrases.** In Jonathan's copy a few additional phrases have been scrawled on the blank last page. It is doubtful that he ever had the chance to use any of them. JBP, Ephemera Collection.

Monsieur le boucher, avez-vous un poulet qui n'est pas mort de la gale? Mr. Butcher, have you a chicken that didn't die of poultry mange?

Excusez-moi, mon ami le fermier français, mais y a t'il des Boches morts dans votre grenier? Excuse me, my French farmer friend, but there are dead Boche in your hayloft.

Je n'ai pas demandé si votre fille était une prostituée; j'ai demandé si cette prostituée était votre fille. I didn't ask if your daughter was a prostitute; I asked if this prostitute was your daughter.

Pouvez-vous nous diriger vers le front? Nous sommes perdus et tres saouls et plutôt gênés. Can you direct us to the front? We are lost and very drunk and somewhat abashed.

Votre char est sur mon pied. Your tank is on my foot.

Quelque chose a pondu des oeufs dans vos cheveux. Something has laid eggs in your hair.

Est-ce la puenteur de la guerre que je sens ou êtes vous tous français? Is that the stench of war or are you all French?

JBP, Ephemera Collection

14. **"I'm going to kill my sister."** Lucile had absolutely no control over her younger sister; Beryl would continue to write to Jonathan pretending to be Lucile until the end of the war. Jonathan got fairly good at distinguishing the counterfeit correspondence penned by Beryl from the legitimate letters written by Lucile, and even came to look forward to them as humorous diversion. What follows is one of Beryl's more obvious efforts at deception. JBP.

April 17, 1918

My dearest Jonathan,

I miss you so deeply that the pain of your absence has manifest itself in a palpable ache in the abdomen that results in frequent bouts of crumpled cramping. You would not wish to see me right now.

Toddy asked me again last night to accompany him to the new Arline Pretty/Douglas Fairbanks picture. I confess that this time I succumbed and accepted his offer. I know that you would object strenuously to the liberties he took with me in the darkened theatre, yet I hunger so much these days for the touch of a man—any man, for that matter—including, but not limited to Mr.

Pamida the unkempt ragman and his daft assistant Squib, and the offensive line of Devanter College's varsity football team.

I left the theatre on Toddy's arm, not because of any abiding affection for the gentleman but because I was undone. He had explored my body with his hands and mouth without intermission, finally leaving my bodice and undergarments in shameful dishabille. He then proceeded to take me to his lodgings on the outskirts of town where I was further disrobed and disgraced and where I do most grievously confess I came close to having my virtue fully compromised.

I must say, dearest Jonathan, that I am a woman whom you would do best to scorn and dismiss, having degraded myself not only with Toddy but with all manner of men, including, but not limited to, Teaseman the manure vendor and his grime-caked, toothless apprentice Happy, and the Wilkinson County Volunteer Fire Brigade.

I do not deserve you.

I suggest that you call on my beautiful and chaste sister Beryl when you return from war service. Beryl has never so much as been touched by a man save one accidental brushing of the hand by Mr. Withers who is forgiven on account of his blindness.

Yes, Beryl is the girl for you, my love. I will the bear the pain of the loss even as I continue to shamefully proclaim my hungry female body open to all comers.

With all sincerity,

Lucile

When Beryl realized that she was losing the battle to steal

Jonathan from her sister, her tactics became even more inventive. She stopped pretending to be Lucile and wrote to Jonathan under her own name. In the letter that follows, she makes one last desperate sortie to win the heart of her sister's boyfriend through pity alone.

October 14, 1918

Dear, dear Jonathan,

The doctor tells me I have only a few weeks to live. I have now gotten the dreaded Spanish flu not once or even twice but three wretched times. I am taxed to exhaustion and have lost weight, for I can keep nothing down but rice pudding and then only if the rice is removed. As I waste away to near invisibility I can only think of how much your presence at my bedside would rally me. If only I could look into your beautiful hazel eyes and be told that you cherish me with a love that far exceeds any love you have ever had for my libertine sister Lucile who as I write this is off with one among a host of young slacker suitors (for she so admires the ingenuity of those who dodge service to their country through feigned illness or pacifistic mollycoddledry).

Perhaps I will see you one last time before the veil is pulled permanently across my young life. Or I shall pray for a miracle—that your mere presence will snatch me from the abyss and my strength be restored in the warmth of your blazing smile. Soon, I pray, I will be gamboling about like a frisky fawn—gamboling with you, my love, with health returned and eternal happiness assured. A miracle it would surely be. And so I live on hope even as life slips out of me like sand from a splintered hourglass.

Get home safe.

Yours truly,

Beryl

15. "After a Chaplin one reeler came news from the front, followed by a two-hanky Gish blubbertale, interrupted by the spiel of one of those dreadful four minute men." In his letter to Jonathan, dated 16 October 1918 (JBP), former college chum and fervent socialist activist Findley Sanders described the theatre's four-minute man's pitch for war bonds as "absolute spread-eagle lunacy." Sanders, who, incidentally, would be arrested only one week later for his antiwar activities, reported that the war booster also urged his audience to give up hamburgers for the "duration" and send all the town dachshunds ("dog-huns") to the local abattoir. Sanders added with undisguised relish that one woman, an obvious inveterate dachshund-owner, made her opinion of this idea known by hurling a box of Cracker Jacks at the man, nearly putting his eye out. She was discourteously escorted from the theatre, and, no doubt, charged with "disloyalty and sedition."

Such was the climate of the times.

16. Jonathan struck up several friendships "over there." Some friendships endured for many years after the war. Others did not. Among the latter was his relationship with Arliss McKeon, whose incredible talent at least deserves brief mention here. Skilled at word-perfect textual recall, McKeon delighted and amazed his fellow doughboys before going on to enjoy several successful years on the Orpheum vaudeville circuit, declaiming as "Mr. Mnemonic" Lincoln's Gettysburg Address, Bryan's "Cross of Gold" speech, and hundreds of other orations he had committed to memory with apparently very little effort. Although he spent most of his later years as a rouged salon palaverer and social sycophant, McKeon continued to perorate from his repertoire right up to the moment of his death in 1972 at the age of 76. Awaiting the arrival of the ambulance following an ultimately fatal coronary arrest, McKeon is purported to have mumbled his way through a good portion of the notoriously lengthy thank-you speech given by Greer Garson at the 1943 Academy Awards banquet, as well as random sections of Richard Nixon's televised "Checkers" speech, his final breaths expelling the haunting words "respectable Republican cloth coat." Lynette Klein, *He Remembered It All* (San Francisco: Puppage and Sons Publishers, 1982) 378-80.

17. **Jonathan saw serious fighting in the last weeks of the war.** Jonathan Blashette to Addicus and Emmaline Blashette, JBP. The full text of Jonathan's letter home follows.

October, 1918

Dear Mother and Father,

I am writing you from the front. I'm not sure when this letter will reach you. We have had a time of it.

I miss you both. I miss dry socks. I miss clean drawers. I miss good eats. (We did finally get some chocolate bars yesterday courtesy of the Y.M.C.A. after a full week of rock-hard French bread, salmon and water.) They also sent along some cigarettes. Yes, Mother, I have begun to smoke. We all smoke. It is what you do here in the trenches. My buddy Max is the exception. Max lost his face yesterday. He offered me his fags as they were rolling him onto the stretcher. "I can't smoke these any more," he said, "because I have lost my mouth." Or maybe I imagined this is what he said. I imagine things a lot. I have not slept in days. The shelling doesn't stop. Whizz-bangs, 77's. The Whizz-bangs come in low. You can't get out of the way. The shrapnel can take an arm off. I can't even describe the concussion.

I am no coward, but this war is hard stuff. I try to think of things that will keep me sane. I try to think of the two of you, of sweet Lucile and funny, funny Beryl who wants me in the worst way! And I try to think how much I want to help win this thing and come home and never have to think of it again. A good buddy of mine was killed yesterday. A Heine sniper picked him off for doing nothing but taking himself a Goddamned stretch. (Mother, pardon moi my "parlez vous.") He wasn't thinking. You don't always think. Sometimes it can get you killed. Sometimes you get killed anyway. Every bullet has a name on it. Some of the bullets find their marks. I don't know if I've dodged mine yet or not.

I want to come back from this war. And all in one piece if that isn't asking for too much. (Unlike these other fellows, I could lose a leg and not be put out too much.) See, I want to start a business. You will laugh. This is the rankest-smelling place on the face of the earth. The stench of death gags you. The waft of mustard gas (even though we haven't faced a frontal assault of the damned stuff yet) makes you want to wretch. Unwashed humanity. B.O. with a capital B. The ladies have their perfumes and their rose water and their Mum-cream. I'm going to make something for the fellows. A deodorizer for the male underarm. That would be a good start, right? I told this to my chum Luddy. He says it's a dandy idea. I say that sounds like a swell name. Dandy. Dandy-de-odor-o.

Sarge says we'll be going over the top soon. There will be an end to this. One way or another.

Your loving son,

Jonathan

18. **"Seein's how they got all us doughboys to wearing those sissy wrist watches, maybe Jonny won't have such a tough time of it convincing us all to perfume our armpits."** Luddy Greco's Diary, 17 November 1918, private collection of the Sherman Greco family.

19. **"Now that the war is over, I have big plans."** Jonathan Blashette to Andrew Bloor, 19 November 1918, private collection of Bloor's grand-nephew Christopher Paton (hereafter referred to as AnB).

20. **Each took a different path.** Though the three trenchmates swore lifelong allegiance to one another, they would ultimately drift into orbits that rarely intersected. Reunited years later at the Bonus March on Washington, D.C., in 1932 (q.v.), the three men came to realize how far they had grown apart, and beyond memory of their crowded hour at Château-Thierry, how little they had in common. Luddy Greco heartily embraced socialism and, later, communism. Fate sent Darrell Delehanty to the opposite political extreme. Both of these men found easy reason to exercise strong suspicion and mistrust of one another, and of Jonathan as well. In Greco's mind, Jonathan had become capitalistic and bourgeois. Delehanty, who would become a rising star in the reinvigorated Ku Klux Klan of the 1920s, found Jonathan, conversely, far too progressive and much too embracing of the "intolerables" for his taste.

Incidentally, I discovered a document that sheds a bright light on Jonathan's strong distaste for the Klan: it is a transcript of an exchange between Jonathan and Imperial Kleagle Edward Y. Clarke, recorded from just outside the door to Clarke's office by Jonathan's friend and corporate lieutenant Harlan Davison. Jonathan had been directed to Clarke for purposes of making a sizable contribution to the Roosevelt Memorial Association (for which Clarke served as officer) and quickly found himself the target of a high-pressure sales pitch for membership in the KKK. True to form, Jonathan quickly shored up his composure, then proceeded to have great fun at Clarke's expense. Davison allegedly shared the transcript with Governor Al Smith during his 1928 run for the White House. Smith confessed to never having been so thoroughly entertained. Harlan Davison's Diary, Harlan Davison Papers (hereafter referred to as HD).

CLARKE: The structural organization is very simple if you'll follow along.

JONATHAN: Where are we going?

CLARKE: I'm going to explain how the Klan is organized so that you may have a better idea as to whether you may wish to become a member.

JONATHAN: I can be a member of both the Theodore Roosevelt Memorial Association and the Ku Klux Klan?

CLARKE: My dear sir, you may be a member of however many organizations you wish. That is entirely up to you.

JONATHAN: Including "Catholics and Jews for Miscegenation"?

CLARKE: I beg your pardon.

JONATHAN: How about "The N.A.A.W.S."?

CLARKE: "The N—Double A what?

JONATHAN: "The National Association for the Advocacy of White Slavery." I would prefer to serve on the Committee overseeing the surreptitious monitoring of the opium dens.

CLARK: Ho, ho, Mr. Blashette, you are pulling my leg.

JONATHAN: You can pull my legs too, but it might keep you busy for a while.

CLARKE: Ho, ho. Now if you'll follow this colorful chart I've set up.

JONATHAN: Did you say "colored" chart?

CLARKE: No, Mr. Blashette, I most certainly did not. Now, here at the bottom we have the Kleagles. The Kleagles are the rank and file of the organization. The foot soldiers, if you will.

JONATHAN: Yes, I see.

CLARKE: We have divided the country into "realms." And each realm is headed by a King Kleagle. And several realms constitute a "domain." The head of a domain is called a Grand Goblin.

JONATHAN: Sounds a little scary.

CLARKE: For a man with Negro blood, I would think so, ho ho.

JONATHAN: Who's this man standing all alone at the top of the pyramid?

CLARKE: That would be *me*, the Imperial Kleagle.

JONATHAN: You've been drawn to look like Teddy Roosevelt.

CLARKE: Have I now? Well, I must confess a certain fondness for President Roosevelt.

JONATHAN: So you asked your illustrator to make you look like him?

CLARKE: It's only a slight resemblance. I didn't think

anyone would mind.

JONATHAN: I don't recall that President Teddy Roosevelt ever endorsed your organization, Mr. Clarke. What's more, I recall that he invited Booker T. Washington, a man of African descent, to have dinner with him at the White House.

CLARKE: It was no dinner, sir. I believe that Teddy and Mr. Washington merely had a hasty sandwich in the scullery.

JONATHAN: That isn't what I heard. Furthermore, I understand that the two men shared a fruit cup following a confusion of spoons that very well could have resulted in the bringing to the president's lips of a utensil that had been thoroughly licked by a blatantly colored tongue.

CLARKE: That is preposterous.

JONATHAN: (interrupting) And at one point…

(*The voices now begin to break and grow in volume as Jonathan is clearly being led to the door to be expelled.*)

CLARKE: I will hear no more of this.

JONATHAN: Alice, the president's mischievous daughter, climbed into Mr. Washington's Negro lap and pretended to be a ventriloquist's dummy.

CLARKE: THAT, SIR, IS AN OUTRAGEOUS MENDACITY!

8

HOW YOU GONNA KEEP HIM
DOWN ON THE FARM?

1. **"Even a week in this ridiculous quarantine was too long."** Jonathan's Diary, JBP. Although Jonathan spent only eight days in the cave, a number of other Pettivillians passed a good part of the autumn and winter of 1918-19 there. True, none of these apocalypse-minded Arkansans caught the dreaded Spanish flu, a pandemic that was hitting this part of the state just as brutally as it was the rest of the world, but many of those who retreated into the cave did endure nasty bouts of scabies as well as the tyranny of Rance Chesler who installed himself as "Cavern King" and issued edicts from his stalagmite throne.

The bizarre tale of this fascinating chapter in Arkansas history is documented in Donna Krell's self-published, yet finely written *Dwellers of the Night: the Story of the Flu Dodgers of 1918-1919* (1993). Curiously, though, Krell chose to engage her daughter Jacinth as illustrator. The stick figures offered by the seven-year-old do not enhance the text, and in some ways detract from it. By way of example, in Chapter 7, as Krell explores the regrets of some of the cavern-dwelling expatriates who articulate their longing for the salubrious light and warmth of the sun, Jacinth offers a group of stick men and women wearing large and irrelevant orange fright wigs, eating multicolored peas.

2. **Lucile took the pledge.** Lucile Moritz like many members of her generation took "the pledge" when she was very young. It went something like this:

I pledge that I may give my best to home and country. I

promise, God help me, not to buy, drink, sell, or give alcoholic liquor while I live. From all tobacco and other harmful things I'll abstain and never take God's name in vain.

Maura Hester, *Love Interminable or Till Death We Shall Not Part: Fifty Great Enduring Love Affairs* (Savannah: Bookmirth Publications, 1975), 47-52.

Her sister Beryl took the pledge as well, but broke nearly every clause on the same day, December 5, 1933—the day Prohibition ended—declaring at a St. Louis speakeasy turned "speakfreely":

Make mine a double, wouldja, barkeep? Hoo! Hoo! Drought's over, boys! Hey, handsome, gimme a Goddamned light.

Bowie French, *How Dry I Am: an Oral History of Prohibition* (Cicero, Illinois: Luck Be a Lady Press, 1947), Preface.

3. **"Will You Marry Me?"** Jonathan Blashette to Lucile Moritz, 24 December 1918, carbon copy, JBP.

4. **"Yes, oh yes, I will be your wife, my Christmas angel!"** Lucile Moritz to JB, 26 December 1918, JBP.

5. **When Lucile did not show up, Aunt Evelyn became worried.** Evelyn Waldron was very close to the "good niece," having served as surrogate mother to both Lucile and her scheming sister Beryl. According to Evelyn's account of the harrowing week that followed, when Lucile failed to arrive at her "Gloucester, Massachusetts retreat" to receive prenuptial pampering and trousseau selection assistance from Evelyn, Jonathan was notified and put directly on the case. He immediately alerted law enforcement authorities all the way from New York City to Gloucester of Lucile's disappearance. In the meantime, Evelyn fell into a morass of fear and agitation and eventually had to be sedated. The

initial anodyne was administered by a Madame Lourdes, a French holistic whose herbs did little more than make Evelyn "feel a little droopy." A second physician was brought in and Evelyn was successfully tranquilized and received the horrendous news in a dull stupor. Interview with Paulette Poole (great niece of Lucile and Beryl Moritz), November 22, 2001.

6. **"Yes, we have a sticky Jane Doe."** It was Jonathan who correctly identified the molasses-covered body. No one can say why Lucile ventured to Commercial Street in Boston's North End while awaiting her train connection to Gloucester on that deadly day in January. But there she was, just as the Purity Distilling Company's huge cast-iron tank burst open and the great swell of raw molasses—more than 2.5 million gallons of it—gushed forth, drowning twenty-one and turning the city of Boston into sickeningly sweet-smelling flypaper for weeks. Patrick Oldeman, *Tears for the Shawmut* (Boston: Old Corner Book Printer, 1995), 223-228.

7. **There was a lacuna in the Luna.** I discovered the full text of the expurgated material from the January 16, 1919, edition of the *Boston Luna* in the paper's morgue.

As Promised: Our Annual Boston Beans Recipe

Nobody knows beans like Boston knows beans.

Soak **1 1/2 cups dried beans**

Cover the beans with water. Bring them to a boil. Simmer them slowly for thirty minutes or more, until tender.

Prepare your oven.

Drain the beans, setting aside the cooking water.

Add:

1/2 cup chopped onion

2 tablespoons or more of dark *molasses* (author's emphasis)

1 tablespoon dry mustard

2 or 3 tablespoons of catsup

1 teaspoon salt

1/2 cup boiling bean water

Place the ingredients in a greased baker. Attend them with:

1/2 lb. sliced salt pork

and bake them at low heat for 6 to 9 hours. If they become dry, add a little

set aside bean water.

Uncover the beans for the last hour of baking.

Mention of the molasses might have been withdrawn but the recipe would certainly have suffered.

8. **Jonathan failed to see the black humor of it.** Nor would he permit anyone to speak of the freak accident that took his precious Lucile from him. It was not until Jonathan had reached his seventy-second year that he finally allowed himself to appreciate the cruel yet cosmically humorous irony of it all. Lucile had fought hard for prohibition. Within a year of her death, rum would become illegal. The Purity Distilling Company would no longer be allowed to turn its vats of molasses into the demon potable. And yet, it was a well-recognized ingredient of rum itself that had

taken a deadly-aimed preemptive shot at Lucile and her temperance crusade. As he approached the end of his own life Jonathan finally allowed himself a good laugh and a good cry and then drank a toast with his manservant Uriah to the memory of his beautiful Lucile. Appropriately, they drank rum. Maura Hester, *Love Interminable*, 55-58.

Postcript: I have no record that Beryl renewed her efforts to win Jonathan's heart, damaged as it was by the loss of Lucile. I note that shortly before Lucile's death Beryl had begun to see a man named Runstein who manufactured anatomically correct articulated mannequins and wooden darning eggs, and was apparently quite devoted to her.

9. **"Our broadcloth patterned dress shirts are over here and thank you for the compliment and no I do not have plans for lunch."** So smitten was Jonathan with the perky little sales clerk in Men's Furnishings at Rosenwasserberg's— downtown Pettiville's very first "full service department store"—that he made daily trips to the store to purchase all manner of men's clothing and accessories, including at least two gold-filled dress sets which he neither needed nor could afford. It therefore came as a blow to Jonathan to learn of Tulip's sudden marriage to Ambless dental student Newbold Osbert. The news may have precipitated his hasty move to New York City a short time later. The cold shoulder he received from his forsaken former employers Izzy and Moe didn't help. Jonathan's Diary, 3 November 1919.

10. **"The bad news of the week is that Tulip and I will no longer be dating."** Ibid., December 10, 1919. The good news was that Ford had just come out with automatic starters for its model T's.

11. **"She left me something to remember her by."** When Jonathan made his permanent move to New York City in early 1920, he carried the poem with him. As it disintegrated

with time and wear, he admitted that simply touching the paper-dust remnant at the bottom of his pocket would conjure up memory of "that pretty little pixie" Tulip McTigue. The text of the poem follows.

Yet Roses Bloom Still in Fields of Woe
by
McDonald Bowling

Even in fields of woe,
Bloom roses still!
Joyful scent revive in me
Some soft rememb'r'd thing.
O!
Halcyon days,
Fragrant days of youth —
Fleeting, fading.
Memory rush of garden promenading.
Tears of loss:
Wash and cleanse.
As I gently touch the rim-hem of that sweet
rememb'r'd thing.
Of that moist, supple,
Peach prim,
Pastwastard.

The poem is obviously marred by Bowling's use of the neologism *pastwastard*. Bowling himself regretted its employment, noting in chatty letters to his urologist (Byron Blackfoot: *Confessions to a Pee Pee Doctor* [Portsmouth, New Hampshire: Towler Press, 1989]) that it was never his intention to include it, but "sometimes you just do a thing, knowing it is wrong, inappropriate, senseless or patently moronic. Like when you eat a piece of fish that clearly isn't fresh or when you admit to a crime you didn't commit." On March 16, 1932, the sixty-three-year-old poet was executed for the murder of Libby Morgan, a woman he had clearly never even met.

12. **"Come to New York."** After learning that his aged father was barely making ends meet by working part time as a moonshine "still basher" in the Ozarks, Jonathan wrote to his mother (13 May1920, JBP), begging her to move the two of them to New York City where Jonathan was certain that his salary as a waiter at a midtown Childs Restaurant would be sufficient to support the three until Addicus could find work locally. Although the letter was never received, we know that it was sent because it turned up in the mailbox of one Atticus Bouchard in Pettiville, Alabama, a philatelist who kept it for the stamp on the envelope: a rare Benjamin Franklin misprint—one of only eight in existence. The image is familiar to most stamp collectors and is valued even more than the coveted "Inverted Jenny." Franklin's mouth is missing and he has apparently been given Thomas Jefferson's hair. Under "U.S. Postage" are the additional words, "U.S. Pastwastard."

13. **"His name is Rodolfo Alfonzo Raffaelo Pierre Filibert Guglielmi di Valentina d'Antonguolla."** Jonathan's Diary, 14 July 1920. Jonathan and the superfluously named Italian-American taxi cab driver were to spend the next several hours together, drinking Allash Kummel and crème de bananes. Although neither was successful in concocting a perfect screen name for the Hollywood-bound cabby who ultimately became Rudolph Valentino, or an eye-catching alternative name for Jonathan's forthcoming deodorant venture (Jonathan was waffling over "Dandy-de-odor-o"), their lists of possibilities for both were varied and colorful, and became even more so as the evening wore on and the men became increasingly intoxicated. There is no evidence to confirm the rumor that the sexually ambivalent Valentino asked Jonathan to share his bed for the night, although

Jonathan, his heterosexual libido perhaps slightly compromised by excessive alcohol intake, did note in his diary that the young man was "too beautiful to be a man, and certainly too beautiful to be driving livery for a living. I wish him well in his film career, and especially in his efforts to get that meandering birth name of his down to a manageable moniker." One wonders if Valentino would have enjoyed the same level of popularity and acclaim had his name been drawn from Jonathan and Rudolph's brainstormed catalogue of possibilities. Box 17, Ephemera: napkins, JBP.

Phil Le'Pierre

Anton Antonioni

Rod Pierre d'Anton

Fonzie Filbert

Jugs Valentine

Ralph Ruggles

Tony Diggs

Gig Frogg

Gorgonzola Antonguolla

Valentino Gofisho

Filbert McNutt

Giggles McGrin

Wallace Beery

Fonzie Fondolfo Fonzarelli

Fluffy Bobo Googoo

Boo Boo Fuzzy Moo Cow III

Among the names the two concocted for Jonathan's startup male deodorant company were:

Stench-not

M' Good Man

Armpit Fresh

Banish

B.O. Blockade

Onslaught

Honey Pits

Whifft

Male-odoro

~~*Corsair*~~*

Scent O' Brawn

Ollie's Factory

Derma-scent for Men

Smell Me Now

* Struck through, perhaps due to its similarity in pronunciation to "Coarse hair"

14. **The death of his mother hit him hard.** Less credible are other stories that circulated at the time, including one that had Jonathan spending long nights staring at his mother's photograph and singing softly the lullabies she taught him in his youth, including a gentler version of a traditional favorite. JBP.

Rockabye baby
In the tree top.
When the wind blows

The cradle will rock.
When the bough breaks
The cradle takes wing
And flies through the winter,
And flies through the spring,
And sets itself down
In the room which you see,
To be near to your Daddy
And near, dear, to me.

15. **Addicus had no choice in the matter.** The conversation as remembered by Jonathan's Aunt Delilah proceeded as follows:

JONATHAN: Father, I'm going back to New York City.

ADDICUS: I'll miss you, son.

JONATHAN: No you won't. You're coming with me.

ADDICUS: I'm not so sure that would be a good idea.

JONATHAN: Mother has gone to be with Jesus. The bank is about to foreclose on the farm. I'm going to start a business in New York. I think you'll be happy there too.

ADDICUS: I've got Arkansas in my blood, son.

JONATHAN: Aunt Delilah, maybe you can talk some sense into him.

DELILAH: Addicus, you go on with Jonathan now. It's for the best. There's nothing keeping you here and it would be nice for you and Jonathan to be together.

Here Delilah's recollections become slightly suspect.

DELILAH (continued): Now, have we settled the

matter? Good. Now, look at my face. People tell me I have a lovely smile. Should I believe them?

ADDICUS: You've always had a beautiful smile, Delilah. And you wear your clothes like a Parisian.

DELILAH: I do, don't I?

JONATHAN: You definitely got the looks in this family, Aunt Delilah.

ADDICUS: *And* the brains.

DELILAH: You stop it right this instant! You're making me blush!

Delilah Blashette Frost, *Scribblings and Babblings* (privately produced mimeograph, 1944). Used by permission of Frost's great-granddaughter Glynnis Kingston in exchange for my noting here that Glynnis, in addition to writing trenchant women's pieces, creates customized wall hangings and has a lovely professional singing voice that has a slightly feline quality, which makes it appropriate for cat litter commercial jingles. She can be reached via her representatives Michele G. Rubin or Nadia Grooms at Authors Hut LLC, 2121 West 26th Street, New York City 10010.

16. **"Childs has taken me back on as waiter and even given me a raise!"** Jonathan's Diary, 31 May 1921, JBP.

17. **She was a dead ringer for Great Jane.** Glover drops the ball with a giant thud here. The short paragraph in his book devoted to Jonathan's association with Kissy Valentine is based solely upon conjecture. He apparently doesn't bother to look at Jonathan's journal entries for the period and seems unaware of the existence of Kissy's lengthy diary, which was published in 1987 by Man Love Press as *Kissy Tell*. Glover was apparently so uncomfortable writing about the

relationship that he painted it with as few brushstrokes as possible. For a biographer usually given to breathless literary hyperbole, he is here emotionally uninvested and descriptively spare.

> *While working at Childs, Jonathan briefly dated a woman named Kissy Valentine who he said reminded him of his former girlfriend Great Jane. Kissy and Jonathan subsequently found themselves incompatible and parted as friends. Kissy went on to a career on the stage. Her favorite soup was potato leek.*

Glover makes no mention of the fact that the incompatibility had much to do with the fact that Kissy Valentine was, in actuality, Wade Kissman, a transvestite and Childs regular who fell in love with Jonathan and who, after revealing her true gender to him, was heartbroken by his inability to reciprocate the affection. Glover is correct when he states that the two remained friends and that Kissy went on to a theatrical career (although technically, as Tallulah Bankhead's dresser, she never appeared on the boards), but he misses a prime opportunity to explore the complexity of Jonathan's ambivalent feelings. Jonathan's diary entry for June 17, 1921, the day of the breakup, is quite illuminating.

> *Kissy is a man! I guess I suspected it all along. But maybe I didn't want to accept it. I did have strong initial feelings, I will admit it. Feelings that, truth be told, haven't disappeared entirely. I want no physical relationship with Kissy/Wade—that is for certain. And yet I am still drawn to the warmth and joy I feel when I am around her. (I still can't stop thinking of him as a her!) It is the damnest thing! Kissy asked me if I loved her. I said, "Not in the way you want me to, but that doesn't mean we can't remain friends." This made Kissy cry. She cried while I waited on tables 17, 21 and 23. Then while I was giving table 27 a coffee refill, the cops came gangbusting in for their weekly*

raid. As per their usual, they hauled off a bunch of the fairy-regulars, including poor Kissy and her "girlfriends" Miss Gloria Swan Song, Is-a-whora Duncan and Nastymova. As per my usual, I contributed to the waiter kitty to bail them all out.

9

THE SWEET SMELL OF SUCCESS

1. **It was a sizable investment.** We can only guess at the identity of the mysterious benefactor. I am inclined to believe it was J. P. Morgen who twenty years earlier had been suspected of having paid Jonathan's legal fees in the lawsuit filed to free him from his indentureship with the Grund Traveling Circus and Wild West Show. In the interim, Morgen had significantly increased his financial holdings through shrewd wartime investments and successful stock and bond trades. There was another reason why the Arkansas businessman might have been a prime candidate to loan start-up capital for Dandy-de-odor-o, Inc.: Morgen suffered from a severe form of bromhidrosis that left him virtually friendless, often emptied corporate board rooms, and on one occasion cleared out a well-attended stockholders' meeting, the hall subsequently requiring fumigation. A strong affinity by Morgen for such a venture would not be an implausibility. One wonders at the same time if Jonathan's battlefield inspiration for Dandy-de-odor-o might have been antedated by a hospital visit from the aromatic businessman on the eve of the boy's scheduled operation, a half-forgotten memory later revived—as olfactory memories often are—as fresh and aromatic as the day of their birth.

For a different opinion, consider Glover and Furman's theory that the money for Jonathan's start-up company came from his academic mentor Andrew Bloor. They posit that Bloor may very well have inherited some of his uncle's estate following the old man's death during the Spanish Flu Pandemic of 1918. There would be some truth to this if Bloor's uncle Cleve MacDougal had, in fact, passed away. (The Spanish Flu was notorious for sparing the very young and the very old, a phenomenon that baffles scientists to this day.) Apparently, neither Glover nor Furman read the *Carpentertown (Arkansas) Gazette's* retraction of MacDougal's obituary. I include it here.

Correction.

We regret to note that the obituary for Mr. Cleve MacDougal that ran in yesterday's paper was published prematurely. Mr. MacDougal is not dead, nor has he ever been dead. He was taken ill with the flu but he is most decidedly on the mend. He wishes everyone to know that he should be up to entertaining visitors by the end of the week and that his sizable estate is still "up for grabs," so all potential heirs are admonished to be on their best behavior.

2. **Jonathan hired him on the spot.** Chief chemist Hiram Diles would remain employed for the next forty-two years in Dandy-de-odor-o's Research and Development Division.

3. **Jonathan hired him half way through the interview.** Chief financial officer Charleton Caldwell would remain a part of the Dandy-de-odor-o corporate family for the next forty-five years.

4. **Jonathan hired him after several months of harassing phone calls, an extensive letter-writing campaign and at least one episode of drunken stalking.** Ironically, it was Harlan Davison who was to become Jonathan's most trusted lieutenant and, in time, his best friend. In his letter to his sister Shirley Watkins, written several months after he was brought on board (19 November 1922, HD), Davison states as much. An excerpt follows.

After several months of harassing phone calls, an extensive letter-writing campaign (please thank all your third graders for their efforts) and at least one sad episode I will not go into here, I am once more a soldier in the army of the employed. I am quickly earning Mr. Blashette's trust and am growing more and more confident that the company will be my home for many years to come. You need worry no longer about your wayward, rudderless younger brother.

5. **Davison was related to Carry Nation.** Griswold Lanham, "Harlan Davison: the Three-legged Business Marvel's Right-Hand Man," *Journal of Entrepreneurial History* 13 (1990): 25-42. In an amazing historical coincidence, Davison was also related to Reid Lowell, the only saloon owner who succeeded in a counteroffensive against Mrs. Nation's reign of terror. While Nation was off on a road trip, taking her whacks at a new crop of demon "rummy houses," Lowell visited Nation's own home and chopped into fine kindling most of its Adirondack porch and lawn furniture with his own sharply whetted hatchet. Pinned to the resultant wreckage was a note that read, "Like you, Mrs. Nation, I did this stone sober. Unlike you, I shall now go and have myself a pint to celebrate."

6. **Bardock joined the firm in the summer.** The name of Jonathan's new accountant was originally Joseph Berdache. When Joseph was six years old, his father was informed by a family friend, a linguist, that Berdache literally meant, "homosexual, cross-dressing American Indian male." A legal name change was immediately petitioned for all members of the family. Ellery Reinhold, *The Story of Dandy-de-odor-o, the Little Company That Could...and Then Did* (New York: Christopher Street Press, 1972), 99.

7. **"Today I introduced Jonny to Winny. It was an instant match."** Davison had known artist Winny Wieseler since the two were kids. His journal entry for the day goes on to say:

I hardly needed to say a word beyond the briefest of introductions. She looked at him and he looked at her and she looked at his third leg and he looked down at his third leg and then up at her and she met his eyes with hers and smiled one of those big goofy Winny smiles and I knew instantly that he knew that this wasn't going to be a problem and he smiled with obvious relief—one of those crooked, face-scrunching Jonathan Blashette grins and then they fell into a conversation originally about beer nuts which I had put out in a bowl on the table but then about everything under the sun and the conversation continued through the afternoon and into the evening and perhaps even well into the wee small hours of the morning (I excused myself after an hour or so). It is an amazing and wonderful thing to see two dear friends hit it off so easily and so completely. I will be patting myself on the back over this one for months to come.

Davison's Diary, 6 January 1923.

8. **"I think she's the finest girl I ever met...and she even likes jigsaw puzzles."** I bow to Lana Leggio, who, in her biography of Winny, *Winsome Winny* (Springfield, Massachusetts: Cohpannamo Books, 1958) evocatively describes the reasons for the attraction:

Jonathan was quite taken with Winny. And it wasn't simply the fact that she loved and accepted him as he was. He embraced everything about her—her commitment to progressive causes (women's rights, abolition of child labor, prison reform), her highly evolved taste in art and music, and her colorful, sustaining friendships. As Winny Wieseler evolved from shy country girl to a thoroughly modern force of nature, Jonathan Blashette eased back and enjoyed the ride, content to let this new and—he hoped—permanent love of his life navigate the couple's destiny—a destiny lovingly shared, its catapult sprung

from the shimmy and shake of those wild, reckless, wacky,
and feckless 1920s.

Nothing sums up better the winning wit and whimsy of
Winny Wieseler than her parody of Edna St. Vincent
Millay's poem "My Candle Burns."

My ice cream cone drips at both ends;

It will not last this heat;

But ah my tummy, and oh my tongue—

It tastes so good to eat!

9. **Winny demonstrated her propensity for protest even as
an outwardly timid and withdrawn young girl.** Safe and
secure behind the private fortress of her correspondence,
Winny pulled no punches, as this, one of many angry letters
she dashed off to those public figures who raised her
youthful hackles, will attest.

March 18, 1907

Dear Ex-President Cleveland,

Today you said that sensible and responsible women do
not want to vote. You said that God in his infinite
wisdom had worked out a social and political hierarchy
with men on top.

Mr. Cleveland, I am only eleven years old but I am old
enough to know that you are a fat, stupid man who
would do well to keep his stupid, fat-headed opinions to
himself.

The day will come when bloated, bullying men like
yourself will be forced to give way to women of wisdom
and fair-mindedness who will take this country in the

right direction.

In the meantime I will continue to remind men like you that such pronouncements make you appear ever the more stupid.

Sincerely,

Winny Wieseler

PS. May I have a picture of you for my scrapbook? Thank you.

There is no evidence that the former president ever responded. Ibid., 14-15.

10. **She was a talented artist, to boot.** Winny was so heavily influenced by the first International Dada Fair in Berlin in 1920 that she immediately framed her next protest for mixed media. Her piece, "Tramp, Tramp, Tramp," displayed at the Günther Gallery in Philadelphia in 1921, depicted a shellacked foot, described by Winny as "a symbol of the downtrodden, trampled upon by those of pride and privilege. I want people to see the foot and think of Sacco and Vanzetti who have feet of their own but who also have hands and hearts and lungs and want nothing more than use those lungs to breathe free and to use their feet to stand tall and unflattened by the boot of corporate greed." The foot on display was Winny's. Literally. She lost interest in the project after two exhausting days of standing behind a black curtain with her right unshod and shellacked foot exposed and extended out upon a pedestal, an inviting target for spitballs and mischievous feather tickles. Ibid., 143-47.

11. **Jonathan was no fan of Coolidge, whom he found to be far too "lazy faire."** Winny expressed similar distaste for the new president in letters she exchanged with Jonathan while on holiday in Cuba with her spinster aunts. Winny's

antipathy for Coolidge had formed a few months earlier when, as vice president, he had accused women's colleges of being hotbeds of Bolshevism. One imagines that the following letter, written on the day after the president's swearing in (August 3, 1923), was received with a nod and a smile. Jonathan Blashette to Winny Wieseler, Wieseler Estate.

Dear Winny,

The invisible vice president is now the invisible president. I understand he was at his father's farm in Vermont when he got the news of Harding's demise. He was supposedly roused from a deep sleep. (Which raises the question: how does one know the difference between Coolidge awake and Coolidge asleep?) Here is how I imagine the conversation went.

SHERIFF: Mr. Coolidge, Senior. I am sorry to disturb you at this hour.

OLD MAN COOLIDGE: What time is it?

SHERIFF (consulting his watch): 7:45.

OLD MAN COOLIDGE: Botheration! Well, we're all up now. What brings you here, Sheriff?

SHERIFF: Is your son—?

COOLIDGE (coming down the stairs, rubbing his eyes like a groggy toddler): Yes, I'm here, Sheriff. What is it?

SHERIFF: I have some grave news, sir. The President is dead.

COOLIDGE: President Harding dead? It is unthinkable.

(A long pregnant silence passes as all parties contemplate

what this means.)

OLD MAN COOLIDGE: I suppose we should make things legal, son. Where's the family Bible?

(The father administers the oath of office to the son. The father is a notary public. The son is now *officially* the President of the United States.)

OLD MAN COOLIDGE: Will there be anything else, Sheriff?

SHERIFF: I suppose not.

OLD MAN COOLIDGE (glancing out the window): The secret service men are mashing my pansies.

SHERIFF: Yes, I see them. I will ask them to move. Goodnight, Mr. Coolidge. Goodnight, Mr. President.

COOLIDGE: Good night, Sheriff.

(The sheriff leaves. Father and son sit for a moment in silence.)

OLD MAN COOLIDGE: I forgot to mention: the vet came to see Bessie today.

COOLIDGE: Teat still inflamed?

OLD MAN COOLIDGE: Not so much as before.

(President Coolidge nods. Another silence.)

OLD MAN COOLIDGE: Cup of Ovaltine?

(President Coolidge shakes his head.)

COOLIDGE: Best be getting back to bed, Pa.

OLD MAN COOLIDGE: Best you should. Long day

tomorrow.

COOLIDGE: Ayah. Good night, Pa.

OLD MAN COOLIDGE: Good night, son.

It should be an interesting eighteen months...if I can stay awake. I miss you.

Love,

Jonathan

12. Jonathan postponed the road trip to follow the Scopes Trial. Incidentally, a second, less publicized "monkey trial" docketed to get under way in Dawes Forge, Tennessee, on August 1 was to have included a brief appearance by William Jennings Bryan dressed in an ape suit. Out of respect for the family of Bryan, who, having concluded his prosecution of the Scopes case, promptly dropped dead of a heart attack, the judge granted both sides a continuance and forbade any references to Bryan or to monkeys at the trial. The case, in fact, never came to trial. Charges were dropped against the town's young evolution-teaching high school biology teacher, Miss Clorinda Pernell, who promised to leave all mention of apes out of her classroom lectures in exchange for either a black Alaskan seal fur coat or an ermine with sable collar. The school board called her bluff and delivered her first choice, tied up with a big pink bow. So attached was Miss Pernell to the coat, that she was known to wear it year-round even as it became threadbare and she a sad, heavily perspiring remnant of her former self. Tightly swagged in the thick coat, she died of heatstroke during the heat wave of 1937. Sporting a thick moustache from an untreated hormone imbalance, Miss Clorinda Pernell, in the end, evolved into a life-drained replica of those very apes to which she had linked us all. A family court order prevented the Dawes Forge Anthropological Museum and Arboretum from installing her embalmed body in its new Primate Display (Miss Clorinda Pernell having sold rights to her corpse to the museum in this last year of her life to feed an obsession for rose water parfum).

13. **U.S.A.: Union of Simian Anarchy.** Jonathan's West Greenwich Village neighbor Cabe Knudsen errs when he decries "monkey trials all over the country." I have found evidence of only these two, in addition to a somewhat heated exchange involving two divinity students in Normal, Illinois, which ended when one of the two young men tried to put out the eye of the other with the business end of a roasting fork. An interesting footnote to a footnote: Cabe Knudsen was deported three months after this conversation following another nationwide sweep for potential anarchists. He claimed Tahiti as his country of origin and happily spent the remainder of his life there, serving for a time as curator of the Gauguin Museum of Art. Knudsen may be familiar to some art scholars as the man who dared to answer Gauguin's haunting "Where Do We Come From? What Are We? Where Are We Going?" His responses respectively: "Stupid Little Monkeys. Stupid Little Monkeys. To the zoo."

14. **"There sat Aimee Semple McPherson, coifed in her signature bob."** If the event were true, it would have constituted one of the most bizarre in Jonathan's life. I haven't found evidence that a single contemporary of Jonathan's assistant Davison believed his story, and Jonathan's diary, tellingly, is silent on the alleged meeting. Davison was apparently acquainted with a female acolyte of the evangelist who committed suicide when McPherson disappeared and was originally feared drowned, a fact that could very well go to plausible motive for Davison's concocting the story that clearly paints the popular

revivalist as liar and schemer and fully disputes her claim that she had been kidnapped and tortured. (She was allegedly burned with a cigar on her knuckles.) I found the following account among the notes Davison had made for an unfinished memoir he was writing at the time of his death in 1971. HD.

I spied her in a dark corner of the hotel dining room. There she sat, coifed in her signature bob. I nudged Jonny and whispered, "The woman in the corner, do you see?"

Jonny peered and nodded. "It's Aimee Semple McPherson. Perhaps her kidnappers allow her to come down to the dining room to take her meals."

"What should we do?"

"Why don't we go over and ask her what's what?"

Jonny, like me, had little patience for women who pretend to be kidnapped and get everybody on the West Coast in a lather over it.

McPherson saw us coming and looked a little unnerved. We had her cornered.

"Excuse me," Jonny says. "Are you the famous, allegedly kidnapped evangelist Aimee Semple McPherson?"

"No, I am not."

She took out a compact and began to powder her nose, hoping, I would suppose, that we would simply go away.

"I must say that you bear a very strong resemblance to the woman," Jonny pursued.

"People tell me that. Now if you don't mind—"

To my surprise, Jonny sat down. Taking his lead, I pulled up a chair and did the same.

"Excuse me, but you are not welcome at this table. I wish to be alone."

"Why did you do it?" Jonny asked, relentless.

"I don't know what you're talking about," she said, nervously. The woman appeared quite undone by our visit. She had powdered her nose to such point that she now resembled a Geisha.

"What if I were to put it thusly?" Jonny replied. "Let's suppose you were Aimee Semple McPherson, what would you guess would be the reason you would be sitting in this dining room eating—what is that?"

"It's pâté of braunschweiger with capers. Would you like a nibble?"

It appeared that she was now attempting to win her release through forced hospitality.

Jonny declined. I took a bite. It tasted like liver cheese.

"Let's say that I am who you say I am—the world-famous founder of the International Church of the Foursquare Gospel."

"Throw out the lifeline," Jonny sang.

Aimee smiled. "Yes, that Aimee Semple McPherson. Let us say that I were she. Well, wouldn't you think I would be entitled to a vacation? It's exhausting work healing cripples all day. Sometimes you think they're totally healed and they start to walk toward you and then they fall flat onto their poor, generally homely faces, and you must return them to their wheelchairs or whatever jerry-

rigged contraptions they have assembled to move them about because they're too poor to afford a decent conveyance. Well, wouldn't I be entitled to a few weeks rest and relaxation here in Carmel? If only for all those tens of thousands of passports I've stamped for entry into the kingdom of gold and myrrh?

Jonny was about to respond but I was too quick: "A young girl killed herself when she thought you had drowned."

"I suppose the poor young thing wanted to join me at the Gates of Heaven."

"But you aren't there."

"Well, I admit, she'd be in for a little bit of a wait."

"Are you aware that two men also died—trying to 'rescue' you?"

"Yes, I do read the papers, but it must have been clear to most with some degree of common sense that I was not out there. Were there cries for help? Was I seen thrashing about in those waves? No, I was not. Because I was kidnapped. I was tied up and kept against my will in an undisclosed location, and at some point, I will have to escape and return to my flock with a fantastic story to tell. Yes, gentlemen, that is what I would say if I were Aimee Semple McPherson, but I am not. I merely favor her. Now, may I be left to finish my appetizer before my boyfriend comes down? I'd rather he not see you here. He is very jealous and what's more, has himself been reported missing by his wife several weeks ago. The poor dear has enough to worry about right now."

Jonny had been holding his tongue through all of this, but now spoke in angry sputters. "What makes you think that I won't go to the police at this very moment and report your presence here?"

Aimee smiled, a caper lodged stubbornly between her upper two incisors. "This is why." At that moment I felt a sharp blow to the back of my head and then I was out. Apparently, Jonny, too, was similarly rendered unconscious. When we both came to, Aimee was gone. All that was left was the faint whiff of her floral perfume and a smudge of pâté upon her plate.

Jonny decided that it would be best not to go to the authorities with our story. "She'll resurface soon. Nobody will buy the story. She'll convict herself the moment she opens her mouth."

Two days later Aimee showed up at the Angelus Temple with one whopper to tell—swallowed hook, line, and sinker by her fawning followers. A story that had absolutely nothing to do with pâté.

15. **Leopold and Loeb liked the scent.** Nathan Leopold to Jonathan Blashette, 4 October 1924. Attempting to expand the market for Jonathan's men's deodorant line, Jonathan and Davison sent free samples to as many celebrated Americans as he could think of—and a few whose celebrity was colored with all the dark hues of notoriety.

16. **Calvin Coolidge wasn't available that day.** The reason that President Coolidge wasn't able to see Davison, or anyone else on that day was because he had cleared his calendar to meet with "Ol' Rip," a horned toad that emerged alive during the razing of the old courthouse in Eastland, Texas, after thirty-one years of incarceration in the building's cornerstone. Few details of the visit have survived with the exception of one transcribed account from *The Amphibian Lovers' Oral History Project: 100 Years of Frogs & Their Friends* (Chicago: S. Elliot and Company, 1982). Coolidge allegedly invited the toad and its human entourage to stay for lunch, during which he hand-fed the toad flies

skewered on toothpicks. The legendarily laconic president is said to have remarked, "My, my. Hmm. Yum, huh?"

It was foolish of Davison to think that he could have gotten a product endorsement from the president in the first place.

17. **"Didn't James Joyce's eye patch used to be over the other eye?"** Jonathan Blashette to Harlan Davison, 1 November, 1924 HD. Jonathan's pub encounter with author James Joyce was the second in a long series of late-night celebrity convives. Many of the individuals whom Jonathan met during his many years of urban night-owling were, like Joyce, well established in their high-profile professions; others, such as Rodolfo Valentina d'Antonguolla, were soon to *be* famous. Most of the encounters, though friendly and even affectionate, never rose to anything sustaining, and generally didn't extend beyond a single, isolated evening of convivial fraternity, soul-baring confession, and/or bathetic beer-basted blubbering.

Still, Jonathan's pantheon of pub pals is impressive. Among those with whom he bonded over brews and spirits, both legal and il-, were popular radio announcer Graham McNamee; at least one of the Dionne quintuplets (Jonathan was too drunk at the time to recall which, but did remember that the young woman imbibed only Shirley Temples, and so was the exception to the elevated blood-alcohol rule); fashion designer Christian Dior (to whom, it is rumored, Jonathan suggested the sack dress); Betty Ford (during her tenure with the Martha Graham Concert Group); contract bridge expert Charles Henry Goren; murderess Winne Ruth Judd (during her years on the lam—"What saw? Oh, *this* saw. Why, Mr. Blashette, I carry this ol' thing everywhere I go. It's my *lucky* saw. Now—enough about the saw *if you know what's good for you*"); mobster Lucky Luciano; record-setting thoroughbred Man O'War ("Who the hell let that horse in here?"); government agent Eliot Ness; saxophonist

Lester Young; German film director Leni Riefenstahl ("I'm going to live to be 101; just watch me, liebchen"); entrepreneur Billy Rose ("Is Fanny Brice in here? She left something on the stove"); crooner Rudy Vallee ("Where's my megaphone? Did somebody pinch my megaphone?"); folksinger and composer Woody Guthrie ("So long. It's been good to know you"); jigsaw puzzle designer Jo LeGood; actor J. Carroll Naish; baseball player "Gorgeous George" Sisler; manufacturer William C. Procter ("I'm looking for a business associate of mine—Jimmy Gamble"); and manufacturer Arde Bulova ("Do I have the time? Sure as tootin' I've got the time."). Incidentally, it was Bulova who originated spot advertising on the radio and convinced Jonathan to give the new medium a shot.

18. **"Things are going well."** The full text of Jonathan's letter to Bloor (10 November 1924 AnB) follows:

Dear Dr. Bloor,

I thank you for your letter. I am happy to report that things are going well. Things, in fact, are going exceedingly well. Dandy-de-odor-o, Inc. has become more successful than I ever imagined. We cannot keep up with the orders that are flooding in; we are already making plans for expanding our plant and are taking on new employees on almost a weekly basis.

It has not been a difficult task. There, apparently, has always been a need for deodorizers for the male underarm. I suppose it was simply a matter of time before someone like me came along to find a way to fill that need. But is it, simultaneously, filling the need within me to make something of my life—something lasting? Something with which I can make a difference in this world? Perhaps not. Yet, I know that the money I make from this business can be put to good use in myriad ways. I would like to found an organization with some humanitarian aspect. I haven't yet decided what that will be. I am still trying to figure out why I am here. You have told me that I have a life mission. I know that selling deodorants is not it. Dandy-de-odor-o, Inc. constitutes merely a rest stop along the highway of my life. To freshen up. To help others freshen up. I will be back on that highway soon—speeding toward my destiny, to be sure.

I have rented a very comfortable little apartment for my father on the Upper West Side of Manhattan. When I first moved him here he had a terrible aversion to the city. Almost daily he would remind me how much he wanted to get back to Arkansas. But now he seems to have settled in nicely. He has made several friends— older men like himself, living alone—with whom he sits in Riverside Park and discusses current events. They debate the merits of various local delicatessens. Last night he told me that he is considering becoming a Jew. He doesn't wear his overalls any more. He is evolving into a true New Yorker.

Doctor Bloor, I am in love. I will speak frankly. Her name is Winny Wieseler and she is smart and funny and beautiful. I cannot wait to see her each day. And when I am not with her, I am thinking about her—constantly. I do not think I dishonor the memory of Lucile by having such strong feelings for Winny. I have simply been blessed by God with the chance to meet and cultivate affection for two most extraordinary women. I cannot wait for you to meet my Winny. Will you be in New York some time soon?

Sincerely,

Jonathan Blashette

---

19. **She was dedicated to public service.** Among the other causes to which Winny devoted herself was working to replace the name of the Dakota School for Crippled and Stumbling Children. Leggio, *Winsome Winny*, 123.

20. **It was no Algonquin.** Of decidedly less collective magnitude than the luminaries who congregated uptown at the Algonquin Hotel, was the literary demimonde that gathered twice each week at the Bowery Hotel "Round Table." (Robert Benchley did wander in on one occasion to use the telephone and was corralled into sharing a drink with the group for a quarter of an hour. The experience included little conversation and much gawking.) And yet the conclave's existence through the twenties and into the early thirties made enough of a ripple in the New York literary and theatrical pond to merit a book by Justin Dunigan, grandson of charter member *New York Clarion* columnist A. Deveer Dunigan. In his book, Justin assembles a number of the quasi-witticisms delivered by participants of the Bowery klatch, among them the effervescent and slightly cheeky Winny Wieseler. A sampling follows. Justin Dunigan, *Wednesdays at Noon, Fridays at One: An Anecdotal History of the "Other" Round Table* (New York: Tabitha Press, 1983).

> *A. Deveer Dunigan*: My paper reports that Nellie Bly has just died. I am more inclined to believe that the woman is feigning death as a means to investigating the undertaking profession.

> *Thomas Marchese* (columnist for the *New York Shoppers Weekly*): She certainly has the coloration down.

> *Cordelia Klempt* (columnist for the *Ladies' Reader*): Nellie Bly—Nellie Blech! Gentlemen, may we please suspend such morbid talk until after the à la mode?

> *Arden Philpot* (drama critic with the *Yonkers Crier,*

regarding an actress whose name is now lost to us): Watching her perform is like observing the purchase of stamps.

Winny Wieseler (on the former President): You can lead a horse to Warren Harding, but you can't castrate the two of them simultaneously.

Enos D. Ryerbach (bon vivant): The biggest difference between men and women lies in the tits, unless, of course, you're speaking of Mr. Philpot here, when one is advised to travel farther south to draw a conclusion!

Arden Philpot (his retort): Enos, you are bile in human form!

Cordelia Klempt: Shut up, the both of you! You're wilting my surprise salad.

Victor Sonderskov (freelance poet, on the recently opened tomb of King Tutankhamen): Tut, tut, tut. I am not moved.

Winny Wieseler (on the launch of Chanel Number Five): I haven't tried the new fragrance. I have, however, worn Chanel Number One and Chanel Number Four simultaneously and would imagine the end result to be the same.

Enos D. Ryerbach (On Coco Chanel): I do not generally endorse women whose names are eponymous with beverages.

Arden Philpot (reviewing Pirandello's *Six Characters in Search of an Author*): I would have preferred to see perhaps two more characters.

Thomas Marchese: What an age in which to live—

Fascists to the right, Communists to the left! And Mr. Kahlil Gibran telling us to love them all! Give me Texas Guinan and a night of liquor-facilitated self-absorption. Give me a plush seat in the Epicurean, hedonistic middle! Give me the bottle of ketchup, Arden, before the grease on my meatloaf sandwich congeals!

21. **"Tomorrow I will ask Winny if she will consent to be my wife."** Jonathan's Diary.

22. **Then, suddenly, Winny was gone.** Lana Leggio, *Winsome Winny*.

23. **Jonathan received the tragic news late that night.** Patrick Oldeman, *Tears for the Shawmut*, 256-66. Fate had indeed played another cruel trick on Jonathan. Once again the setting for tragedy was (amazingly) Boston. Whereas six years earlier Lucile Moritz's young life had been snuffed out by a tsunami of molasses, Winny was now meeting her end in a different, yet equally freakish Beantown accident. Like Lucile, Winny was in the wrong place at the wrong time. Jonathan knew that she liked to dance, but was unaware that the Charleston had become such an obsession with her that her frequent travels would inevitably draw her inexorably and often foolhardily to the hottest night spots in town. 1925 was the peak year for the popular dance, and Winny (as Leggio notes in her biography) made a special effort to get to the Pickwick Dance Club—*the* hot spot in Boston for "doin' it, doin' it."

The official post mortem was unequivocal: the roof collapse was attributed to "unnatural stresses" placed upon the building's structural members by the feverish, swiveling, swaying, flailing and knee-knocking of hundreds of monkey-limbed dancers, among them one Winny Wieseler from New York City by way of Heppleville, Illinois. Poor

Winny—artist, writer, progressive activist, lover and friend to Jonathan Blashette—had literally danced herself into an early grave.

A postscript: Jonathan vowed never to return to the city that had claimed his two fiancées. He refused even to sell his deodorants there, in retribution. "I hate this town more than any man on this planet, save probably Babe Ruth," he told a reporter in 1927. "It killed two women who meant the world to me, and murdered my hope for any future happiness. The men of Boston can stink with b.o. till the cows come home!"

10

LIFE AFTER WINNY

1. **The grief slowly receded.** The loss of Winny clearly haunted Jonathan for the rest of his life. His near-obsession with her death resulted in a number of strange attempts to either perpetuate her memory or, conversely, to force closure through some radical acknowledgment of her passing. According to Harvey Freeman in his article, "Jonathan Blashette; Inside the Man," for *Body Fresh* Magazine, a trade publication put out by the Deodorant Council of America (July/August issue, 1972), Jonathan commissioned well-known portraitist Ely Wochna to do a painting of Winny, which Jonathan then hung in the study of his Greenwich Village brownstone and which remained there for the rest of his life. What made this commission odd is the fact that Jonathan requested that its artist return to his home every year upon the anniversary of Winny's death to retouch the painting, subtly aging the face, neck and hands of its deceased subject, so that with the passage of years, the late Winny would, in effect, age along with her extant paramour Jonathan.

Freeman elaborates:

> *Comparisons to Wilde's Mr. Dorian Gray are without merit. Unlike the portrait of Mr. Gray, which was transmogrified by the unseemly acts of its owner, here was a painting physically modified by the painter himself, under specific instructions from its owner. Deprived of the permanence of youth—that blessed state customarily granted by the artist's brush—denied the reward of immortality by a man who did not wish to age alone, Winny was required to grow old, to wrinkle, to sag,*

perhaps even to bruise and scar, should one presume that the head in its dotage might encounter sharp airborne objects, or perhaps duck too slowly beneath a drooping oak branch or spinning windmill sail, or swing carelessly toward an unacknowledged lamppost, thereby incurring cutaneous abrasion, although one suspects that it was never Jonathan's intention to see the face of his beloved Winny vandalized by the years, but merely to have her grow old with grace and dignity, in quiet company with the man who loved her.

The painting disappeared from Jonathan's home shortly after his death. One imagines that the family felt it simply too macabre to include in the public estate sale. Those who saw it last will attest to the artistry of its painter; its subject looking appropriate for the age she would have been, had she lived. Curiously, in her last "years" her head had acquired a simple red babushka. One wonders as to the reason for the suspected hair loss, but an explanation has never been given.

An even more bizarre (and uncorroborated) attempt to address Jonathan's grief over the death of Winny comes to us from Davison. According to his diary both he and Jonathan spent the fifth anniversary of Winny's departure in the home of a spiritualist who made a good faith effort to communicate with the deceased through the "thick curtain of mortality." She did not succeed. Although a connection was made, it was Harry Houdini who allegedly took the celestial call that night and who asked Jonathan to get a message to his wife, who he understood had been trying to reach him since his passage (per their pre-mortem agreement). The message was this: "Yes, there is an afterlife. Yes, I love you still. The secret of the Water Torture Cell: false rivets."

2. **Jonathan lost touch with Klempt after Winny's death.** Winny's best friend Cordelia Klempt (charter member of

the Bowery Hotel Round Table) gained some notoriety in her sunset years for defying the community of Desert Hills, Arizona, to which she retired in 1965, by xeroscaping her front lawn, much to the distress of her bermuda grass-loving sixty- and seventy-something neighbors. Cordelia's response to the harassment and fines from the community board that followed was that she "lived in a &*%# desert and intended for her &#%#!* lawn to reflect that fact." Despite being denounced and ostracized for wanting to ban water-greedy turf and deciduous plantings from her yard, she stayed put for another twenty years, and in the drought of 1970 had the pleasure of watching all her neighbor's lawns go ugly-brown and brittle from stringent water restrictions. Still, she faced the likes of the following for much of her stay in the community. *Desert Hills News*, 27 September 1967.

"Do You See What I.C.?"
by
Community Columnist I.C. Lavington

Cordelia Klempt continues to thumb her nose at us all as she shoves yet another unsightly cactus into that abortion she calls her front yard. She persists in forcing all of us to stomach that unsightly abomination of an eyesore every time we drive down Yucca Crest or turn onto Dry Mesa Parkway. It is noticeable, I might add, from as far away as Saguaro Circle and Sagebrush Lane.

One is inclined to say to the aesthetically-retarded Miss Klempt—this is America, my dear stupid woman, not the Soviet Union. Here we uphold beauty in all its plush, dewy greenery, in its riot of floral color. Your yard of rocks and sand and thirsty, gnarled desert succulents mocks your neighbors, mocks your community, mocks this very nation for which blood was spilled (and is currently being spilled as we do battle with the vicious V.C. in that land of rice paddies and coolie hats) so that we might live in peace and prosperity among beauty and ample verdancy. Who are you to move to the desert and infect your property and our community with that selfsame desert? You are the most insidious form of Anti-American subversive.

Obviously, none of us endorses the placement of that burning cross in your front yard last weekend. But perhaps we can understand the anger that motivated it.

What is wrong with grass, Miss Klempt? And what is wrong with trying for once in your long rebellious life to fit in?

3. **"I want you to meet a young friend of mine: Jasmine."** Much too young, it turned out. Jonathan came to realize that Davison's first inning "Winny" home run had been a total fluke. A long series of matchmaking strikeouts followed. Eventually Jonathan had to ask his friend to stop fixing him up. Lanham, "Harlan Davison," *Entrepreneurial History*, 13 (1990), 25-42.

4. **Jonathan dated Jasmine for five weeks.** The relationship was doomed from the start, and not only because Jonathan was rebounding badly from the death of Winny. Jasmine, a dead ringer for Clara Bow, was a typical young, indefatigable, devil-may-care flapper. She exhausted thirty-eight-year-old Jonathan, even as she divided her attention among all the other men whose names crowded her dance card. Here is an excerpt from the only existing letter from Jasmine to her soon-to-be-ex-beau (written on a sorority-sponsored road trip). Jasmine had only a few days earlier met one Reginald Grayson III, a Varsity-dragging John Held caricature, even down to the raccoon coat and Stutz Bearcat roadster. JBP, 2 May 1926.

He's a cakeater, Jonny, a real jazzbo but I'm no dumb Dora. I say, 'You might be the big cheese in these parts but

I'm stuck on my Jonny, see? My Jonny, he's the bee's knees, the real McCoy. That's what I tell him. I make nice with Reggie, you understand, but if he gets the least bit fresh, I go all hardboiled, I'm not bunking you. I can hold my own with jellybeans like him, you better believe it.

He does have IT, though. Positively, gotta admit it. But so do you, *my little snugglepup. Just a little more crags 'round the edges, dat's all. And I'd have it no other way. You are my sheik of Araby, and don't you worry your turbaned head, my dear. Tres copacetic, things is. Sheba —yours for life.*

You are absolutely the berries!

(A couple of days later Jasmine phoned to say she was engaged to Reginald. Jonathan was never to see her again.)

5. **"You got your pung cows and you got your chow cows."** Ellery Reinhold, *The Story of Dandy-de-odor-o, the Little Company That Could…and Then Did*, 101-03. Edders, the company's new senior vice president for investor relations, had earned so much money shipping calf shin bones from his Chicago slaughterhouse to China to be made into Mah-Jongg tiles, that he was able to retire at age forty-one in 1928. When Jonathan snatched him up, he was happy to be going back to work again. Having invested heavily in the stock market (including sizable holdings of Dandy-de-odor-o), Edders was hard hit by the Crash of '29. He suffered a nervous breakdown and spent the remainder of his life in modest circumstances in a small Forest Hills, Queens, saltbox, picking up the occasional royalty check from verse he wrote for the Holiday Hearts greeting card company. When his mind began to fail, Holiday Hearts began to reject his work out of hand. One really can't blame them if the following versification, unearthed from the company's archives, is representative of the obtuseness and

offensive nature of his later efforts.

On one's birthday:

> One year closer.
> The grave draws nearer.
> But that doesn't make you any the less dearer.
> Hugs and kisses and voices a' trill.
> But if you don't mind my asking:
> Where is the will?

On one's anniversary (husband to wife):

> Many years ago
> In days of yore,
> I gave my troth to an erstwhile whore.
> I cleansed your womb of its former employ,
> And gave you some measure of marital joy.
> I forgot and forgave
> And all was near bliss
> Notwithstanding the blindness (from the syphilis).

On graduation from high school (from parents):

> Graduation day.
> Hip hip hooray!
> Now go away.
> And stay.

6. **"I'm Famine. This here's Pestilence."** Jonathan would have liked to have met all four of Notre Dame's famed "horsemen," immortalized by sportswriter Grantland Rice, but only Stuhldreher and Miller were dining at the hotel that night. Describing the chance encounter in a letter to his friend Toby (the Monkey Boy) Brancato (family papers), Jonathan noted that he might have lingered at the table all night, but, true to his name, Stuhldreher really was "quite

famished" and couldn't digest with someone hovering about.

7. **There followed a long series of mismatches and romantic misfires.** Furman, *The Story of Jonathan Blash—[ette]*.

8. **"I have a prolapsed womb. Would you still like to date me?"** Author's interview with Charmian Campbell, granddaughter of Lavinia Hudd.

9. **"Can we postpone our first date until I get out of traction?"** Author's interview with Bridey Burmeister, granddaughter of Astrid Csizmadia. Incidentally, Astrid broke her hip when the leather belt of her Vibro-Slim snapped and she fell backwards onto the living room floor.

10. **"Please don't touch me there. It's only our first date."** Author's interview with Eustacia Hodgdon, granddaughter of Ona Hodgdon. The body part in question was Ona's arm.

11. **"First name's Delicia; last name's Everest. Would you like to mount me?"** JBP, "Hooker Encounters" Notebook.

12. **She never emerged from her coma.** Author's interview with Lotta Patois, great niece of Marie Ward. This fact was disputed by one of the attending nurses who entered the room late one night to find Marie sitting straight up in bed and playing solitaire. The nurse was about to go to the phone to share the good news with Marie's family (one evening with Marie at the newly opened Stork Club didn't qualify Jonathan to be contacted) when she noticed a move that Marie had missed. The nurse quickly became engrossed in the game, and Marie, happy to be conscious and to have liberated all of her aces, invited the nurse to sit next to her in quiet, nocturnal communion. Only once did either speak to the other. Marie allegedly turned to her companion and remarked, "It's so nice to have conscious brain function,

isn't it?" After a few more minutes of thoughtful card play, Marie's eyes suddenly rolled back in her head and she returned to her previous comatose state. The nurse plumped her pillow a bit, wiped a tiny thread of saliva from her chin, and then finished the card game for her. Many years passed before she mentioned the incident to anyone. She finally decided to share the story with her pastor, the Reverend Boxer Seale, who, not being Catholic, was under no ecclesiastical directive to keep it to himself, and so included it in his *When We From Sleep Awake* (Henderson, Kentucky: Joey Gee Books, 1975), a collection of anecdotes about resurrection, coma emergence, and rudely broken reveries.

13. **Jonathan resigned himself to lifelong bachelorhood.** Jonathan's Diary, JBP, 9 August 1927.

14. **These were dark months for Jonathan and Dandy-de-odor-o.** The slump in sales may have also been attributed to a statement made by actor Wallace Beery in *Behind the Screen*, a popular Hollywood fan magazine. Tough guy Beery bragged, "I don't need no sissy perfume-counter dabby-doo under my arms. A man's supposed to smell like a man, not like some guzzied dame in a flower shop." At the same time Jonathan and the Dandy-D board of directors were hearing the first of a string of charges leveled by the investigative press that the company's assembly line equipment was unsafe. Reinhold, *The Story of Dandy-de-odor-o*, 156-57.

15. **The company was in the red due, in part, to blackened business practices** Perry Jennings' exposé on defective assembly-line equipment at Dandy-de-odor-o's Queens, New York, factory represents only a small fraction of this investigative journalist's prodigious reportorial and literary output. Never achieving the stature of such muckrakers as Tarbell, Stannard Baker and Sinclair, Jennings in his hard-

hitting pieces did reach a wide readership, most notably through his monthly contributions to *Jest Kids*, a periodical for boys and girls (although his wrenching accounts of child labor practices in the textile industry resulted in a severe drop in subscriptions to the magazine). A monthly cartoon to which he several years earlier contributed text and ongoing story lines, "The Continuing Adventures of Li'l Lame Nell, Six-year-old Loom Operator," was a catalyst for the passage of legislation by the Georgia General Assembly…to ban sales of the periodical within the state.

Late in his career, Jennings' credibility was undermined by a series of articles for *Guv'ner's Magazine* in which he fabricated the existence of feline sweatshops in Lynn, Massachusetts, wherein sweaters and other knit garments were manufactured through energy generated by cat treadmills—the heavily catnip-drugged grimalkins trotting until collapse toward tantalizing mechanical mice-on-sticks.

In his lifetime Jennings also wrote fourteen novels, thirteen continuing the saga of the toothless Gum family which settled in central Nebraska and sold consommé. His fourteenth novel *Things My Wife Did to Me* was a very loosely veiled account of Jennings' rocky marriage to silent screen actress Velma DeGraaf, apologist for and possible paramour of doomed comedic actor Fatty Arbuckle and coiner of the tag line "Take your grimy eyes off my sheen."

Jennings' last two books, both memoirs published post-humously and heavily revised by widow DeGraaf, sold fewer than two hundred copies in their only printings. In fact, existing copies of *Things I Did to Myself* and *My Life as a Wife-slugging Bastard, with Afterword by Roscoe "Fatty" Arbuckle* each now commands a high price in the rare book market. A copy of *Things I Did to Myself* was exhibit "A" in a lawsuit filed in 2001 by Mauvourneen Heyer, who, when told of the value of her mint condition copy by a book dealer on the television program *Video Flea Market*, lost consciousness and cracked her skull on a rare Queen Anne highboy being caressed at the time by both of the Keno twins.

16. **Accidents and other odd happenings plagued the plant.** No one has any idea how Elwin Lyster got inside the box. One moment he was observed by co-workers at his usual station in Section 17B on the assembly line. The next moment he was gone. Elwin was later found curled sleepily among packing material and deodorant sticks. A co-worker recalled that Lyster's face was beatific, "as if he had been to a wonderful secret place mortals don't generally get to visit." For years thereafter Lyster would eagerly relate to those he'd meet all the details of his fifteen minutes in "a place difficult to describe without assistance from the clergy." Unhappy with the adverse publicity generated by those who found such individuals socially menacing, Blashette would eventually be forced to fire the former game warden and butter-and-egg man without severance or apology, although Lyster was allowed to keep the box, which he nicknamed "My Portal to Paradise" and more informally "Roy." Reinhold, *The Story of Dandy-de-odor-o*, 162-66.

17. **Soon they were crawling out of the woodwork.** Dandy-D seemed to attract individuals like Bucky and Mr. Scrum who must have assumed that factories run by men with three legs could be havens for their alternative approaches to life. Jonathan didn't help matters by hiring many of these strange characters himself and without any form of background check. Among the other oddball workers whom Blashette found himself eventually cashiering or sending off for reorientation sessions at Miss Love's School of Conformity was conveyor operator Chigger Farrow, who would hold his breath at random moments and occasionally lose consciousness, then topple off the milk stool his mother

had given him for the express purpose of mitigating damage to his head and spine when he took his tumbles. Blashette also employed slow-talker Hoyt Spivak and horse-reviler Algernon Accola, Carmine "The Weeper" Morrow, as well as Dabney Whalen, Mormon father of twenty-three who was not only married to seven women simultaneously but who had troubled unions with each of them. Ibid., 166.

18. **"Something's got to be done with this company or we're going under. All we need now is a major economic downturn and we're sunk."** Memorandum from Charleton Caldwell to Jonathan Blashette, 15 April 1929, Dandy-de-odor-o Corporate Records.

19. **"Stocks Collapse in 16,410,030 Share Day"** *New York Times*. 30 October 1929.

20. **"Wall Street Lays an Egg"** *Variety*, 30 October 1929.

11

BROTHER, CAN YOU SPARE A DAME?

1. **"I've seen one blue tit before, but never two at the same time."** Jonathan would not realize until much later that his drinking companion for the evening was an amateur ornithologist who was referring to the old world titmouse *Parus Caeruleus*, distinguished by its cobalt-blue crown. Jonathan's Diary, JBP, 2 November 1929.

2. **"It was a fabulous party."** The story is totally apocryphal. There is no evidence that T. E. Lawrence, Ted Shawn, E. M. Forster & Bill Tilden had ever met one another, let alone devised plans to gather at Jonathan's home in his absence to look at magic lantern slides of wrestling Muybridge male nudes.

3. **Oliver Hardy was one of the few well-known actors Jonathan never had the chance to meet.** The closest he ever came was once mistaking the popular orchestra conductor Paul Whiteman for Hardy in the lobby of the Blackstone Hotel in Chicago. The two men strongly resembled each another and were often confused, especially when Whiteman did his Oliver Hardy impression.

A side note from a sideman: Jonathan was never a big fan of Paul Whiteman. He felt that the "King of Jazz" while embracing and exploiting the black jazz idiom, should have, at the same time, demonstrated his gratitude by racially integrating his orchestra. Jonathan sympathized with those African American jazz musicians who felt that Whiteman was either a racist or too much the coward ever to make the attempt. One trumpeter whom I interviewed several years ago for a book I never completed about the Harlemphiliac author and photographer Carl Van Vechten (and whose name I withhold at the request of his family), passed along this story of his stage door confrontation with Whiteman after a performance by his orchestra in New York City: "I asked the fat lily white ass why he wouldn't hire any of us Colored folk for his orchestra, especially since he's always playing our music. He just giggled and did that funny flippy-doodle thing with his tie like Oliver Hardy always does in them Laurel and Hardy pictures. Then when he realized that I wasn't digging this, he got real serious and said, 'Look here, my Colored friend. I'm not in the business of losing money by putting any Negroes in my orchestra. Plain and simple. Besides, the name is Paul *Whiteman*, boy. That's *Whiteman*, not *Blackman*. Now if you will kindly move aside, I have reservations at the Cotton Club.'" Furman, *The Story of Jonathan Blash—[ette]*, 133-34.

4. **"We can weather this storm."** Memorandum from Jonathan Blashette to Dandy-de-odor-o employees, 12 February 1930. Corporate hatch battening began with the sale of the product itself. Jonathan, determined to keep Dandy-D afloat, slashed the wholesale price of the deodorant by half. Joked vice president for marketing Vinton Kalet, "We've got those damned deodorant sticks so cheap now, they're probably using 'em for lard down in Appalachia." (Reinhold, 175-77.) Other means by which Jonathan hoped to tough out the hard economic times involved cutting employee salaries by 25 percent and significantly reducing overhead. "You won't find this company going belly-up, no sirree," he stated with resolve. "Even a guy with a hole in his sole and a soup kitchen crust in his hand's got a right to smell like a swell. And knowing that fact, he'll scrape up whatever he can to purchase our product." With the exception of radio, advertising expenditures were also trimmed. Reinhold contends that it was the popularity of radio that saved the company.

5. **"You won't find a job if you smell like a slob."** The jingle reached its peak in popularity in the mid-1930s. However, as late as 1947, the slogan was ad-libbed by Bob Hope in the only Hope/Crosby "road" picture to be dubbed an inarguable "stinker" by American film critics. *Road to Irkutsk* was shelved after its premiere in Hollywood and all prints subsequently destroyed. According to co-star Dorothy Lamour in an interview with *Sinematic Confessions* magazine (12, No.4 [1970]:34), Hope accused Bing Crosby of having never heard of deodorant, and Lamour came close to making an unkind comment or two herself, the heavy woolen uniform the comedic crooner wore unleashing wafts of male apocrine unpleasantness "to the detriment of all of us who value an unpolluted work environment."

6. **The new director of product planning limped to the easel and took the pointer.** Reinhold, *The Story of Dandy-de-odor-o*, 184. Arnold Haverty's left leg had been mangled in a childhood game of blindman's bluff. After local toughs crashed the eleven-year-old boy's birthday party, he was blindfolded and walked right off the small bluff that marked the boundary of the backyard meadow in which the game was played. The young bullies confessed that they were only tangentially familiar with the rules of the game. The same excuse was offered following an earlier game of Snap-the-Whip, which resulted in Haverty's young cousin being flung up into a tree.

7. **Haverty had a bit of the devil in him**. Ibid. Among other popular pranks perpetrated by mischievous Arnie was sneaking into Sally Rand's dressing room at the 1933 Chicago World's Fair and replacing the stripper's body balloon with a dangerously smaller inflatable.

8. **"I liked Haverty's laugh. I wanted to emulate it."** Jonathan described it this way: "Homph, homph, heh, hickle, heh, homph." Jonathan's Diary, JBP, 1 March 1930.

---

9. **"In the sum of it, a most delightful evening with the three-legged man."** Evelyn Waugh did, apparently, enjoy his late-night encounter with Jonathan at the Kensington Pub, taking the opportunity to unbosom himself of a number of deep-seated regrets and concerns. The satirical British novelist confessed profound disappointment over being forced by his publisher to excise most of the homosexual, pedophiliac, and incestuous references from his *Decline and Fall*, adding, as he became bolder in his admissions to Jonathan, that an earlier draft of the manuscript containing, as well, a scatologically defiled tea party and an orgy involving several English schoolboys and two crippled milch cows, could have made for a much more controversial book. It was all, according to Waugh, simply a matter of "mores and taste. You see, I prefer a few more seasonings in my literary spice rack." That evening Evelyn also expressed regret over having the same first name as his wife. It made for a number of confusing marital moments, especially on those occasions during which self-critical monologues were overheard and misunderstood by wife Evelyn, to the cruel delight of the hired help. Private notes, Waugh Papers, Cramlington University. U.K.

10. **It was during his visit to England that Jonathan met Clara Gleason.** Jonathan Blashette to Addicus Blashette, 15 March 1930, JBP.

11. **"I didn't care for her at first, but she does have a way of growing on you."** Ibid., 19 March 1930, JBP.

12. **The old die young.** Clara's contempt for anyone over the age of fifty is best summed up in the poem which follows. Published by *The Young Set*, organ of the British Society for the Abolition of the Aged, "Buckie Biddle" caused an outcry at the time. Clara was sent hate mail from angry seniors throughout the world (including Jonathan's father, Addicus, who, exercising his new Yiddish vocabulary, pronounced it

meshuga) and from every demographic subset, including a centenarian who mailed her his befouled bed sheets and called her a "snot-nosed ninny." Harsh British reaction in particular was one of the reasons Clara ended her lengthy literary sojourn in England and returned to the States with Jonathan.

Buckie Biddle

Buckie Biddle made a piddle
In her panties,
In the middle.
Down her leg, dribble dribble
While down her chin wind streams of spittle—
Droolly mewlly little
Dots and spots of spinky spittle.
Spitty splat and splatter spit,
Plinking pink and wrinkly tit—
Down bony chin, jutting brittle
To droopy tit, a splishy puddle.
Buckie blinks and squints and prattle
Blurts and spurts, a mumbly muddle.
Murmur Murmur reminisce.
Buckie's brain:
Addled mess.
Buckie's life near to end—
Broken life, no hope of mend.
So fluids flow,
Recede and dry.
Then desiccated Buckie die.

13. **"I love her because she's dangerous."** Jonathan's Diary, 18 March 1930, JBP. The effusive entry continues:

I love her because she grabs life by the horns, by the short hairs, by the ear lobes and doesn't let go. She hangs on to life, wrestling with it, thrashing it about, flinging it from side to

side like a terrier with a death-destined woodrat. She takes
life in her hands as if it were some great sopping sponge from
which she must wring out every last drop. She holds it over
her beautiful upturned head and she squeezes the salty
liquid from its pores and it spills into her open, thirsty
mouth and she drinks of it in great happy gulps as it rivulets
down her sweet, softly curved chin, from her gaping,
grinning, giggling mouth. And I want to take her in my arms
and celebrate her celebration of that celebratory instinct
within us all. I want to lay tongue-active kisses on her winks,
on her saucy secretive smirks, on her sloppy, full-barreled
assaults on a world gone stale, gone dry on the vine, a world
gone greedmad or complacent or afraid without cause. She
stands back and whoopbelts: "Why this? Why not? Why
worry? What, me worry? Where is my life? Here it is!
Splayed before you to be wholly engaged. To be put into gear.
I will address the starter and watch it go. And I will adjust
the setting to 'high' and I will fly!" My Clara—climber of
mountains and spinner of dreams, untempered, uncorralled,
undeterred. My glorious free spirit. My ClaraDelicious.
I love her for all these things. I love her too, perhaps most of
all, for waking me to my own potential.

14. **"Doctor Bloor, Clara will show me how to bring purpose to my own life."** Jonathan Blashette to Andrew Bloor, 21 March 1930, AnB.

15. **"For heaven's sake, Jonathan, don't let her go to Boston."** Andrew Bloor to Jonathan Blashette, 4 April 1930, JBP.

16. **Clara came with baggage.** In addition to her son Hunter and her niece Margreta whom she was raising following a burro collision in the Grand Canyon that permanently juggled the brains of her sister Ida, Clara brought with her four dogs, two cats, Clara's Aunt Love, Clara's Aunt Love's iron lung, Clara's Aunt Love's nurse Miss Puntz, Nurse

Puntz's extensive collection of japonaiserie, a sheep named Orville (for the wool), a goat named Snickersnee (for the cheese), and the famed engineer and bridge designer Bascom Caruthers. Merry Mintz Figel. Research notes from unproduced stage production *Clara! The Musical,* c. 1965.

17. **One of Bascom's ears had been badly disfigured in a botched candling episode.** Ibid.

18. **Among the other habitués of Clara's literary "salon" were Dorothy Musgrove and Carter Wendt.** Carter was perhaps genetically predisposed to poetry and light prose as the grand-nephew of poet Damon Wendt who, befriended by Walt Whitman at a Camden dry goods store as the two men found themselves laying claim to the same flannel work shirt, was inspired to write in the style and spirit of the hoary celebrant of the common man. (With all correspondence between the two having been burned by Damon's sister and Carter's great aunt Edith Puggs, upon Damon's death and her discovery that he had deliberately called her in order of frequency, "Pigg," "Porker," "Priggy Pig" and "Ham Hips"), we are left with only Damon's clearly derivative poems as evidence that Carter's great uncle not only shared Whitman's "invert" nature, but sought to incorporate the predilection into his poetry in an even more overt manner than did his friend and fellow flannel-wearer. An example is the following, from his self-published collection, *Blades with Stalks.*

Paean to the Packing House

O men of meat!
With rippled sinew, with muscles spread thick and bared,
To push, to pull, to swell, sweat-moistened, to haul and heave
and thrust—hips forward hips back, a rush of man-work,
This place of heft and husky, hirsute manhood.
This abattoir of dust and dank and blood.

Blood of beast, sweat of man.
O pageant of manhood!
I gaze upon the scene and within me a beast awakes, stretches, yawns, fisting his eyes and viewing carnage civilized by the muscular men of meat.

Hear the throaty cries of the barrelmen of beef and brawn who carry the weight of commerce upon their massive, undulating shoulders.
Throats that hunger for the taste of meat cut, meat uncut.

I sing my joy of the packing house.
I am singer in a place queer in its blood-lock, yet sustenance-sustaining,
Carnivorous, cacophonous cavern of the deep, the dark, the dangerous, the men of meat.

I brush the young one lightly, gently, my hand searching, tentative in its touch.
To touch the shoulder, the hocks, the lumber limbs of the one with the astral eyes.

He pushes me back, a look of warning, a look of one who becomes master even in his youth.
Hands unsuppled by the work of the trade.

His baritone cry, warm and felt-lined, deep in the timbre of youthful man-gruff: "Stop looking at me.
Stop touching me.
You're standing in a blood pool, you old fool."

Fool I am but fool I be.
I touch him again, softly, a gentle stroke across the sullied apron pulled taut against his, no-doubt, fur-tuft chest.
Another push in answer.
In furrowed scorn.

"I told you to stop touching me. Touch me again, and I'll pop you with this calf carcass."

I laugh.
I embrace the folly of my petulant spirit, and am again about the pursuit of this fine avatar of male youth who carves the meat with the sheer brawn of his musky man-paw.

My hand reaches out again...

   And is met by the darkness of day-sleep, of sudden
somnolent ensilencing.
The flame of consciousness doused.
   Upon my back I enter the Packing House of Dreams.
Where men welcome my wandering touch.
These men of meat!

A side note about Dorothy Musgrove: the poet moved to Washington, D.C., in 1932 and soon became a permanent, albeit minor, fixture in the "den of power" as she liked to call the city. Trading Clara's literary salon for a political one, she enjoyed frequent invitations to sup with D.C.'s "living monument" Alice Roosevelt Longworth and other capital celebrities. Her low profile generally kept her name out of the local press.

The one notable exception occurred in 1936 when Dorothy found herself the victim of Seattle Congressman Marion Zioncheck's drunken joy ride through the streets (and sidewalks) of downtown Washington. Struck in the head by an airborne trash can lid, she declined medical attention and proceeded to the home of Mrs. Longworth where she was expected for an intimate dinner party. With her head bloodied from the accident, she launched into a send-up of Teddy Roosevelt's legendary address following the nearly fatal attempt made upon his life during the 1912 Presidential campaign, parodying Teddy with precision: "I want you all to be very quiet. Perhaps you're not aware that I have been hit in the head by the lid of a garbage can knocked skyward by a drunken Congressman." According to Dorothy's recollection of the evening, "fun-loving Alice was reduced to hysterics, dropping to the floor and pummeling the boards in a fit of apoplectic mirth." (Dorothy Musgrove, *Things I Remember*, [Baltimore: Boysenberry Press, 1960], 137-40.)

19. **"This is my brother Lyndon."** Clara's younger brother Lyndon Tosch Gleason was equally literary and best known for his *Fork Creek Collection*, (Redding, California: Di Prisco Press, 1955), taking as its inspiration, Edgar Lee Master's *Spoon River Anthology*. The work, originally mistaken for parody, was, in fact, a sincere effort to tell the encapsulated stories of the inmates of a large state institution for the intellectually challenged. Exhibiting the cruel insensitivity of its day, the asylum was officially known as the Illinois State Institution for Imbeciles, Idiots, Cretins, and Morons, and more informally as "Dummy House." The book sold few copies, for it was nearly unreadable. An example follows:

Mickey Spenders

> I got porridge! Yum. Mumyum. Porridge!
> I like porridge. Sugar it. Sugar it. Yum.
> More more porridge!
> Timmy!
> Hey Timmy, get porridge!
> Thatzit.
> Thatzit.
> Now Timmy got porridge!
> In the mouth, Timmy! In the mouth!
> Uh oh.
> Timmy got porridge hair.
> Yee yee yee yee.
> Hey, hey, hey, hey!
> Hug me.

20. **On April 20, 1930, Clara and I were married by a justice of the peace in Reno, Nevada.** Jonathan Blashette to Andrew Bloor, AnB.

21. **"So, you're finally tying the knot at the boyish age of forty-two!"** Bloor knew that he would not approve of Clara when they finally met. His intuition was confirmed on a

visit to New York two months later. Bloor wrote in his journal that "as suspected, I found her to be totally lacking in charm and grace," and "a regular foghorn with hips." Still, it doesn't appear that he ever revealed his true feelings to Jonathan, apparently aware that when the relationship finally soured (as Bloor was sure it inevitably would) he would not wish to be among those dancing the "I-told-you-so shuffle"—a dance which, Bloor noted, is never flattering and often "puts one at risk of being removed from the dance floor altogether." Bloor's ostensible (but privately grudging) approval of Jonathan's wife seemed, however, to endear Jonathan to his mentor all the more, the two growing even closer, their correspondence much more frequent and illuminating of their emotional lives during this period. Andrew Bloor to Jonathan Blashette, 27 April 1930, JBP.

22. **Jonathan kept his Greenwich Village brownstone as a pied-à-terre.** It was an ideal arrangement. The old farm house in Wallywaycong, New Jersey, was large enough to hold Clara, her family and hangers-on and all her creatures great and small. The house in the city served as the perfect "get-away" when Jonathan needed a quiet break from the "Clarathrong."

23. **"What do I do with my arboreal stepson?"** Jonathan's Diary, 18 July 1930. Granted, it seemed that half the boys in North America were going for the national tree-sitting record in 1930, but fourteen-year-old Hunter's choice of Wallywaycong's venerated Founder's Oak, which stood on the front lawn of the county courthouse, was a controversial choice. Even when following the crazes of the day, Jonathan's stepson had a taste for rebellion that placed him in a category by himself. Climbing the oak may have looked to some like a simple act of youthful mischief, but to others it represented a disturbing offensive against tradition and authority.

I have found wildly conflicting accounts of the events surrounding town historian Fitzhugh Dowdy's hospitalization for nervous exhaustion on the day that Hunter was finally "de-treed." I am more inclined to believe Dowdy's own—albeit heavily embroidered—account, passed down to us through his diary (Dowdy Family Papers). If nothing else, the entries pertaining to the tree-sitting episode shed some light on the man's fragile mental state at the time.

> *Saturday, July 19, 1930. I rise and hurry to the courthouse to find that the monkey is still there—still ensconced in that tree, desecrating it by his very presence, with the three-legged monkey stepfather doing nothing whatsoever to remove the child. Nor do any of the county commissioners seem alarmed by his presence. Damn them all. No tree—but especially this, the most cherished in our city—deserves such a fouling. I have a dunker and coffee while glowering up at the intruder. The dunker and coffee are too much for my weak constitution. As I stand retching without product, I watch the boy through rage-filled eyes. Between undulating body heaves I rail and remonstrate and command the vile man-cub through the most easily decipherable gesticulation to remove himself. Yet he does not. Moreover, he taunts me, audaciously asking me with mischievous gloat to catch the bag containing his evacuants, because his chum Mikey has yet to arrive to cart the foul-smelling effluents off. I find that I am having trouble standing erect from the enormity of it all, and I crumple beneath the tree and weep for its spoiled beauty and I weep for the rich history it represents that the boy has besmirched and I pinch my nose from the stench of the bagged evacuants that the boy dangles with most cruel malice over my exposed head. It is the darkest morning I can ever remember with the exception of that in which Poppy threw me into the river with all the kittens I had sought to save.*

Sunday, July 20, 1930. I rise and rush with a tripping,
stumbling gait to the Founder's Oak only to find that the
devil boy is still there, with father nowhere in sight and no
one but me exercising any concern whatsoever for all that
the beautiful tree represents. The sheer weight of this most
horrible realization is simply too much for me. Suddenly
the world darkens and recedes and I feel my whole body
slipping into the abyss of unconsciousness. When I awake
I am in a hospital bed taking an injection in the buttocks
by a nurse who says it will calm me. Soon I feel a soft
solace enfolding me. Shortly thereafter I am visited by Mr.
Blashette who assures me the boy will be down by the end
of the day. And I rejoice with tears and a strange hula-like
movement of the arms which I seem to do spontaneously
and to my intense mortification.

24. **Clara's literary circle continued to expand.** Figel,
research notes from *Clara! The Musical.* A frequent visitor
with adjunct status was poet Davy Kreis who several years
later, inspired by the free verse epic *Paterson* by William
Carlos Williams, wrote the three-volume nearly unreadable
Bayonne. It received the 1949 Mrs. Delwood Dandle
Poetaster Prize. I sought a copy of the encyclopedia length
poem to excerpt, but was unsuccessful. The New York Public
Library's Rare Books Division reportedly had a set in the
early 1950s. It vanished at some point during the
intervening years. It is hard to know the exact date of its
disappearance, since it was never requested. Librarian John
Rathe remembers that the volumes had at one point been
used as improvised stepladder to assist diminutive
researchers in reaching the division's water fountain.

A side note: Mrs. Delwood Dandle is considered by some to
be the world's worst published poet. It has been surmised
that her only book of poems was given a limited printing by
Caven-Mulgrove Publishing to satisfy publisher Brennan

Mulgrove's gambling debts. Delwood (also known as "Squeaks"), a loan shark of the Damon Runyon school, worked out a deal to prevent Mulgrove, with his well-documented weakness for long shots at Belmont, from getting his legs broken.

A selection from her poem, "Little Birdy" follows.

> Little birdy, why doth thou sing
> So sweet thy song of mirth?
> The sunny morning smileth.
> Is that not enough?
> Thy song is gilding
> to a lily white.
> Little Birdy, banish night.
> Morning come.
> You maka me hum.
> Sweeta little birdya.

Mrs. Dandle never explains why her narrator suddenly lapses into a harlequin Italian accent. Equally inexplicable is Dandle's decision to illustrate the poems with pictures from the children's book *The Five Chinese Brothers*.

25. **"The Cossacks' names were Douglas MacArthur, George Patton, and Dwight D. Eisenhower."** Luddy Greco's Diary, 28 July 1932. Jonathan had arrived at the Bonus Expeditionary Force's encampment in Washington, D.C., only hours before the World War I veterans who had gathered there to demand early payment of the soldier's bonus due them in 1945 were routed by forces led by General MacArthur under orders from President Hoover. Former doughboy-pals Jonathan, Greco, and Darrell Delehanty were in the midst of trading war stories when 700 troops, aided by tanks, cavalry and machine guns, drove the three, along with thousands of unemployed veteran protestors (and many of their families) from their nation's capital.

Jonathan promptly returned to New York, writing in his own diary the next day only the words, "Dark day for America."

Luddy, scarred by memory of that day, became a Communist, and eventually moved to the Soviet Union.

Delehanty remained silent.

MacArthur and his majors Patton and Eisenhower went on to serve their fellow citizens with distinction in the Second World War, their part in the brutal Bonus Army pogrom all but forgotten.

26. **Caldwell wasn't mathematically gifted.** Reinhold, *The Story of Dandy-de-odor-o*, 202-205. Dandy-D's chief financial officer's oft-repeated claim that he had "no head for numbers" was a constant source of frustration for Jonathan who worked hard to convince shareholders and the business press that Caldwell loved nothing more than pulling the public leg. My research has revealed that Caldwell's lack of confidence in his own numerical abilities can be traced to an incident in the summer of 1934 during a family vacation trip to Atlantic City. As the C.F.O. dozed on the beach, one Vivienne Falconi (a vacationer from Newark) accidentally dropped a copy of *Anthony Adverse* upon his head. Caldwell lay hospitalized and comatose for two days. (Hearing of the unfortunate occurrence, the 1,224-page best seller's author Hervey Allen sent a get-well card that read, "Perhaps I should have written the thing in installments.")

Regaining consciousness, Caldwell came to the horrible realization that he had forgotten the number between six and eight.

Asked to count to ten by the attending physician, he would

either leave out the number seven entirely, or replace it with one of many nonsense words, e.g.: "four, five, six, fish-twaddle, eight." Eventually Caldwell and the number seven were reacquainted and he came to utilize it just as extensively as he had before the accident. But a happy ease and total comfort around numbers for one of Jonathan's most trusted lieutenants was never to return. Jonathan didn't seem to mind. The following exchange from 1937 is recounted by a window washer who happened to be conveniently stationed within earshot. Buddy Browar, *Eavesdropping on the Captains of Industry: Thirty years of Soap and Corporate Dope* (Cincinnati: Mayer Z. Oats Publishing, 1946), 129-132.

> *"Your mistakes notwithstanding, Caldy, we're still in the black. That's all that matters. Hey, maybe I ought to drop a few books on some other heads around here. Lately, Dougherty has been cruising for a big ol' head-butt with Margaret Mitchell."*
>
> *To which Caldwell jocularly responded, "All one thousand thirty—"*
>
> *"Seven," Jonathan inserted, helpfully.*
>
> *"Yes. Seven. Pages of it. You thought I was going to say 'fish twaddle,' didn't you?"*
>
> *A nod. A chuckle. An affectionate cuff under the chin for President Blashette's odd little C.F.O.*
>
> *It is here that my presence was detected and the blinds hastily drawn.*

27. **Dingleberry also proved to a be problem.** Reinhold, *The Story of Dandy-de-odor-o*, 218-19.

28. **The antisocial behavior continued, then abated.** Ibid.,

219. However, on occasion, something would set off Dandy-de-odor-o's director of personnel, and he would return to the periphery of his early sociopathic behavior. As late as March 1975, Dingleberry was roughly escorted from a suburban multiplex theatre after hurling a boot at the screen upon which the critically panned film musical *Mame* was being projected. Although he quickly retrieved the boot and apologized to those nearby who felt threatened by it, Dingleberry's continued mumbled imprecations against Gene Saks and Lucille Ball for "this protracted cinematic fart," clearly showed that the man continued to live on the narrow brink of rage.

29. **There was little doubt that Jonathan was snubbing Nelson Rockefeller.** Diary entries and correspondence detail the reason for Jonathan's refusal to shake the young businessman's hand at the gala. Jonathan, though no fan of Lenin, felt that Rockefeller's "baby with the bathwater" approach to resolving the issue of whether Diego Rivera should be allowed to include the image of the Soviet dictator within the massive Rockefeller Center mural, was pure aestheticide. It set a dangerous precedent, opening the way for the destruction of any art with which those in positions of power did not agree, the end result being the loss of artistic freedom for all.

Winny had taught him well.

An important postscript to this story: The day the sledgehammers came out, Jonathan called Rivera and offered to commission the Mexican artist to paint a mural for the corporate offices of Dandy-de-odor-o. Rivera politely declined, but did eventually accept a financial contribution from Jonathan, which compensated him in part for work he did on another mural: a brazen reaction in colorful fresco to the Rockefeller Center debacle. A small private library in Harlem had the honor of Rivera's gifted services. "You Americans view all states outside your own Capitalist-strangled system as imperfect, while you blind yourselves to your own blemished history," Rivera is said to have screeded (in Spanish) as he embarked upon this new commission. "Perhaps it is time to remind you how far your nation has to go in reaching that pinnacle of perfection to which you smugly think you have already ascended."

I have found no visual record of Rivera's anti-American library mural, which was inadvertently painted over in the seventies. (The wall now depicts a cavalcade of American presidents up to Gerald Ford as imagined with African American features.) However, I have read descriptions of some of the images incorporated by Rivera into his mural in Geraldo Rivera's controversial *The Story of My Grandfather Diego*. Together they form a frightening indictment of an America rejecting the very ideals upon which it was built:

• American soldiers issuing Small Pox-infected blankets to Indians in the 1870s. (Interestingly, Rivera had touched upon one of the world's first acts of bio-terrorism!)

• The U.S. Supreme Court declaring unconstitutional in 1918 the nation's first federal child labor law. (Rivera supposedly has the justices using the backs of young babies for footstools.)

• The racially motivated attack on off-duty Black Union officers by citizens of Zanesville, Ohio, near the end of the Civil War.

• There was also an unflattering picture of a snoozing, pot-bellied J. P. Morgan, his nose painted the size of a cant-aloupe, and another of Andrew Carnegie building libraries with the bones of steel workers who had unfortunately gotten within firing range of the philanthropist's hired strikebreakers.

• And finally, for no reason other than, perhaps, mischief, an image of Frida Kahlo seated before her vanity mirror, grooming her famous eyebrow.

Incidentally, a Ms. Ruby Towers, whom I met in Harlem, tells me that she has a photograph of the lost mural in her possession but would not let me see it unless I helped her "honey-voiced" granddaughter Shauneequa get on the television program *American Idol*. This I could not do.

30. **In time Jonathan and Hunter grew closer.** Jonathan's improved relationship with his stepson is evidenced by this letter home from summer camp. Hunter Gleason to Jonathan Blashette, July 5, 1934, JBL.

Dear Dad,

Greetings from Camp Chaubunagungamaug! Camp Chaubunagungamaug is everything that you said it would be! Thank you so much for sending me here! Everyday I go swimming in Lake Chaubunagungamaug or me and the other fellows go hiking in the Chaubunagungamaug Forest and look for nuts or trail markers left by the Chaubunagungamaug Indians who lived here in days of old. It is a swell place and I am making many new friends here. I hope that you send me back to Camp Chaubunagungamaug next year. Oh well. Time to go fishing. You guessed it. Lake Chaubunagungamaug. I hope I catch a big one!

Give my love to Mom.

Sincerely,

Your stepson, Hunter

PS. Tomorrow the Chaubunagungamaug Forest rangers are going to let some of us fellows go up to the top of the Chaubunagungamaug Forest lookout tower to see if there are any forest fires in Chaubunagungamaug Forest or around Lake Chaubunagungamaug. I hope not, because then they'd have to evacuate Camp Chaubunagungamaug! Gee, this letter took an awfully long time to write!

31. **Davison was dubious midwife at the birth.** I cannot substantiate Harlan Davison's claim that he was present at the creation of Alcoholics Anonymous. True, Jonathan's trusted Man Friday was in Akron on a Dandy-D business call the very same night in 1935 in which William Griffith Wilson and Dr. Robert Holbrook Smith brainstormed together until dawn, but neither Wilson nor Smith mentions his presence in their personal accounts. Still, among Davison's papers I have found what might have been his ultimately unsuccessful contribution to the evening's session, "Twelve Steps to Sobriety." The two pages are coffee-stained. (Legend has it that Wilson and Smith each drank fourteen cups of coffee that night, could not sleep for days, and surgeon Smith, in particular, was so jittery as a result that he allegedly had difficulty the next morning placing a patient's rejected gall bladder into the organ pan.) If the document is authentic, it is easy to see why it was dismissed by the two founders, since it incorporates none of Wilson and Smith's dependence upon the power of religious faith, and at times the spiritually untethered Davison rejects divine assistance altogether. I have found no mention of either the document or Davison's possible participation in the birth of AA within Jonathan's papers, nor in any of Davison's correspondence. Therefore, I draw no conclusions and submit the following document in its entirety without further conjecture or commentary.

Twelve Steps to Sobriety
A draft
by Harlan Davison

1. We admit that we are presently powerless. We embrace the fact that our lives are controlled by the demon liquid spirits.

2. The existence of God still open to question, we look for a power greater than ourselves with a more temporal address. A respected uncle, an admired high school football coach, President Franklin Delano Roosevelt, and Clark Gable are all good choices. A good choice for women would be the ever-popular Dolores Del Rio.

3. We make a decision to turn our lives over to that power greater than ourselves, unless in the case of Clark Gable, he does not answer our correspondence with anything but an autographed picture of himself as Fletcher Christian.

4. We take a good, long look at our lives, where we have been, and where we have gone wrong. We do not take this inventory in a saloon because it may prove counterproductive.

5. We are specific about what we have done for which we should be ashamed. We make a detailed list. If necessary, we purchase additional Big Chief notebooks.

6. We make the decision to remedy defects in our character that have diminished the lives of others. This step does not necessarily involve the removal of unsightly facial moles.

7. We drink strong black coffee whenever possible, many cups of it. Our teeth become stained but we bear the stains as proud emblems of our sobriety, for lips that taste coffee do not taste liquor, Irish coffee excluded.

8. We make a list of all the people we have hurt. We prepare to make things right with them all, excepting those who have passed away, and in such cases we then prepare to make things right with their children, and if they died childless, we prepare to make things right with a close neighbor or perhaps the family butcher.

9. We make our amends to all those we have harmed in order of the grievousness of the offense. Maiming others with our automobiles would be highest on the list. At the bottom, perhaps, would be making a sarcastic comment to a newspaper vendor when he greeted us innocently and cheerily, only to have our sour mood darken for a moment his beautiful sun-kissed morning.

10. We look deep within ourselves and find those things requiring change, and we change them for the better and when we are wrong we admit it promptly, even if this admission involves chasing after the wronged party and wedging him between furniture to get our point across.

11. We drink more coffee. If necessary, we chew and swallow the grounds. We reek of the stench of coffee, but we rejoice in it, for it represents the essence and incense of our rejuvenation.

12. We share these steps with other alcoholics in need. We come together in groups and say our name and drink coffee and smoke cigarettes and eat lard-shortened doughnuts and sugar fry cakes and acknowledge that we are men and women on the road to sobriety and health through fellowship and mutual support. We celebrate our rebirth as alcohol-freed Americans, ready now to make sober contribution to the life of this great nation, and so we go clear-headed with raised chin and elevated spirits, and with renewed determination to get ourselves off the breadlines and into a job. And Clark Gable willing, we shall succeed.

32. **It was all over but the shouting.** Even on the best of days Dandy-D's vice president for international marketing William B. Worthington would shout his opinions and instructions in a voice so deafening that Jonathan was forced to put an Ear, Nose, and Throat specialist on staff to administer to the injured. Eventually Worthington left to go to work for a turbine manufacturer. In a raised voice, the departing company man confessed that he could not help himself; he came from a long line of shouters, mostly ministers. There is a rich history of bellowing from the pulpit, the phenomenon, curiously, the subject of perhaps the longest book title in American publishing history: *Shouting: Genuine and Spurious in All Ages of the Church, from the Birth of Creation, When the Sons of God Shouted for Joy, until the Shout of the Archangel: with Numerous Extracts from the Old and New Testament, and from the Works of Wesley, Evans, Edwards, Abbott, Cartwright, and Finley, Giving a History of the Outward Demonstrations of the Spirit, Such as Laughing, Screaming, Shouting, Leaping, Jerking, and Falling under the Power &C.*, by G. W. Henry (Oneida, New York, 1859).

33. **Clara could bear no more children.** As disappointed as Jonathan must have been to learn that the surgery would prevent Clara from giving him the biological child he had always wanted, his feelings go unregistered both in his diary and in correspondence from this period. Furman wonders if this might not have been a silent acknowledgment of the fact that the odds were already working against him; even without the fibroid tumors, Clara might still have had difficulty conceiving, given that Jonathan was in possession of an undescended testicle—a condition that generally reduces sperm count and the odds of "hitting the target." Or as Odger delicately put it, "See, ol' Jonny was born with three legs but only one ball. Ol' Tweedledee was tucked away up in his stomach somewheres. Back in those days, why, the

doctors they didn't generally go about the business of dropping those suckers into the oat bag. And even if this had been standard procedure, they'd probably have been too distracted by that extra danged leg to notice that the boy was one nut short of a Mars bar."

34. **"Clara and I have decided to adopt."** Jonathan Blashette to Andrew Bloor, 28 March 1935. AnB.

35. **"Clara says he's the most beautiful baby she's ever seen. Even famed engineer and bridge designer Bascom Caruthers left his blueprints to come down from the attic to give him a look."** Jonathan Blashette to Andrew Bloor, 17 May 1935, AnB.

36. **"We are going to call him Addicus Andrew, after my father and a very dear friend."** Ibid. Bloor's response, coming only a few days after his retirement from Oberlin College, was touching. The complete letter follows. JBP.

May 21, 1935

My dear Jonathan,

You have moved me to tears. I am watermarking my stationery with this shameful welling of my lachrymal glands! I was never blessed with a marital union and so I have never known the joy of fatherhood. You are finally, in your forty-eighth year, partaking of that experience and I wish you all possible happiness.

I have just remarked that I have never known the joy of fatherhood. That is not entirely true. For I have come to think of you as my own son. You have opened your life to me as has no one else and I feel each day the ligature of that special bond we have forged. Yes, like that of father and son. I hope that your birth father will forgive me for trespassing here, but it is true.

I wish all good things for you and Clara, and for little Addicus Andrew Blashette.

Next month I will be moving to Omaha to take up residence with my sister Evetta and her husband Sven. I will not know what to do with myself. Teaching was my life. I will wear the mantle of "emeritus" proudly, but will so miss the classroom and all my students.

Evetta is a blessed soul. Her husband, Sven, however, often tries my patience to the extreme. On my last visit, he brought his catch of the day boastingly into my bedroom and dripped fish water upon my bed. He is illiterate and frequently requests that I read product labels to him. These readings seem to entertain him in a way that I cannot comprehend and I am often required to recite a particular label more than once and employ different voices, especially highly pitched ones that remind him of women from the Orient. I refuse to do this in the presence of my sister. It is an act of humiliation I reserve for Sven alone. Yet sometimes when the recitations are over, I feel strangely invigorated and eager for our next session. I do not understand the reason for this.

Congratulations again on the adoption. I look forward to seeing the child on my next visit to "Chez Blashette."

Give him a little hug for me.

Your friend always,

Andrew Bloor

37. **"Adopted Son of Deodorant Executive Kidnapped. Family had the child for only six days."** *New York Dispatch*, 23 May, 1935.

38. **"God, oh God, what did I do to deserve this?"** Jonathan's "Letter to God," JBP.

12

THE SHIFTING SPOTLIGHT

1. **"I just heard the news."** Nydia Blashette to Jonathan Blashette, 24 May 1935, JBP. Jonathan's Aunt Nydia, sensitive to the emotional toll the kidnapping was taking on Jonathan and Clara, continued to write to the couple, often including verses of inspirational poetry she had penned during stolen moments from her job as hash-slinger at the Fort Ituska Logging Camp Mess Hall. Far from being the balm to Jonathan and Clara that Nydia hoped they would be, the verses served only to sharpen the pain of loss that the couple felt. It is not difficult to see why Jonathan and his wife found the poetry so objectionable, as illustrated by the following excerpt.

You cry for the child at night.
I know.
I hear the whimpers, like the warbly whimpers of the whimperwill.
Like the moping murmur of the moany bird.
Custodian of the empty nest—
A nest robbed of chirpy chick
By the clawed swipe of the thievy rascally rat.
A silent nest where no young one sings—
Where stillness settles heavy, dulled and dampened by the leaden ache of a mother's loss.
A pining and keening among the oaken branches of a family tree
Unnecessarily
Pruned.
A pining, keening, wail-warble
For the happy child who once dwelled within this
Nest of love and twining tangly tendertwig.

Where, oh where is that child-chick so fair,
So young, so soft
So loved.
You cry for the child at night.
Tears that do not dry with the break of day.
In company with the flitter-flutter of the
Mourning Dove,
Newly arrived upon your sill.
Coo.
Coo.
Addy Andy, where are you?

2. **"Did Hauptmann have a brother?"** Nydia Blashette to Jonathan Blashette, JBP. The letter, which I include in its entirety below, prompted Jonathan to direct his local postmaster to return all correspondence from Nydia "to sender," and to temporarily sever ties with a woman who obviously meant well but had a strange way of showing it. Addicus had been estranged from his younger sister for years, and had counseled Jonathan to avoid her as well. It seems that Jonathan finally took his father's advice.

June 18, 1935

My favorite nephew Jonathan,

Nearly a month has passed and I know that the FBI has given you very little hope of ever seeing your little Addy Andy again. I keep thinking of that Mr. Hauptmann who killed the little Lindbergh baby and I have to wonder, did Hauptmann have a brother? Though the handwriting in the two ransom notes is very different, it is my hope that it is the brother who took your child and I will tell you why. Because I believe that unlike the first Mr. Hauptmann, this Mr. Hauptmann could be a different sort of man entirely—one who will hold little

Addy Andy somewhere safe and warm. Perhaps he conveys his baby captives to some secret nursery where they are suckled and dandled and cared for with a gentle Germanic hand. That would be a wonderful thing to learn, would it not? I believe that if one brother is bad, it does not have to follow that the other will also be bad. I would think that there are many brothers who would want to make up for the bad in the evil, murderous sibling. I know, for example, that after John Wilkes Booth assassinated President Lincoln, his brother Edgar who was also an actor, often played the clown at children's birthday parties and sometimes pretended to be Rip Van Winkle and would sleep until time for cake when he would rise up like a big ol' gobble bear, much to the delight of all the little ones. His name could have been Edmund. Or Eduardo.

I have spoken little of myself during these past few weeks. I will say that I am well and except for the mosquitoes here as large as humming birds, the harsh, damp winters, the uncouth behavior of these Paul Bunyan-pretenders (little boys at heart playing at being big burly men) I am happy to be here. Alaska is the last frontier and your aunt is ever the trailblazer.

Perhaps some day I will be able to see you again. It has been many years since we have been together—many years since I was sent away to deliver in anonymity and without scandal that bastard child that grew arrogantly within me.

Your loving aunt,

Nydia

3. **"Cannot thank you enough for helping to bring the child home."** Jonathan Blashette to Special Agent Vaughn

---

Dobbs, June 30, 1935, Correspondence Files, Records of the Federal Bureau of Investigation. It took three days to find someone able to decipher the letter that was safety-pinned to Addicus Andrew's little sailor suit, and then three days more to find someone who could translate it successfully. The language, an obscure Mediterranean dialect spoken by only a handful of natives of the Isle of Fish off the coast of Portugal, posed such linguistic difficulty for Cape May University Mediterranean language scholar Gaffer Hurd that his early attempt at translation into English was roundly dismissed, and the search was renewed to enlist someone more versed in "Piscianeté." Fortunately, this early effort wasn't permanently discarded; I found it nestled safely in Blashette's papers. (Box 71, folder 18), and offer it below in its entirety as curious sidebar:

Dear Mr. and Mrs. Blashette,

Jackle Weebe, my husband (or brother or male cousin or village prelate disguised to look like a beggar-man) got the boy (or baby boy or baby crib mobile or overstuffed box lunch or bucket of mashed fish meal), wrote give-give letter (or ransom note or telegram or thank-you card sent upon receipt of an invitation to an oyster-shucking party) for to give-give us money. I hold the boy (or baby boy, etc.) but Jackle go (or left, or will leave, or is leaving, or will have left—tense unclear here) and me alone with boy (or baby crib mobile, etc.). I wait and wait (or squat and squat, or pace back and forth on one leg like an impatient heron) but take good care of infant (miniature adult, brave little man, wax figurine resembling a weeping Saint Francis of Assisi) and wait so long, I say enough of this! and bring back Avicus Andoo to you with money. I think (I am cognizant, I make a cerebral stab, I choke on the enormity of life's huge portions) that Jackle got eye-big (scared, frightened?) and left me holding the bag. (Or left the cake to be eaten alone. Or left the umbrella open in the sunshine. Or left the clock without a horological function.) So here the little one is. I bought him the sailor suit (or seaman's lucky biscuits, or pipe fitter's line-axe or sequined codpiece). It isn't necessary to reimburse me. (Or don't pay me twice for a deed done once. Or dance, little monkey, dance and I will pay you only with monkey kibble and kindness.)

Best wishes (or sincere regrets, or remembering you always as if the years were pebbles on a vast beach, each stone smooth and distinct and beautiful, yet constituents of the myriad wondrous whole, dear friend).

Rondonia Filette

4. **The kidnapper's name was Jack McKevitt Weebe.** One theory as to why Weebe escaped suspicion for so long is entirely plausible; with his fingerprints having been abraded from years of working in pumice mines, little Addicus Andrew's kidnapper left FBI agents only a tracing of sock lint and a single curl of unassigned body hair by which to track him down. The case wasn't cracked until a bright young investigator not even assigned to the case, Hermes Gasparian, hypothesized that the reason no fingerprints were left at the scene of the crime was not because the culprit had taken special care to wear gloves but because he did not, in fact, possess fingerprints. Weebe was subsequently brought in for questioning along with an old friend of Blashette's from his circus days, Torso Timmy, (a.k.a. Timmy Briggs), the latter quickly released with apologies.

5. **Winny would always remain Jonathan's favorite artist.** Winny's powerful aesthetic influence on Jonathan lived on long after her death. Because of this now deeply ingrained

love of art, Blashette cultivated friendships with artists whenever he could and served as chief patron of the droll and mischievous Fiona Fareed who began her career as a muralist with a penchant for nautical scenes, especially those in which sea vessels take on human characteristics, venture on land, and dance together to happy porcine jug bands. Fareed spent her last years scandalizing the art world by putting flesh and sinew on Georgia O'Keeffe's skeletal bovines and deliberately misspelling Okeeffe's name in her weakly written, meandering apologies.

6. **"Clara has asked for a divorce."** Jonathan's Diary, 15 January 1936. The rest of the entry says, simply, "She doesn't love me anymore." One suspects, though, that there was much more to it than that. The kidnapping had obviously left Clara wrung out, nerve-jangled, and no longer comfortable with the clutter of her life, a domestic chaos that included a high-profile business executive husband whose colorful coterie of friends and associates had become a daily vexation. (It was also an open secret that Clara detested the profusion of partially completed jigsaw puzzles scattered on surfaces throughout the house.)

The trauma of the kidnapping had apparently transformed Jonathan's wife from brassy, gregarious, full-bosomed earth mother to a far more subdued and less spirited brand of hausfrau. I wonder, as well, if the presence of so many paintings of Jonathan's dear departed Winny hanging about the house (not to mention the painting-in-progress of Winny herself staring appraisingly down at Clara on each of her not infrequent visits to the Greenwich Village brownstone) was a factor in the unraveling of her ties of devotion to her husband. It could also be that Clara had come to realize that, for all his professions of affection, Jonathan had never truly loved her with anything even approaching the intensity with which he worshipped Winny (or even Great Jane or Lucile for that matter). Whereas Jonathan and Clara might have been marginally content to recline among the plush cushions of an easy and respectable domestic union, Clara quickly came to embrace a different scenario, one in which she had the bed all to herself, with all the oddball associates who used to enliven her days and nights, now kept at safe distance.

7. **"Reno giveth and Reno taketh away."** Jonathan Blashette to Andrew Bloor, 1 July, 1936 AnB.

8. **Jonathan encouraged his best friend to pursue other interests.** In late 1938, Davison, inspired by the success of Carnegie's *How to Win Friends and Influence People*, Dorothea Brande's *Wake Up and Live*, and Walter Pitkin's *Life Begins at Forty*, decided to write his own self-help book. Jonathan agreed to assist him in finding a publisher, should it be an effort that he found worthy of publication. The end result was *How to Pick Up Women and Keep Them...Until Morning*. The manuscript was never published. The following selection gives ample evidence as to the reason.

Four Sure Fire Ways to Grab Her Attention

1. Compliment her on her hat. (No matter how much you dislike it.) Women like to be complimented on their millinery. Keep your comments simple and direct and do not offer an excessively detailed appraisal. To speak too knowledgeably about the hat's appeal will have her mistaking you for Edward Everett Horton or one of his mincing ilk. She will invite you to afternoon tea but never to her bed.

2. Be topical. Show that you respect her interest in current events and public affairs by commenting casually on some news item that may have come to her attention. Do stay away from the following conversation killers: Hitler and

Mussolini (*unless you are to criticize them roundly and impugn their medieval stands on womanhood*), electrophotography, coelacanths, or Kate Smith (*because you will inevitably make some unkind comment about her size, and this may, in one of many ways, come back to haunt you*).

3. *Touch her gently on the shoulder as you speak. Women like to be touched in conversation should the contact be friendly and chaste. It demonstrates that you are warm and winning. Do not venture beyond a light tap, and use such only for punctuation. Do not use the touch to fill a break in the conversation, for it will draw far too much attention to itself. Do not touch her repeatedly or she will think that you are palsied or battling* delirium tremens. *Do not brush her clothing with the hand, or she may think that she has clothed herself in a garment that is attended by lint. In her mind, your effort to remove this phantom bit of fabric fluff will demonstrate that you believe she is unable to keep herself clean and kempt in public. Finally, do not—I repeat DO NOT paw her or allow the fingers to move independently of one another. You will be mistaken for a masher, lothario, or Ed Wynn.*

4. *Ask her if she would like to join you for a cup of coffee. Add that you are on your way to have a cup of coffee yourself, so the invitation need only reflect a desire to continue a pleasant chat with no additional expectations incumbent. Should she agree to join you, do not under any circumstances offer to buy her anything beyond the java. Purchase of a doughnut for the young woman will indicate a level of interest that may discomfit her. A doughnut by its shape carries Freudian implications that will only serve to create an atmosphere of subliminal discomfort. The following cautionary tale should serve to warn you away from all thought of food in this initial*

encounter: A young man offered a beautiful young woman he had just met a cup of coffee, and once seated at the lunchroom counter, a doughnut as well. She accepted the offer. He placed the order for the doughnut while at the same time ordering for himself a frankfurter with mustard and relish. The man, at one point, found both the doughnut and the frankfurter in his possession, and, exercising a shameful lack of tact, proceeded to insert the processed meat log into the inviting hole of the doughnut with short rapid thrusts, its entry amply lubricated by the slippery mustard and relish paste. The woman, horrified, fled from the lunchroom, and was, in fact, never seen by the man again. The man did not realize his error until much later. By then it was too late to make amends.

9. **However, there is little evidence that the two ever met.** I could find no mention in Jonathan's diary of his meeting with Lou Gehrig a week before the ballplayer's poignant farewell address at Yankee stadium. But Davison does note in his own journal:

Last night Jonathan said he spent a couple of hours at O'Grady's tossing back brews with none other than Lou Gehrig. He said that Lou ended up asking his help with a speech that wasn't quite there yet and was grateful that Jonathan had edited out quite a bit of the foam.

In Jonathan's papers I did find a yellowed scrap of paper, with the scribbled heading "L.G. Goodbye Speech, July 4, 1939." A good thirty to forty percent of the text had been lined through. A section follows (with elision noted in brackets).

I'm lucky. When the New York Giants, a team you would give your right arm to beat, and vice versa, sends you a gift, that's something. When everybody down to the groundskeepers and those boys in white coats remember you with trophies, that's something. [When the fellows in the press box pitch in to buy you a shiny new toaster, that's something too. So is getting a three-speed blender from your shoeshine kid who doesn't have two pennies to rub together on the best of days. And when that woman who sits in the bleachers and sounds like a crow gives you cookie jar shaped like a fat chicken, that's something that will make a fellow sit up and say, "Gee! A chicken cookie jar from the crow lady!" And when the guy who lives over your stoop with the Homburg and the caterpillar brows leans out his window and yells, "Hey, Lou—take this egg poacher—and oh yes, this 'Champion' Croquet set with weatherproof varnish, and this 'Waldorf' Wardrobe Trunk with vulcanized fiber binding and built-in shoe pockets! That sure is something too. I'll say it again.] I consider myself the luckiest man on the face of the earth.

10. **Jonathan changed his mind about converting to Catholicism.** Fate would treat Father McNulty none too kindly. Several years after his highlypublicized sanity hearing, the priest was defrocked for trying to exorcise an epileptic maid-of-all-work. I should note that Jonathan maintained a close friendship with McNulty in spite of all of his difficulties, and even as Jonathan began to take his first tentative steps toward a full embrace of secular humanism, which at this stage involved working the punch ladle during the refreshment portion of meetings of the Society for Ethical Culture.

It has also been alleged that Jonathan's decision not to join the Catholic church can be traced, in part, to Adam Powers's scathing anti-Catholic treatise *178 Questions You Should Ask Yourself About the Catholic Church*, which received a ringing endorsement by the Indiana Ku Klux Klan, although all of their copies were accidentally burned in the infamous Hoosier Book Bonfire of 1928.

Dismissing the publication publicly, Jonathan admitted privately to finding some merit to questions 3, 45, and 79. Only one copy of this notorious tract is known to exist, and it lives in the heavily restricted "Bad and *Very* Bad" vault at the Notre Dame University Library. I gained access only through heavy cajoling and the bribing of a particular sweet-toothed librarian with a dozen of my Grandmother Sally's tasty miniature apple pies (called "teeny pies" in family parlance). I've noted those questions below:

#3 Why do only Catholics and never Protestants see the face of the Madonna in lumber knot holes and the bubbles of simmering cheese fondue?

#45 If the Catholic Church believes that in Heaven all men and women will walk in equality in the warmth of God's beatific gaze, why does it bar female participation in the echelons of its terrestrial church above the station of nun or rectory maid?

#79 What's with the funny Bishop hats? What's that all about?

Adam Powers went on to write a number of other controversial and offensive pamphlets—each praised by extremist elements of the political and religious right. They include the following titles:

Dark Skin, Dark Heart

The Insatiability of the Oriental Woman, Fully Illustrated

Why the World Needs Bubonic Plague

Tchaikovsky Was an Aesthete; Thirty Cautionary Tales of Famous Aesthetes, Fairies, and Limp Wristed Polly Pusill-animitors with Extensive Glossary & Foreword by YMCA Chaplain William "Parson o' the Gridiron" Huggins, author of

The Muscular Christian.

11. **"I am not dating. I am merely spending pleasant evenings with pleasant women whom I meet."** Jonathan Blashette to Andrew Bloor, 4 September 1939, AnB.

12. **Sharine had lived a hard and checkered life.** According to descendants of Sharine Picotta whom I was successful in tracking down, and who would talk to me for a price—specifically tickets to see Tanya Tucker performing in Blaine, Missouri, and several pieces of pristine Revere Wear—Ms. Picotta was not a prostitute in the technical sense. Her handsomely remunerated services were strictly limited to the erotic art of adult wet-nursing, and her clientele among the rich and famous was reputed to have included Wallace Beery, Clark Gable, and German Field Marshal Erwin Rommel.

The fact that Jonathan saw Sharine for only one week may indicate a lack of interest on his part in "lactal lovin.'" Jonathan's Diary, 12 September 1939.

13. **Me be tarsing through the crevettes with the Bim-Bom-Bee.** I have no earthly idea what this phrase means. HD.

14. **"I asked if he was Judge Crater."** Jonathan had every right to ask. The man behind the counter of the small fishing purveyor's shack looked very much like the famously missing Judge Joe Crater. It is unlikely, though, that the lure salesman was, in fact, Crater, the 1930s judicatorial version of Jimmy Hoffa. Nor is it conceivable that his nonagenarian companion was the equally missing newspaperman Ambrose Bierce, although Jonathan inquired about his identity as well. According to Jonathan's diary, the Crater-look-alike responded to Jonathan's inquiry with a sarcastic, "And Amelia Earhart's in the back doin' the dishes, ain't cha,

Fly-girl?" From the rear of the house came a woman's voice, sheared with attitude: "Yeah, gonna finish these pots and pans and then go kiss me some damned clouds!" Jonathan's Diary, 12 October 1939.

15. **"I got the damned runs three days straight! Believe it or not!"** Jonathan met Robert Ripley in the public men's room of the New York Public Library.

16. **"I put on the fez, and I get head-hives. I take off the fez and the head-hives disappear."** Davison was never again to wear a fez. One wonders why he felt the need to put one on in the first place.

17. **She was trampled in the Wilmington nylon riot of 1940.** Barbara Sadler, *Nylon Riots: An Exhaustive History, Volume 3* (Chicago: Sartorial Press, 1953), 255-57. Hiram Diles' wife, Cassia, recovered within a couple of weeks. Her sister Magda required surgery and two years of intensive psychological counseling.

18. **"German pansies are on the war path."** Here, I think Davison means German *panzers*. Davison's Diary, 1 November, 1939, HD.

13

BEI MIR BIS DU PRETTY

1. **"I have been thinking about Great Jane a lot lately."**
Jonathan Blashette to Andrew Bloor, 13 November 1939.

2. **"You should go down and see her."** Andrew Bloor to
Jonathan Blashette, 17 November 1939, AnB.

3. **"I have done one better: I have brought her back to New
York."** Jonathan Blashette to Andrew Bloor, 24 November
1939. Although both Jonathan and Great Jane had
understood that their restored relationship would be chiefly a
platonic one—the reanimation of an old and dear friendship
facilitated by close proximity and, in Great Jane's case, a vast
improvement in life-style—the decision was not easily
understood or accepted by Davison, who wrote in his diary:

*…Apparently the woman was living on the street. He
won't tell me the whole story. Eating out of garbage cans—
that sort of thing. It was sad. But what does Jonny do?
Leave her some money for food, for her to get her own
place? Get her checked into some sanatorium or hospital
somewhere? Nope. He brings her all the way up to New
York and sets her up right in his house.*

*I just don't get it. He's opened his home to this sorry
looking creature with an Arkansas delta accent so thick I
can't understand half of what she says (and that's when
she's got the teeth in) and for what? So he can fret and fuss
over her the rest of her life? Like he owes her something?
What does he owe this woman? They didn't make a go of
things years ago and believe you me they aren't going to
make a go of it now with all those open sores and what
have you. She's a sick, beat-up old woman who's probably*

going to funk him out every day she's there. Which could be years, or hell, she could kick the ol' bucket tomorrow, and send him right into Depression Valley thinking of what he might have done to save her.

That's the thing with Jonny. He wants to save everybody he meets and with his dumb luck he loses more than his share. And I really can't get through to him. So I just keep hands off.

And worry.

4. **"Could you pick up Great Jane after her appointment at Elizabeth Arden?"** Undated note in JBP.

5. **She seemed to bloom in Jonathan's daily company.** Glover, *Three Legs, One Heart*, 189.

6. **Jonathan introduced the former prostitute to penicillin.** Ibid., 191.

7. **"Great Jane is back in my life. I am a happy man."** Jonathan Blashette to Andrew Bloor, 14 December 1939, AnB.

8. **"I told that man, 'you couldn't get elected dog catcher in this town!'"** Taped interview with Amory Gumbert, Ottawaugus Oral History Project. After winning election as dog catcher in Ottawaugus, the small upstate New York town where he had purchased a summer home a few months before, Jonathan learned to divide time between the corporate board room of Dandy-de-odor-o headquarters in Manhattan and the shady lanes of Ottawaugus, where he chased errant mongrels to the delight of locals who'd never seen a three-legged dog catcher before.

The job was not without its perks. Jonathan fell in love with a sassy, long-lashed Chihuahua, which also fell in love with him, and which he named Señor Smalls.

9. **He came within a hair's breadth of winning the big prize.** In Davison's defense, the winning "musical question" on the radio program *For Pete's Sake! I Know that Tune!* was a riff selected from Mexican classical composer Carlos Chávez's torturously named concert piece *Xochipilli Macuilxochitl.* Previously, Davison had impressed Jonathan and others in the audience with the breadth of his musical knowledge and his on-microphone aplomb. In his article on Davison, "Harlan Davison, A Man Who Means" written for the journal *Entrepreneurial History* (13 [1990], 25-42), Griswold Lanham writes:

> *Davison, in an obvious pickle, could only respond with, "For Pete's Sake! I know that tune! I just can't pronounce it!"*
>
> *"Well then," the host rejoined, "can you spell it?"*
>
> *"What do you think I am—an Aztec? Jeez Louise!"*
>
> *"Well, that's a shame," said the host, handing Davison a box of Oxydol detergent as his consolation prize. Had the Dandy-de-odor-o executive answered correctly, he would have gone home with a check for $75,000 and extensive bragging rights.*

Later that night Davison nursed his disappointment with four double bourbons and eventually decked the barkeep when the man ran out of beer nuts. Jonathan bailed his best friend out of jail and let him sleep it off on his sofa. "At least you found something you're good at," Jonathan said consolingly over breakfast the next morning, and raised Davison's spirits by singing the song that had gotten him into the finals the night before. Davison soon joined in as did Great Jane who trilled away from her bubble bath down the hall while little Addicus Andrew merrily galloped to the beat upon the impromptu hobby horse of Jonathan's three knees—the house rocking with the joyous lyrics:

Hollywood party
At Hollywood and Vine!
Motor on over.
Ain't it too fine?
Roll up the sidewalk—
Break out the booze!
Trip it, don't skip it—
It's tomorrow's news!
Starlets and bar-flits
And tinsel tycoons
Are swinging and singing
Those Hollywood tunes!
Hollywood Party!
Come join the throng.
Trip it, don't zip it.
We're all going strong!
Hollywood Party—
The thing to do.
Champagne service
Straight from the shoe.
We're waiting,
We're waiting,
We're waiting
For you!

The world was beautiful again...for the moment.

10. **"The Japanese have bombed Hawaii. We are at war."** Jonathan's Diary, 7 December 1941.

11. **Hunter was first in line.** Another reason for Jonathan's stepson Hunter's eagerness to fight for the Allies in the European Theatre had its origins in his childhood. Hunter's

eighth-grade homeroom teacher, a Frau Brunhilda Röhm, was a cruel martinet who delighted in humiliating her students. She was also German. Proud of her heritage, she was known to administer harsh punishment to any student who wrote her name without the umlaut. A rebellious child, as we have already seen, Hunter refused to employ the umlaut on more than one occasion, and on more than one occasion was punished by being forced to wear brightly colored lederhosen at intramural wrestling matches. The mortification he endured fed his hatred of Miss Röhm and by extension of Germans in general.

And of wrestling.

Hunter would later lose his life on Utah Beach during the D-Day Normandy Invasion. "He was a brave kid," Jonathan wrote in his diary a week later, "a pain in the ass, but a pain in the ass I'm really going to miss. God rest him."

12. **On the secretary's left buttock cheek was a small tattoo of a little baldheaded man peering over a fence.** Cloris Kern, *Kilroy Was There Too* (Daingerfield, Texas: Brenda Books, 1984), 132.

13. **It was one of Davison's life goals to see the Andrew Sisters naked but for tasseled pasties and crotch patches.** Reinhold, *The Story of Dandy-de-odor-o*, 245.

14. **Addicus died after a brief illness.** A curious side note: Though Jonathan's father never converted to Judaism, he had, by the time of his death, earned a special place in the hearts of his many Jewish friends and neighbors on New York's Upper West Side. "Addicus, the Methodist Jew of Amsterdam Avenue" was honored with a six-day Shiva and a namesake sandwich at the Seventy-second Street Delicatessen. The "Addicus Blashette" Arkansas-Pulled-Pork-on-a-Bun remains on the restaurant's menu to this

day, but has never actually been served in this strictly kosher establishment.

Jonathan had been among those who had gathered at the old man's bedside to say their farewells. Continuing a family tradition, he notes his father's last words in his diary (3 January 1942):

You've been a good son, made your papa so proud. Look at you: successful businessman. And such a nice suit. Although Manny could have gotten it for you wholesale. This I should tell you?

15. **"We will call her Molly Chang."** I have found no evidence that Jonathan ever took Davison's idea seriously. It seems clear that Jonathan had always preferred to sponsor or co-sponsor an established radio program (and spot advertising was begun later that year, chiefly during the broadcast of major sporting events, and generally those in which participants tended to perspire heavily). Still, it is interesting to note to what degree Davison felt his idea had merit, even to the point of preparing the following memorandum to Jonathan and Dandy-de-odor-o in-house advertising personnel.

TO: CEO Blashette, et al.
FROM: Harlan Davison
RE: Radio program sponsorship
DATE: February 11, 1942

Gentlemen,

The undisputed popularity of *Fibber McGee & Molly* and *The Goldbergs* makes it clear that Americans are eager to listen to radio programs that follow the trials and misadventures of hyphenated-Americans named Molly. I therefore, contend that the time is right, and in fact, long overdue for Dandy-de-odor-o to sweeten its investment in this lucrative advertising medium, through sponsorship of a Molly-centered program of its own. Whereas Molly McGee is Irish, and Molly Goldberg of the Jewish persuasion, our program will feature the indomitable Molly Chang, owner of a small Chinese eatery in some fictional American city with a sizable Chinese-American community. She will be warm and maternal and will dispense Confucius-like pearls of Oriental wisdom, much like a female Charlie Chan. In fact, she will have a son, not unlike Charlie's number one son—very worldly and American, a real wiseacre, who, when we first meet him, will be wearing a zoot suit. (Blind Uncle Chin-Tang will accidentally sit on the boy's slouchy fedora.)

The program will be comedic and will feature guest appearances by such radio luminaries as Charlie McCarthy and Deanna Durbin. On occasion, though, Molly will become very serious and talk about the war and the struggle of the Chinese people against Japanese aggression. Perhaps W. C. Fields will ask her how she feels about the Rape of Nanking.

I think that she should be played by Loretta Young. For publicity photos she should be made to look like Luis Rainer in *The Good Earth*.

I am open to any additional suggestions you might have about this program idea.

Dandy-de-odor-o Corporate Records. Davison Files

16. **"Great Jane has become Lady Jane."** Jonathan Blashette to Andrew Bloor, 23 November 1942, AnB. The full text of the letter follows:

Dear Dr. Bloor,

I am sorry to hear about your spasms but happy to know that the doctor thinks they will subside with bed rest. Thank you for your sister Evetta's recipe for lemon trout. I will pass it along to Miss Cook and ask her to prepare the dish this weekend. (It is so convenient to have a cook with the name Cook. I asked her once what her first name was and she said, without cracking a smile, "Lovetah." She's a find, that one.)

Great Jane has changed her name. Great Jane has become Lady Jane. And she truly fits the part. I knew the transformation was complete when she asked for season tickets to the Metropolitan Opera. She already has a close circle of female friends with whom she plays contract bridge each week. And she continues her work with an organization that finds steady employment and housing for hoboes (a mission very close to her heart).

I cannot tell you how heartening it is to see the woman's life turned around like this. Her complexion has cleared. She grows stronger with each day, her respiratory troubles having nearly disappeared.

And she has also become a valuable member of the Dandy-de-odor-o corporate family, assisting me here and there with projects as needed. Next week she will be taking her first solo flight on behalf of the company— meeting with sales representatives in Portsmouth, New Hampshire. (We are trying to make inroads with the U.S. Navy, but for some reason American sailors still refuse to use deodorant.)

Best wishes as always,

Jonny.

17. **"Her train doesn't go through Boston, does it?"** Andrew Bloor to Jonathan Blashette, 28 November 1942.

18. **"300 Killed by Fire, Smoke and Panic in Boston Resort—Dead Clog Exits."** *New York Times*, 30 November 1942.

19. **The final death count at the Cocoanut Grove was 491.** Patrick Oldeman, *Tears for the Shawmut*, 301-10.

20. **Many of the bodies could not be identified.** Ibid.

21. **"Jonathan is a basket case."** Harlan Davison's Diary, HD. The full entry for December 3, 1942, follows:

Jonathan is a basket case. This morning he got word that Lady Jane was at the Cocoanut Grove on Sunday night. She had decided to stop for the night in Boston on her way to Portsmouth so that she could visit with a friend whose daughter was a performer at the club. The friend, who got out through the front door before the bodies began piling up, lost sight of Jane in the panic and did not see her again. (Her daughter was among eight chorus girls who leapt from the second floor into the arms of two male dancers!)

Jonathan had warned Jane of the Boston curse. Apparently she didn't take it seriously. And now she lies in some Suffolk County, Massachusetts, morgue charred beyond recognition. It is a horrible thought and one that is taking a terrible toll on Jonathan. He has eaten and slept very little since learning of the tragedy.

22. **"I am changing my name to Job."** Jonathan's Diary, 5 December 1942.

23. **"I am going to sell the company and buy a small island in the South Pacific and live the rest of my life in mourning beneath wind-ruffled palm fronds."** Ibid., 6 December

1942.

24. **"Nix on the South Pacific; the palm trees will only remind me of the Cocoanut Grove. It was an ignited artificial palm that supposedly started the fire."** Ibid., 7 December 1942.

25. **"I am moving back to Pettiville and retire there."** Ibid., 8 December 1942.

26. **"Nix on the Arkansas idea; the place will only remind me of all those I loved who once lived there."** Ibid., 9 December 1942.

27. **"I am going to drink myself into oblivion and maybe take some strong narcotics."** Ibid., 10 December 1942.

28. **"Now why would you want to do that?"** Scribbled query in the margin of Jonathan's diary, 10 December 1942. Apparently heeding the call of nature, Jonathan had left his diary to go down the hallway to the bathroom. Moments later, Jane entered the house through the door to the utility room. Assuming that Jonathan was uptown at his office, she did not call out his name. As she passed his study, she noticed evidence of occupancy: a burning cigarette, a cup of steaming tea, and the open diary. With affectionate mischief, she scrawled these words upon one of the exposed pages, then ducked into the closet. Jonathan returned to his study and to his desk. As he recalls the moment in his next letter to Andy Bloor,

> *The handwriting was unmistakably hers. I thought that I was being visited by a ghost. And then the ghost appeared. She opened the closet door and presented herself—soiled and bruised but generally intact. "Are you real?" I asked, so frightened I could hardly get the words out. She nodded and grinned. "I am real. I am alive. The curse, Jonny, has*

been broken."

Lady Jane had rescued herself from the flaming nightclub but had been knocked senseless when a panic-stricken marine sergeant dived out a window and directly on top of her. When she came to she had forgotten who she was. ("I thought that I might be Eleanor Roosevelt. It was important for me to find a mirror.") Jane wandered in this state of shock and temporary amnesia for ten days, drawing unconsciously from her former street-savvy survival skills. When she finally chanced upon a billboard for "Dandy-de-odor-o—the Deodorant Men Trust. Pick up a stick today. Not available in Boston" the veil of amnesia suddenly lifted. Jane knew at that moment who she was and why she was there. Most importantly, she knew that she had to get home. Back to New York. Back to Jonathan.

Jonathan wrote in his diary that he held her for a very long time, weeping uncontrollably.

29. **"The war is over. Long live the peace!"** Jonathan's Diary, 2 September 1945.

14

BUSINESS AS USUAL, AND BUSINESS UNUSUAL

1. **"Computers are the future."** Louis Krull, "Prominent Businessmen Cogitate on the Computer" *Scientific U.S.A.*, 1946, No. 1, 120-27, 179-85. Davison was misquoted and therefore not nearly as prescient as some give him credit for being. The misquote is followed by its correction.

I see a day in which the Electronic Numerical Integrator and Computer will be light enough to hold in the hand, powered not by 18,000 vacuum tubes but by a few transistors and conducting chips.

I see a day in which the Electronic Numerical Integrator and Computer will be miraculously powered by only 16,000 vacuum tubes and weigh only twenty tons! Instead of taking up one very large room, I am confident the day will come when it will fit snugly into a slightly smaller room, yet leave space for a chair and a very thin filing cabinet.

2. **It was one of Jonathan's less memorable saloon encounters.** Playwright Bertolt Brecht refused to answer the committee's questions and fled to Europe. The members who remained made up the now infamous "Hollywood Ten." Beverly Hillard (known to his close friends as Beverly Hills) spent the balance of his days reminding whoever would listen (including Jonathan) that he, as the forgotten member of the group that challenged the witch hunts of an industry gone Communist-phobic, had been equally maligned and maltreated. Jonathan records their late-night conversation in his diary.

October 28, 1947

After ordering another mai tai, Beverly proceeded to explain that he was being subjected to a more subtle form of persecution. Although the studios continued to solicit his services as hairdresser, all but a few of the stars whose hair he curled and teased refused to speak to him, enduring their time in his chair with grimaces and groans and over-absorption in current issues of Photoplay *and* Modern Screen *magazines, brightening only when they chanced upon photographs of themselves that seemed to successfully capture some special quality that normally remained elusive.*

"I feel like a piranha, an absolute piranha."

"Do you mean pariah?" I asked.

"Yes. What did I say?"

"You said piranha, the Amazonian man-eating fish."

"No, I don't feel like a fish. Is that dart board spinning?"

"I think you've had enough to drink, Beverly."

"Please. Call me Beverly."

"Maybe I should get you home. Where do you live?"

"George Cukor's guest house."

As I was walking Beverly out to my car, he returned to the topic of the evening: "It's because they all think I have Communist ties, see? If they could shun me any more they would. But they need my services. I am indispensable. But yes, they treat me badly. Helen Hayes won't even look at me. Even when I say, like I did last week, 'Helen. Please. You are the first lady of the American stage. Can you not even find it within your heart to make momentary eye contact?' She just shook that prim head of hers, her eyes never leaving the copy of Photoplay *in her lap. The magazine was opened to a picture of Joan Crawford in an apron, making waffles for her two adopted children. The waffles appeared scorched, but the children wore expressions which said, 'We are resigned to eating these, no matter what.' No, I'm not blacklisted in the official sense, but they're blacklisting me all right. In their hearts."*

3. **"A toast to the Blashette Foundation. Just think of all the good you will do now!"** Andrew Bloor to Jonathan Blashette, 15 November 1947.

4. **Within the first two weeks several checks had been written.** Some of Jonathan's many causes and charities were simply too strange not to earn at least passing mention in these notes. Among them was donation of over $10,000 to the Goebel Art Company and Siessen Convent in the Swabian Alps to silence a blackmailer who threatened to besmirch the good name of Sister Maria Innocentia Hummel, the Franciscan nun responsible for the delicately hand-painted porcelain child figurines of the same name that even today command respectable collectible prices. In late 1947 the blackmailer, whose name was either Cutberth or Cuthbert, sent Sister Hummel photographs of a "hummel" that had recently fallen into his possession—one which displayed none of the jolly innocence that characterized her work—yet one that had apparently been signed by the Sister and stamped with Goebel's distinguishing "bee" trademark. The piece depicted a young girl sitting at the knee of a very obvious Satan—pitchfork, spiked tail and all. It is hard to tell from the photograph I came across just what the young girl is doing to the devil's hooves. She may be buffing them or she may be measuring them for shoes. Whatever is taking place, the girl seems

happy to be performing this service for the Prince of Darkness.

No one knows how this double-figurine found its way to Cut(h)bert(h). Was it a counterfeit, or did Sister Hummel, in some dark night of the soul, craft it from a nightmarish vision of Satanic thrall? However it came into being, its existence threatened an enterprise that was making a great deal of money for the Siessen Convent and creating thousands of fans throughout the world. The "devil's hooves" hummel, had it come to the world's attention, would have had disastrous consequences for all concerned. Jonathan's money, along with—it is believed—a large contribution from the Vatican, kept this from occurring.

Along these same lines, Jonathan is reputed to have spent $35,000 in 1960 for a painting of two young girls with very tiny dots for eyes, allegedly painted by Walter Keane on an off-day and potentially so offensive to devotees of Margaret and Walter Keane and their big-eyed offerings that Jonathan took no chances and destroyed the painting upon purchase. "It would have ended my career if word of that painting had gotten out," a very grateful Keane supposedly confessed to Jonathan. "Why didn't you just dispose of it yourself?" Jonathan asked. "I needed the 35 g's," Keane allegedly responded. "I need paint and canvas for my new series—all the American presidents, each with large sad eyes." (Interview with Patsy Esposito, former president of the North American Keane Fan Club, 14 August 1998—two weeks after her family's successful intervention.)

5. **The Blashette Foundation rarely declined a legitimate request.** One of the rare occasions on which Jonathan did turn down a legitimate application for financial assistance involved the Chamber of Commerce of Truth or Consequences, New Mexico, definitely not, in Jonathan's opinion, one of the legendary Seven Cities of the Cibola.

The businessmen of the town had sought his help in financing a public swimming pool for use by the town youngsters. "It gets so hot here, especially in the summer, you understand," wrote a member of the Chamber, "and the kiddies would appreciate whatever generous gift you might offer to help us provide them with a cool place to splash and play when the mercury licks the tip of the thermometer." To which Jonathan, according to Rowan, is said to have responded, "I don't send money to idiot towns that name themselves after stupid radio programs. Go put the squeeze on Ralph Edwards."

Sybil Rowan in her 'Tis Better to Give: The Story of Twentieth Century Philanthropy (Tucson: Holiday-Hays Press, 1981) contends that Jonathan had never been a fan of Edwards. The story, probably apocryphal given that Rowan's corroborating source is untrustworthy, is that Jonathan had been nursing a grudge against the radio and television personality ever since Edwards allegedly spattered urine on Jonathan's shoe as the two men stood at side-by-side urinals in Radio City Music Hall men's room following a screening of The Farmer's Daughter. According to the men's room attendant who supposedly shared the story with Louella Parsons (it was unearthed years later in her "Not for publication" file), Jonathan pointed out to Edwards that he had just peed on his foot. "Which one?" Edwards had replied. "You have so many." Jonathan, peeved and now somewhat ammonia-smelling, left the washroom in a huff, but not without flinging on his way out, "Don't do my life. You put me on This is Your Life, you big giggle-turd, and I'll tell the world you piss on shoes. Don't you dare test me on this."

I can't believe that Jonathan would have demonstrated such animosity toward a man so loved by millions, and especially given the fact that Jonathan was known to urinate on his own feet on occasion when his mind would wander. Nor do

I find Jonathan to have ever been the vindictive type. My guess is that he simply felt the Chamber of Commerce could easily raise money for the pool on its own.

In any event, Jonathan Blashette was never a featured subject of *This is Your Life.*

6. **"Je *suis* debout."** "I *am* standing up." The four-foot ten-inch Miss Piaf didn't see the humor.

7. **This was followed by another visit from Mister Zoster.** The shingles was much more localized this time, confined almost entirely to the right testicle.

8. **Davison left the lunch meeting much later than the others.** While Jonathan was battling his third outbreak of shingles, Davison was experiencing a new bout of dietary priapism, a condition which generally kept him in phallic straights for several hours at a time. Especially troublesome was the fact that the causal meal took place in the dining room of the Manhattan Tennis Club and Davison hadn't had the foresight to change out of his tennis shorts. Abashed and dangerously crotch-tented, Davison was eventually able to draw a favorite waiter into his confidence and enlist the gentleman in securing an accommodating sweatshirt—in this case one that had been left on the premises by either Sydney Greenstreet or Alfred Hitchcock. However, the rescue wasn't effected without a little good-natured fun at Davison's expense. "Trick knee acting up again, Mr. Davison? Can't get up?" "That's right, Manuel. It's hard. Very hard. Now will you hand me the damned sweatshirt before I get myself arrested?" (Cubby Tertwillinger, *Victual Viagra: Fifty Stories of Dietary Priapism, Fully Illustrated* [Knoxville: Ogilby and Bibb, 1999]).

9. **"How often do you masturbate?"** Jonathan's Diary, 13 February 1948. The question came out of the blue. Jonathan responded by removing himself to a seat on the other side on the train. It was several days later, after reading an article in the newspaper, which was accompanied by a photograph of its subject, that Jonathan was able to identify the man as Indiana University professor Alfred C. Kinsey, author of the recently published *Sexual Behavior in the Human Male*. The question, as it turns out, had been strictly and innocently academic.

10. **Other investors in the group were Darwin Crawley, grocery store chain magnate Owen Sampson, and Benito Jannuzzi.** Rowan, *'Tis Better to Give*, 28-46. Friendships with both men were short-lived. Sampson succumbed to a heart attack while attending a performance of Haydn's *Surprise Symphony*. Jannuzzi disappeared at sea while attempting to disprove Thor Heyerdahl's theory on the ancestry of the Pacific Island peoples. Heyerdahl set out in his rudimentary "Kon-Tiki" to show that Peruvians could very well have sailed and paddled their way to, as Jannuzzi contemptuously put it, "Bali Ha!" According to Jannuzzi's more intriguing theory, Polynesians originally came from France. Jannuzzi's hand-hewn boat, the "Funny, Little, Good-for-Nothing Mimi" went down somewhere off the island of Cyprus in the Mediterranean.

Jannuzzi, incidentally, was the husband of Naomi Fillcrest Jannuzzi, best remembered for walking up to General Patton at a London fish market in late 1943 and slapping him silly with a fresh cod. "That's for the shell-shocked boy you struck, you insensitive cabbagehead lout," she snarled as bobbies dragged her away from the red-faced general. Patton allegedly shrugged off the incident, although some witnesses noted that the surprise attack had the unfortunate effect of loosening his bowels.

11. **Each new undertaking proved more interesting than the one before.** Ibid, 56-57. Another project from which Jonathan drew special satisfaction was the commissioning of a piano concerto for his fellow World War I trenchmate, Adam Hines. Hines, whose hopes of a career on the concert stage were nearly dashed, courtesy of a Hun-launched minnie, asked Jonathan for money to fund a unique commission. Inspired by one-arm pianist Paul Wittgenstein (also a "Great War" casualty) who commissioned composer Maurice Ravel to write a piano concerto for left hand only, the result being the now legendary staple of the classical repertoire, *Concerto for Piano and Orchestra in D major for the Left Hand*, Hines made an even more audacious request. Having lost all of his left arm and all but one digit on his right hand, Hines proposed what would eventually, through the genius of French composer Henri Bagatelle (member of the junior varsity "Les Dix"), become the "Concerto for Thumb of the Right Hand." The piece was unevenly received in its premiere performance in Paris on June 13, 1947, although *Le Monde* was effusive in its praise, hailing it as a "triumph of the human spirit, a testament to artistic ingenuity and brio in the face of missing limbs and digits."

Despite infrequent performances, a tradition has evolved over the years. In lieu of applause, audience members customarily offer a Caesarian thumbs-up or thumbs-down at the conclusion of the performance.

12. **Though he was an avid collector of American art, Jonathan's preference for the esoteric and unusual placed him, nonetheless, outside the mainstream.** I had an opportunity to examine the painting in question, which now hangs in the conference room of the national headquarters for the American Association for the Elderly in Grove Dells, Wisconsin. The folk art primitivism and unnatural perspective of the colorful, well-populated

landscape make it doubtful that *Frolics in the Spring* could have been painted by anyone but Grandma Moses. But another hand—a clearly mischievous one—is also evident, and Jonathan's charge in an undated memo to Interim Foundation Director Alva Block that someone may have perpetrated a little artistic vandalism is a plausible one.

In the top left corner behind a barn, two tiny naked figures appear to be engaged in some kind of close body contact that may or may not involve copulation. At top center someone has endowed a draft horse with an abnormally oversized equine phallus. At bottom right, a Boschian devil figure with a trident is chasing a cow. Hanging from the roof of a small farm house is a Salvador Dali-like droopy clock.

I asked the Executive Director for AAE, Lemuel Boychoir, if he had ever noticed these anomalies before. He scratched his head and said, "Well, no." Then he leaned in and examined the painting a little closer and said, "Oh, goodness."

13. **He was laid out for several days with a bout of hepatitis.** Davison believes he contracted the disease from a tainted Bloody Caesar he drank at a family wedding reception. Davison's diary, 20 April 1948.

14. **The rash covered his entire body.** Jones's case was an exceptional one. Failing to settle the matter on his own, Jonathan dashed off this final letter, then turned the complaint over to his attorneys.

> *DANDY-DE-ODOR-O*
> *388 Park Avenue*
> *New York City*

May 31, 1950

Mr. Leon Jones
1515 Higbee

Jacksontown, Illinois

Dear Mr. Jones,

I have offered you more than enough money to cover the cost of your visit to your physician and the prescribed ointments, which, though initially ineffective, have now done the trick. The rash is gone. You are a well man.

I refuse to make an additional payment to you for "pain and suffering." Even a fool knows that you could have avoided this full body rash if you had simply applied the product as directed—to underarms only. It was your own ill-thought decision to heat the product to a state of viscous goo, then slather great globs all over your body that resulted in the pervasive rash. A part of me wonders if you knew full well the potential for this allergic reaction, but made the application, nonetheless, for the sole purpose of wringing from me a large legal settlement.

Well, think again, Mr. Jones. You would be an idiot on both counts.

If you choose to proceed with this threatened lawsuit, I am prepared to defend myself by whatever means possible.

I stand behind my product and its safety and efficacy under normal use. Only fools (or tort twits) would employ it as you have. I refuse to reward your idiocy and/or greed.

Sincerely,

Jonathan Blashette
President and Chief Executive Officer

Dandy-de-odor-o, Inc.

15. **The deposition took three days.** Jonathan's relief upon completing the grueling examination by the plaintiff's attorneys was short-lived. Upon receipt of the transcripts, plaintiff's counsel immediately moved for the presiding judge to force Jonathan to be redeposed. The court reporter assigned to record the original deposition, a frustrated dramatist, had invalidated Jonathan's deposition by turning his testimony (and the questions posed by opposing counsel) into a full-fledged play script. A "scene" follows. JBP.

PLACE: OFFICES OF WILLARD, WILLARD AND VOORHEES, ATTORNEYS AT LAW

TIME: THE PRESENT

DRAMATIS PERSONAE:

<u>Percival Willard</u>, counsel for the plaintiff, nattily dressed with patrician bearing.

Jonathan Blashette, three-legged corporate executive and defendant, pensive, world-weary.

<u>Cyrus Tammey</u>, counsel for the defendant, bulldog store-front type.

<u>Court Reporter</u>, ruggedly handsome, rakishly charming, exuding confidence and imperturbability, and possessed of a certain *je ne sais quoi* that women of taste find seductively irresistible.

AT RISE: A law office conference room. A deposition in progress.

WILLARD (retrieving a piece of paper from co-counsel): Mr. Blashette, I now call your attention to this document, which we will mark "Plaintiff's Exhibit 14." Do you recognize the document?

BLASHETTE (with obvious disdain): Yes, it appears to be some form of correspondence.

WILLARD (with obvious smugness): And you contend you've never seen it before?

BLASHETTE (bristling): I receive hundreds of letters a year, Mr. Willard.

WILLARD (arching an eyebrow, somewhat wryly): Hundreds of letters of complaint?

BLASHETTE (shifting uncomfortably in his seat): Some matching that description, yes.

WILLARD (obviously finding it hard to conceal his delight in having Blashette "on the run"): But never about a defective product? Perhaps someone didn't like the design of your package. Perhaps you ran an offensive advertisement—perhaps placed a Colored Pullman porter too prominently in the photograph. That sort of complaint, yes? But never, never about a defective product.

TAMMEY (rising from his seat): We can do without the sarcastic, racist commentary, Willard!

BLASHETTE (to Tammey): It's all right. I'll respond. We make a good product, Mr. Willard. But a small number of our customers have allergic reactions. There is not much we can do about that.

WILLARD (animated): That wasn't what I asked, Mr. Blashette. I asked if this letter—the one I hold now in my hand—(He brandishes the letter)—may, in point of

---

fact, address the very complaint which my client has made. Perhaps *each* of these letters—(now holding up several pieces of paper in his other hand)—calls the safety of your product into serious question.

BLASHETTE (angry, defensive): We sell Dandy-de-odor-o to millions of men. A few hundred letters of complaint represent a negligible percentage of our sales.

WILLARD (thundering): **YOU STILL HAVE NOT ANSWERED THE QUESTION!**

TAMMEY (with growing belligerence): Mr. Willard, my client, who I'm certain resents this assault on his character—

(BLASHETTE nods.)

—is not going to sit at this table and admit to you that his product is defective on the basis of a handful of letters from an allergic few. Because it is not. If the product *were* defective, Mr. Blashette would not be here. Mr. Blashette, sir, would be out of business.

WILLARD (very nearly a growl to Tammey): The question is still a valid one—is still of paramount importance to our pursuit of this claim. Let's be frank. Dandy-de-odor-o gives men rashes. Even President Truman admitted to such a rash.

BLASHETTE (angrily): He most certainly did not—

WILLARD (interrupting): That isn't what Bess told the distaff members of the White House press corps!

BLASHETTE (rising): Are you here for purpose of discovery, Mr. Willard, or to take shots at me and my company? (Pulls his extra leg up onto the table.) Why don't you make fun of my subsidiary leg while you're at it?

TAMMEY (helping Jonathan remove the leg from the table): We've made our point, Jonathan.

WILLARD (snide, to Tammey): It appears that your client has had a bit too much coffee this morning.

BLASHETTE (exploding): OH, YOU THINK SO? Then, why don't you finish my last cup? (He grabs up his cup of coffee and flings its contents at Willard.)

WILLARD (crying out from contact with the liquid): **AHHHHGGGG!**

TAMMEY: Let's take a break. We all need to calm down.

WILLARD: **I'M SCALDED, YOU FREAK BASTARD!**

BLASHETTE: You aren't scalded. It wasn't even luke— say, what did you just call me?

WILLARD: Freak. Bastard. **FREAK BASTARD!**

(BLASHETTE snatches up Tammey's cup of coffee and flings it at Willard, as well.)

WILLARD: **AHHHGGG!** He did it again! He did it again!

(BLASHETTE settles back in his chair, a self-satisfied grin upon his face.)

WILLARD (turning to the court reporter as co-counsel endeavor to mop up some of the spatter of coffee from his neck, suit jacket and shirt collar): Court Reporter will note that Mr. Blashette has tried to scald Plaintiff's attorney with coffee. Twice!

COURT REPORTER (with a smile): Already noted.

BLASHETTE (breaking into laughter): Homph, homph, heh, hickle, heh, homph.

16. "I asked him, 'Don't you think you've had enough? Can you get home?'" Jonathan's Diary, 10 November 1953. Failure to prevent Welsh poet Dylan Thomas from imbibing that fateful eighteenth straight whiskey at the White Horse Tavern left Jonathan feeling guilty and depressed for days. He subsequently made a pledge to suspend these sodden encounters with the great, the pre-great, and the post-great by avoiding all public drinking establishments for the remainder of his life. Jonathan never lost his taste for alcohol, but he had lost his tolerance for public drunkenness—demonstrated not only by others but also by himself. His vow was put to the test on several subsequent occasions. The following observations (some of suspect veracity), which I have taken from journal entries made during the last eight years of his life, speak to the strength of his commitment. Without a single exception none propelled him, in spite of obvious impertinent curiosity, to accompany the participants and thus go back on his promise.

• Singer Harry Belafonte arm-in-arm with British actor Arthur Treacher, singing "The Banana Boat Song" as they stumbled into Philadelphia's Top Hat Bar and Grill.

• Economist Milton Friedman pressing his nose against the window of the L&L in Chicago, licking his lips, patting his pocketed wallet and proceeding into the warm smoky duskiness of the bar's interior.

• French premier Charles de Gaulle, singer Maurice Chevalier, molecular chemist Linus Pauling, Brazilian soccer player Pelé, anthropologists Louis and Mary Leakey, and comedian Morey Amsterdam moving in a large boisterous clump into the Oak Bar of New York's Plaza Hotel.

• Actress Elizabeth Taylor flying out the door of the Brown Derby in Hollywood, followed by an angry Debbie Reynolds, swinging a large handbag and snarling epithets.

• Deposed Cuban dictator Fulgencio Batista, rock balladeer Roy Orbison, television newscaster Chet Huntley, Ethopian marathon runner Abebe Bikila, singer Ethel Merman, and Harlan Davison glimpsed through the window of the St. Elmo Steak House in Indianapolis, drunkenly pelting one another with handfuls of beer nuts.

17. **"I like bikes. I don't like Ike."** Jonathan supported Eisenhower until June of 1953 when the president refused to commute the death sentence of the Rosenbergs. Jonathan Blashette to Senator Estes Kefauver, 2 January 1954, carbon copy in JBP.

18. **It was another missed opportunity.** Davison was never able to tell southern writer Flannery O'Connor how fond he was of her work. Walking up to her house in Milledgeville, Georgia, he tripped over one of her ubiquitous peacocks and was shouted off the property. Davison's Diary, 28 February 1954.

19. **Nor was he able to tell Vladimir Nabokov the same.** Settling into Nabokov's living room Davison knocked over a glass case containing a portion of the controversial novelist's prized blue butterfly collection and was shouted out of the apartment. Through the heavily accented barrage of profanity, Davison caught the sentence, "Flannery warned me about you!" Ibid., 3 March 1954.

20. **"I am the Tenzing Norkay of this organization."** The reference was to Sir Edmund Hillary's sherpa guide on his successful climb to the summit of Mount Everest. Davison compared his contribution to the health and success of Dandy-de-odor-o, Inc. to that of Mr. Norkay, who, in

Davison's opinion, was equally unacknowledged and unappreciated. Memo to Jonathan Blashette, 12 March 1954, Dandy-de-odor-o Corporate Records.

21. **Davison did it again.** Griswold Lanham, "Harlan Davison," *Entrepreneurial History,* 13 (1990), 25-42. As Davison's behavior become more unpredictable, Jonathan's unshakable allegiance to his right-hand man became increasingly difficult to defend. While none of the Dandy lieutenants ever suggested either publicly or privately that Davison should be asked to resign, they never hesitated to bring his mishaps and increasingly bizarre corporate strategies to the boss's attention. The following letter found its way to Jonathan's desk on May 3, 1954.

I REMEMBER MAMA

April 27, 1954

Harlan Davison
Executive Assistant to Jonathan Blashette
Dandy-de-odor-o, Inc.
388 Park Avenue
New York City, New York

Dear Mr. Davison,

Thank you for your letter of April 20. I have reviewed your suggestions and shared them with Mr. Nelson and the producers of the television program *I Remember Mama.* We, like you, are happy that sponsorship of our show has been a successful undertaking for your company, and we look forward to continued success in the future.

We cannot, however, endorse any of the story suggestions you offered in your letter. Without exception, all would be ill-suited for the program, and in some cases creatively counterproductive. As you know, *I Remember Mama* is a warm and gentle look at an immigrant Norwegian-American family living in San Francisco at the turn of the century. The story line of each episode is carefully crafted with respect to established characters and milieu, and in accordance with network standards and practices. I am happy to state our specific objections to each of your requests.

1. *"Papa should die. Mama, now a widow in reduced circumstances, will be forced to let rooms for the needed income. Thus, opportunities will abound for bringing popular guest stars on the show and for creating many opportunities for shenanigans and hi-jinks. Milton Berle, for example, could play Uncle Oofda, a fishmonger with a penchant for tomfoolery."*

We have no desire to lose the character of the father. He is an integral part of the story. Nor would Milton Berle's participation be wise. His enormous popularity notwithstanding, he would, no doubt, hijack the program and put everyone in frocks.

2. *"Katrin, rather than opening every single episode by leafing dreamily through her family album, should on occasion 'remember Mama' from a sudsy, sultry bubble bath."*

The idea of turning wholesome Katrin into a sex-kitten is one with which none of us would be comfortable.

3. *"You have dodged the bullet for far too long. The time has come to put your characters through the event that historical accuracy dictates must certainly have occurred at some point during Katrin's remembered youth: the San Francisco Quake of '06. It is inconceivable that Katrin would remember so fondly the rich details that defined the*

day-to-day lives of Mama and Papa and young Nels and Dagmar, yet resign to lifelong amnesia the catastrophic carnage that could not help but rip to ribbons the fabric of this close-knit family. You do your viewers a great disservice by pretending that the lives of these San Franciscans were conveniently untouched by one of the greatest tragedies of the early 20th century. Should you wish a less overt approach, I might suggest the following: an episode which takes place before the tragic event in which Mama has a terrible premonition that the town is about to experience carnage on a grand scale. She will be sent to a doctor for counseling but he will dismiss the forewarning as simple dyspepsia. However, in the last minute of the show, the rumbling will begin. It will be a chilling moment. Katrin's voice will be heard, hauntingly: 'I remember the time that Mama was right. Dead right.' The following week we would see the family sifting through rubble.

Mr. Davison, our program is set in a different San Francisco. A San Francisco in which earthquakes **do not** occur. A San Francisco that does not even rest upon a single seismic fault line. This is our choice. Our viewers do not tune in each week to witness "catastrophic carnage." They can get that by watching the Roller Derby.

With all best wishes,

Frank Gabrielson

22. **"I fired Davison today."** Jonathan Blashette to Andrew Bloor, 3 May 1954, AnB.

23. **"I have lost my best friend."** Jonathan's Diary, 3 May 1954. The estrangement lasted eighteen months and took its toll on Davison. In addition to being his friend, Jonathan

also served as both rudder and fender for Davison, whose interchange with the world often left a deficit of understanding for all concerned. Rather than receding from a society from which he felt alienated, Davison often found himself shoved front and center, there to be ridiculed by a press that had come to dub him "The Wrongway Corrigan of the Eisenhower Era." Typical of Davison's struggles in this harsh public light is the "Levittown Incident." The account which follows comes from *The Long Island Courier*, August 4, 1955.

Wandering in the Levittown Wilderness
by Kerr Barabas

Levittown resident Harlan Davison, former executive assistant to Jonathan Blashette, three-legged president and CEO of Dandy-de-odor-o, Inc., had a little trouble making his way home on Tuesday night.

"We were in the middle of dinner," reports Levittown resident Eddy Rubio, "my whole family and me—and all of the sudden the front door opens and in walks Mr. Davison. He goes straight to my favorite chair, kicks off his shoes and settles himself right down with a *New York Newsday*."

It appears that Mr. Davison was unaware he had entered a Levittown bungalow that clearly was not his own.

This scene was repeated three additional times as Mr. Davison sought without success to find his own home amidst hundreds of look-alike dwellings, each with an identically landscaped front yard.

A postwar American dream for many had for Harlan Davison become a personal nightmare.

"It would help if I could remember my address," a

noticeably embarrassed Davison told police as he was being led away to look for his home.

Blashette could not be reached for comment regarding his erstwhile employee. A spokesman for Dandy-de-odor-o did say, "Davison never had trouble finding his office when he worked for us, but he once confused Barbara Bel Geddes with Nancy Olson at a product launch party, unfortunately in the presence of Barbara's father Norman, who was being wooed to design packaging for a new deodorant product."

24. **"I'm not sure which is worse—having Davison here shambling things up, or having him out there where I can't help him."** Jonathan Blashette to Andrew Bloor, 21 October 1955.

25. **"Then hire him back and bring someone on board to look after him."** Andrew Bloor to Jonathan Blashette, 26 October 1955.

26. **"Shall we set that fence aright?"** Jonathan Blashette to Harlan Davison, 1 November 1955 Davison Papers. The full text of the reconciliation correspondence follows.

Dear Harlan,

I know an old fence that's been in need of mending for three long years. What say I bring my tool box and you bring yours and we'll set that fence aright?

Jonathan

***

Dear Jonathan,

I'm already there, tool box in hand! I don't quite know where things went wrong. I know I've made some mistakes along the way and I know you've been a real trump and let me off easy. I guess the mistakes just got too big to keep brushing aside, huh? I can't tell you why my brain doesn't work the same way as everybody else's. Maybe it's because I got kicked in the head by that mule when I was fourteen. Maybe that jumbled everything up and left me looking at the world a little crossways. (Or it could have been that second kick when I was seventeen. Can't really put my finger on which one did the most damage.)

But I keep thinking back to that day you fired me from Dandy-D. I can't think of what it was I did that could have provoked you more than the usual. Unless it was that comment about the Ink Spots and the Mills Brothers. Maybe that was the last straw. I'm telling you, honest, Jonathan, I've always had a little trouble telling the difference between those two groups—there wasn't any malice toward you (because I know you're partial to one of them although I can't remember which) or to Negro singers in general. You know my grandmother was probably a Negro, so why would I cast aspersions on my own people?

I know this all happened around Winny's birthday and I know it always puts you in the emotional crapper when any of those Winny anniversaries roll around. But you know what? At least you had a Winny. And you have Lady Jane and she's turned into a really special gal. I'm not saying this to get any kind of pity from you. I'm just stating fact. You have loved and been loved back. The revolving door of *my* love life has spun far too fast for me to know how I felt about any of those dames (or vice versa). And the one chance I did have of walking down the aisle with one of them I pretty much botched up by getting the wedding day wrong and going fishing. It would have been nice to have had a Winny or a Lady Jane, if only for a short while. To trade in that revolving door for the kind that actually opens and stays open. Or maybe one of those Dutch doors where you can open the top part and not the bottom or vice versa just for the fun of it.

But there *is* a consolation. Friendship. Friendship with my ol' pal Jonny, restored to its former shine. I've got that toolbox, Jonny, and we're going to get that fence looking good as new. It's a nice old fence, and nicer still, to find us both working on the same side.

Your friend,

Harlan

***

Dear Harlan,

It's a deal. I'll call you this weekend.

Jonathan

27. **The cause of death was congestive heart failure.** In accordance with her wishes, Great Jane was buried in a simple pine box in the Calvary Baptist Church Cemetery in her home town of Chucking, Arkansas. It was not a well-attended burial service. Yet, in New York City, three weeks later, over 250 people came to her memorial, which was held at Washington Square Methodist Church in Greenwich Village, this number including many employees of Dandy-de-odor-o and at least twenty former Time Square prostitutes whom Jane had reformed and persuaded to enroll in secretarial school. Great Jane had made a lot of friends in the Big Apple. Glover, *Three Legs, One Heart*, 222-25.

28. **"Goodbye, my Lady Jane. I love you so."** Interview with Cassia Diles who overheard the words spoken by Jonathan at the burial site.

29. **Damage to Jonathan's art collection was estimated at nearly $3,500,000.** Cary Bormet did not limit his destruction and vandalism to art work held in private hands; in his rampage he destroyed and variously defaced pieces on display in public collections as well. He is most notoriously remembered as the man who relieved himself in Marcel Duchamp's urinal, "Fountain." Adding insult to insult, the art-phobic Mr. Bormet made a point of eating three dozen stalks of fresh asparagus two hours before perpetrating the deed.

30. **"And the days dwindle down to a precious few."** Many remember that Walter Huston's version of "September Song" was among the handful of those songs that Jonathan held most dear in the last years of his life. Few knew that this shortlist also included several of what he called his "silly songs." JBP.

"Bongo, Bongo, Bongo, I Don't Wanna Leave the Jungle"

"The Too Fat Polka"

"Good-bye, Mama, I'm Off to Yokohama"

"Does Your Chewing Gum Lose Its Flavor on the Bedpost Overnight?"

"Chica Chica Boom Chic"

"We're Going to Balance the Budget"

31. Jonathan ordered the Happy Family in Ginger House. Others in the dinner party were more adventurous. Davison got the Surprised Squid in Scallion Panties; Caldwell ordered the Plum Duck and Crispy Chicken in Fragrant Pas de Deux; Diles had the Accommodating Prawns in Discourteously Demanding Lobster Sauce; Haverty had the Sauteed Baby Abalone Mushrooms Kissed and Tongue-stroked by Puckered Snow Peas and Honey-coated Testiculoid Walnut Chunks. Bayer, the bravest of all, tried, and nearly finished, the Kong Style Simpering Slippy Shrimp in Velvet Scallop Squirt Curd, Dragged through a Math of Brazed Beef Tailings. Jonathan's Diary, July 12, 1956.

32. This period saw a number of major celebrity endorsements. Reinhold, *The Story of Dandy-de-odor-o*, 188-90. Among the many media personalities approached by Davison was Greta Garbo, who he contends gave serious consideration to ending her long retirement by appearing in a television ad for Dandy-de-odor-o. According to Davison's journal (10 September 1956), Garbo was also considering two other offers at the time, one for the American Beet Growers Council and the other for Whip it Whipped Oleomargarine. All three scripts exploited Grusinskaya, the angst-ridden prima ballerina character Garbo made famous in the film *Grand Hotel*.

Dandy-de-odor-o:

GARBO (to an overly perspiring young male companion who has just ended a strenuous game of tennis): I vant to be alone…that is, until you shower and make liberal application of that wonderful male deodorant product Dandy-de-odor-o.

COMPANION: Roger Wilco! See ya in a jiff, Grets.

The American Beet Growers Council:

GARBO (to a waiter in a restaurant): I vant to be alone… with this big plate of sliced beets.

WAITER: Yes, ma'am. Anything else?

GARBO: Bring me some tripe.

Whip-it Whipped Oleomargarine:

GARBO (to her maid after nibbling a cracker): I love the taste of butter.

MAID: Au contraire, Madam. It is Whip-it Whipped Oleomargarine.

GARBO: What insolence. Go away, Cosette. I vant to be alone. (After the maid has departed. To herself.) Mmm. Whip-it. That's a name I'm sure to remember. (Turning to the camera.) And you will too. Just ask your grocer for *Whip-it!*

History will record that Garbo never came out of retirement. Some of Davison's journal entries I find highly dubious; others are easily corroborated by other sources. This one falls somewhere in between. Indeed, Jonathan's entry for the same day notes:

> *Davison is trying to get Greta Garbo to appear in one of our commercials. That would be a coup. Or does he mean the comedienne Greta Gabor with the pop-eyes?*

33. **This also included sponsorship of the Miss United States Pageant.** Griswold Lanham, "Harlan Davison," *Entrepreneurial History*, 13 (1990), 25-42. Davison was also instrumental in winning sole commercial sponsorship for the inaugural (and ultimately only) television broadcast of the Miss United States Pageant, a brief rival to the popular

Miss America Pageant. The contest was expressly organized by its eccentric producer Barclay Harwood to determine the most beautiful and talented young woman in all of the forty-eight states except Ohio. Davison felt that the broadcast would be an ideal opportunity to advertise Dandy-de-odor-o's new deodorant line for women, Dandeene.

As with almost all of the advertising ventures shepherded by Davison, this one backfired. The stumble created one of the largest customer backlashes in the history of mid-century American commerce. Residents of Ohio, angered over their state's exclusion from the pageant, staged a boycott of all of Dandy-de-odor-o's products, including "Dandy fresh swabs," a product being test-marketed in Columbus and Cincinnati at the time.

Harwood's hatred of Ohio was legendary, but still to this day inexplicable. It resulted in a highly publicized altercation with the chairman of the Indiana state pageant and its winning entrant to the national pageant, Barbara Jane Midkiff. The contretemps served as inspiration for a memorable comedy sketch on the television variety program *Laffin' Loud with Leila and Lee*. I obtained a copy of the script from the Museum of the Media in Toledo, Ohio. An excerpt follows:

> *HARWOOD*: Miss Indiana, it has come to my attention that you are a resident of College Corner.
>
> *MISS INDIANA* (shaking her head): *West* College Corner, Mr. Harwood.
>
> *INDIANA CHAIRMAN*: Which last time I checked was in Indiana.
>
> *HARWOOD*: Interesting. Because I have it on good

authority that the young lady *isn't* from West College Corner, which, yes, is in Indiana, but from *College* Corner, which happens to be in…in…(His eyes suddenly roll back in his head and he loses control of his saliva.)

INDIANA CHAIRMAN: Mr. Harwood, are you unwell?

HARWOOD (now perspiring and shuddering uncontrollably): In…in…

INDIANA CHAIRMAN: I can assure you, Mr. Harwood, the girl who stands before you is a Hoosier. She's always *been* a Hoosier, haven't you, Miss Indiana?

MISS INDIANA: Always? Well…*no*..

HARWOOD (regaining his composure): May I ask, then, when it was, exactly, that you moved to the Hooter state?

MISS INDIANA: I beg your pardon.

HARWOOD: I *said*—

INDIANA CHAIRMAN: Mr. Harwood, I believe that you just referred to Indiana as the "Hooter" state.

HARWOOD: I did?

(Miss Indiana nods, scowling. She folds her arms guardedly across her chest.)

HARWOOD: I'm terribly sorry. My point is this: my sources tell me that you moved to Indiana only three months ago. And for one purpose only: to qualify as a contestant in the Miss United States Pageant!

MISS INDIANA: It's true, you're right. But I simply *had* to! You've made it quite clear that you'd accept no contestants from…

(Harwood slaps his hands over his ears, and begins to hum loudly the theme from *Magnificent Obsession*.)

MISS INDIANA (continued):...the Buckeye State. And why should I be penalized for this? Look at me. Am I not worthy of this pageant? Look at these hips. (Dropping her arms down to their sides and throwing out her chest.) Look at these *hoosiers*.

HARWOOD: I'm sorry, my dear. Your beauty and shapely figure are invalidated by the fact that you are from...from...(He goes into a seizure and collapses).

INDIANA CHAIRMAN (to Miss Indiana, as he works the end of a pencil into Harwood's mouth to prevent his swallowing his tongue): Face it, Babs, it just ain't gonna happen. We should notify your first runner-up. Where is she?

MISS INDIANA: Back home with her folks. In Cleveland.

INDIANA CHAIRMAN: Oy!

34. **"High expectation begot profound disappointment, as if a much anticipated Beaujolais revealed itself to be, in sad fact, aged to the point of insipidity, such is my feeling over the failure of this merger."** Jonathan's Diary, 17 April 1957. Jonathan was never more ready to step off the corporate stage, the merger with Gallico Industries permitting his release to pursue, full-time, his interests in venture capitalism, philanthropy, and the search "for my place in the universe." He writes in his diary at length of his devastation over the turn of events. Davison's journal also records that Jonathan was not himself for several weeks. Had Jonathan known that Gallico's anchor product, "Stenchaid," a groin-directed atomizing cannon, would be

ultimately discredited and maligned by the same industry that had earlier touted it as a revolutionary Godsend for obese, wheelchair-bound victims of unaerated-thigh space, Jonathan would not have spent so much time and ink bemoaning the sudden contractual reversal.

35. **"Father, I am ready to take the reins of this swell company."** Addicus Andrew Blashette to Jonathan Blashette, 3 May 1957.

36. **"I would like to groom my son to take my place."** Jonathan Blashette to Andrew Bloor, 5 May 1957. The letter that Andrew Bloor sent in response has been lost. My guess is that Bloor was cautiously supportive. Addy Andy had just turned twenty-two. His experience at Dandy-de-odor-o, Inc. up to this point had been limited to part-time mail-room clerk and warehouse stock boy. Yet the young man was eager to learn the ropes of his father's business and move quickly up the corporate ladder. And Jonathan seemed unwilling to elevate anyone else. "This isn't about creating a family dynasty," he explained at a board meeting a few days later. "The boy is smart. He's got the makings of a good businessman. I won't pass the reins until I think he's ready." Minutes of the Board of Directors meeting, 10 May 1957, Dandy-de-odor-o, Inc., Corporate Records.

37. **"He's ready."** Memorandum from Jonathan Blashette to all employees of Dandy-de-odor-o, Inc. *Fortune Magazine* crowed, "Tot of twenty-two takes the helm of multi-million-dollar deodorant company. Wall Street scratches its head today. Will it be scratching its underarms tomorrow?" Company stock value plummeted the next day and did not rebound for several weeks. Jonathan, incredibly, knew what he was doing. By July, Addy Andy's new youthful suntan oil line "Dandy Andy's Shimmer and Shine" had become the runaway product hit of the summer and the wunderkind of the deodorant industry was on his way to corporate prodigy

greatness.

One of my greatest regrets in preparing this book was the missed opportunity to interview at length Jonathan's son, Addicus Andrew. The CEO and president of DDO Industries gave me all of fifteen minutes of his time, this micro-interview taking place in the back seat of a limo on its way to LaGuardia Airport. Subsequently, I made numerous attempts to schedule a second, more leisurely, meeting between the two of us, but was ultimately thwarted by "scheduling conflicts." I do not fault Blashette for assigning such a low priority to seeing me; I understand from his secretary Paulette Karlstrom that he had been very unhappy with Cordell Glover's book about his father *Three Legs, One Heart* and also by Glover's interviewing technique, which often involved sitting cross-legged on Blashette's desk "like a chunky chanteuse sprawled upon an overtaxed grand piano lid." I wish that I had somehow found a way to gain Blashette's trust after this experience, but such was not to be.

15

SETTING SUN

1. **Beauaeuregard Taylor called the meeting to order.** The name of the new director of the Blashette Foundation is spelled correctly. Sybil Rowan notes in her book, *'Tis Better to Give*, that the spelling of Taylor's first name was a "personal frustration" and he wished on hundreds of occasions that his father hadn't been "potted on corn squeeze" the day the birth certificate was filled out. After spelling his name aloud for a college registrar, Beauaeuregard Taylor was instantly accused of being a "wiseguy" and slapped across the face by the man's glove. Why the registrar was in possession of a single, pearl-studded opera glove was never explained.

2. **He was also an established author.** Rowan, *'Tis Better to Give*, 278. This was actually Taylor's fourth novel. He had previously written *Hedgehog's Ball*, *Dancing with My Shadow*, and *No Prayer for Suzie*.

3. **Jonathan stopped going to Café Ennui, complaining that the service was too slow.** Harvey Freeman, "Jonathan Blashette; Inside the Man," *Body Fresh Magazine*, 24, No. 7 (1972): 22-38.

4. **"They are the pretty twinkle stars of my twilight years."** Jonathan's Diary, 2 September 1958. Among the female companions who brightened Jonathan's final years was Venetia House. Not only was the young woman a self-described "jigsaw junkie," but she also shared Jonathan's love of dogs. In fact, it was one canine in particular that played an important role in Venetia's strong religious faith. For many years, including those during which she knew

Jonathan, Venetia was an active member of a small Christian sect that believed that Jesus Christ, as lover of both man and beast, had a pet collie, which accompanied Him during His last months on earth. Among Jonathan's uncatalogued effects I chanced upon a book published by Venetia's denomination, which includes illustrations of the dog being fed table scraps by Jesus at the Last Supper, dog-paddling behind Jesus as he walked upon the waters of the Sea of Galilee, and howling plaintively at the foot of the cross.

I also came across a letter from Venetia to Jonathan in which she apparently addresses his skepticism. The book referenced below is apparently the one I discovered.

Dear Jonny,

I know you think it foolish for me to believe that Jesus had a collie. I know that collies come from Scotland. But is it really inconceivable that the dog could have made his way down to the Holy Land to be with our Lord and Savior? Collies have covered far greater distances, I assure you. And who is to say that Jesus did not, himself, go to Scotland, and find the dog among the heather? The Mormons believe that Jesus crossed the Atlantic Ocean to spend time in the American West, so to me it is entirely believable that He could easily have found Ruggles in the Scottish highlands and brought him down to the land of milk and honey.

I find the pictures in the book very moving. I agree that there are perhaps a couple that should not have been included. I don't think that Jesus knew lawn bowling; I think the author and illustrator should have devoted themselves only to known events from the life of Christ. And I still believe that on the day that Jesus performed the miracle of the loaves and fishes, there were no gnaw-bones in that basket. It was not customary in that day for people to take their dogs to public events. But these are minor objections. *Our Holy Savior and His Dog* is a good book and I would recommend it to anyone.

People who do not understand our faith sometimes laugh. I recall that you could not hold back a chuckle when you saw the picture of Ruggles licking the face of Lazarus to help Jesus wake him from the dead. But let me assure you, that for someone who believes as strongly as I do in Jesus' canine companion, it is no laughing matter.

It is all a matter of faith, as you can understand.

Yours,

Venetia

5. **Other bizarre friendships enlivened his retirement.** Author's interview with Odger Blashette. Among those within that small subset of friends who didn't happen to be seeking philanthropic or entrepreneurial sponsorship from Jonathan was Roger Tierney, an inmate at Washington State Correctional Center. Tierney had originally written Jonathan in error, thinking he was setting up a long-term pen-pal exchange with a Jacqueline Blasset (Not to be confused with the actress Jacqueline Bisset who would have been much too young at the time to be corresponding with an incarcerated felon). Jonathan courteously redirected the letter, but this kindness only prompted Tierney to begin corresponding with Jonathan as well, especially when he learned that his inadvertent pen pal had overcome a disability to become a leader in the male deodorant industry, and did so without breaking any laws.

Tierney's notoriety, was, in fact, well known to Jonathan. Twenty years earlier the felon had kidnapped several contract-bridge-playing residents of the Setting Sun Senior Center in Bellingham and removed them all to a remote logging camp in British Columbia. Here the eight women were forced to participate in a grueling birling competition to the delight of Tierney and his logging buddies. The muscle-sore senior citizens were rescued by Canadian Mounties within a couple of days, and returned home safe and sound, but the crime drew Tierney stiff sentences from both the Canadian and American judicial systems, following jurisdictional wrangling that ended in joint penal custody. "It was worth it, though," Tierney once admitted to Jonathan, "seeing them old ladies spinning those logs like the jacks do. I even noticed a smile on a couple of their rosy faces. 'Bet they never thought they'd be coming up on the end of their lives and get to roll themselves a danged log!"

6. **Jonathan began to see more of Helga and less of Venetia.** Author's interview with Helga Houston. Helga was the sister of Maylene Houston Carmichael, who spent much of her adult life trying to discredit the "Refrigerator Mother" theory of autism put forth by psychologist Bruno Bettelheim and embraced by most of the members of the American psychiatric community in the face of mounting evidence to the contrary. Considered by Maylene and her supporters to be yet another misogyny-motivated attack on motherhood, Bettelheim's belief that autistic children were created by cold and unloving mothers was never recanted by the famous psychologist and was only slowly (and one imagines, mostly reluctantly) surrendered by his colleagues. Maylene's frustration (she was the mother of an autistic son) and rage against Bettelheim knew no bounds, and resulted in one particularly unpleasant incident in which she mailed mice feces to him at his office at the University of Chicago's Sonia Shankman Orthogenic School for Disturbed Children, disguised as a giftpack of gourmet peppercorns. It is not known if Bettelheim ingested them.

7. **Davison often turned up in the strangest of places.** There isn't much doubt in my mind as to the identity of the older man hurling the large rock in the foreground of the photograph. The question, though, is what Davison was doing among the Peruvian demonstrators who had taken to pelting Vice President Nixon's car with stones during his 1958 Good Will Tour gone bad. Davison's diary is frustratingly silent on the whole episode. None of the correspondence I have examined from the period indicates why he took the side trip from Buenos Aires, Argentina, where he was scheduled to attend a meeting with South American patent officials on Jonathan's behalf. In fact, there is no indication from any of the sources I have consulted for this period as to just how Davison felt about the U.S. vice president at that moment, although two years later during the 1960 presidential election he remarked that Nixon reminded him of a druggist he once knew who used to chase teenaged pocket thieves out onto the sidewalk with an extended grocer's claw and who was also thought to have a lifelong addiction to Carter's Pills.

8. **"Her name is Charette. Jonny, I actually think she's the one."** Harlan Davison to Jonathan Blashette, 14 May 1958.

9. **"Sorry. My mistake. She isn't the one."** Harlan Davison to Jonathan Blashette, 15 May 1958.

10. **Charette was a cruel mother.** According to Griswold Lanham's article "Harlan Davison" in *Entrepreneurial History* (13, 1990, 25-42), Davison's girlfriend purchased a Betsy McCall doll for her daughter's birthday in June 1958, then refused to buy it clothes. "Betsy lives in a nudist colony," Charette told Davison in a voice that reminded him of an overly peckish Eve Arden, "and by the way, it ain't really none of your beeswax."

Feeling sorry for young Vicki, Davison bought a wardrobe

for the doll himself and delivered it to the little girl at her grammar school. Vicki's second-grade teacher, a Miss Wingfield, thinking the clothes were for Vicki, chastised Davison in front of the class for not knowing the girl's size. Vicki came to the defense of Davison, whom she had begun to fantasize as war hero, fireman, and/or possibly even her birth father. Having forgotten the name of the naked birthday doll, she pretended that the clothes were, indeed, intended for her. When she attempted to pull one of the little dresses over her head; it became snagged about the forehead. "I've made a real mess of things here," Davison is reported to have apologized. "Come on, Vicki. Let's go get some ice cream." With avuncular tenderness, Davison took the little girl by the hand and guided her to the door, respecting the fact that the Betsy McCall dress draping her head partially obscured her vision. The result was a bit of stumbling that to some of the children resembled a funny dance. Davison and Vicki were blocked at the door by Miss Wingfield, who proceeded to blow her recess whistle painfully close to Davison's left ear. Amidst a wash of playground-minded elementary school children flooding out of their respective classrooms and into the hallways, followed by angry teachers glaring at Wingfield, harumphing, and tapping their watches, Harlan was escorted to the principal's office by two officious safety patrol boys. He was held there until police arrived to book him for attempted kidnapping. In the confusion Vicki disappeared and was later found alone, seated on the down end of a stationary teeter-totter, clutching tightly to her chest the doll clothes Davison had given her and singing softly and wistfully a song she had made up about ponies.

Eleven years passed before Davison saw Vicki again. Now a young woman, she visited him at his home in Levittown during spring break from her studies as sophomore at the Massachusetts Institute of Technology. "You're the closest thing to a father, war hero and/or fireman I've ever known," she confessed, kissing the old man affectionately on the cheek. "By the way, I'm so sorry I'm late. I had trouble finding the house." Then she volunteered to rake up all the leaves in his yard. Touched by her offer and even more so by the visit itself, he replied, "You didn't come all this way just to rake my leaves. But if you like…maybe you could clip the hedge." Together Davison and Vicki spent the afternoon doing yard work and rekindling a friendship.

The two stayed in touch for the remainder of Davison's life. Although he had never gotten himself a wife, Harlan Davison had, in a way, found himself a daughter.

11. **"I Took a Spill."** Jonathan Blashette to Andrew Bloor, 4 February 1959. An excerpt from the letter follows.

You know, Dr. Bloor—I never thought I'd be one of those old farts who go and break their hip as soon as they turn seventy. (In my case, I suppose I got a ten month grace period!) When did these bones get so brittle? How is it that you, several years my senior, haven't had an equally difficult time with the ravages of advanced years?

I have had to do what I never thought I'd do and that is hire a live-in valet or nurse or what have you. A gentleman was recommended to me by the name of Uriah Hensley—a good man, very active in the Negro equality movement. I commend his efforts and those of his son Zachary who is quite a mover and shaker in Civil Rights.

Still, I have never been comfortable with servants except for Miss Cook. I suppose I am basically too much the egalitarian. And how be you these days, sir?

12. **"I, too, took a spill."** Andrew Bloor to Jonathan Blashette, 8 February 1959. An excerpt from Bloor's response follows.

Were we, Jonny, at one point joined at the hip? A very frangible hip, I might add. Yes, I also took a spill, and am likewise incapacitated. You are right. It is a depressing development (although Evetta is taking good care of me), serving only to remind me of my easily verifiable mortality.

For goodness sake, man—if you must have a man-servant, don't spend your days apologizing to the gentleman. He expects to be treated as employee and expects you to comfortably assume the role of employer. Anything less will throw the whole universe out of balance.

And speaking of the universe, have you figured out your place in it, yet?

Just curious.

13. **Zachary Hensley's commitment to civil rights was undisputed.** Zachary's involvement in the Freedom March from Selma to Montgomery and his participation in other historic moments of the Civil Rights movement of the fifties and sixties were complemented by his instigation of the Taylorville, North Carolina, Barbecue Pig Hut sit-in of March 3, 1960. Inspired by the sit-in at the Greensboro Woolworth lunch counter a month before, Zachary and five college compatriots settled themselves down at the whites-only service counter of the barbecue establishment only to be instantly threatened and harassed by the regulars. Hensley's quick thinking turned what might have been a violent, unilateral food-fight into a strong statement for racial tolerance. Learning that one of their number had a

white grandmother, Hensley negotiated a service stance for the young woman next to her stool with one hand permitted to touch the counter and the other hanging at her side. For a young man who was half-black and half-Asian, successful bargaining from Hensley resulted in the man being allowed to sit on the stool in alternate three-minute segments. Another young woman, one quarter Cherokee, was allowed to stand behind her half-Asian Freedom-fighting comrade and be fed by him in small modest bites, each followed by understated chewing. Hensley did not fare as well when it came to his own requested allowance. He left the restaurant wearing a headdress of barbecue sauce. Parker Noell, *Claiming our Stools: History-making Sit-Ins of the Civil Rights Movement* (Los Angeles: Locklear Kun and Sons, 1988), 88-98.

14. **"Her name is Silvana. Jonny, I actually think she's the one."** Harlan Davison to Jonathan Blashette, 22 March 1959.

15. **"So sorry. My mistake. She isn't the one."** Harlan Davison to Jonathan Blashette, 23 March 1959.

16. **Davison saw very little of Silvana after that.** Georgia Neilson, *When Advice Columnists Go Bad* (Los Angeles: Pepper Plum Publishing, 1975), 267-73. Despite widespread syndication throughout the U.S. and the inevitable comparison to popular advice columnists Ann Landers and her twin sister Abigail Van Buren, Silvana Lichtenstein was promptly dismissed and her column deep-sixed. Davison seems to have pounced on this opportunity to break up with the two-hundred-and-fifty-pound, sixty-two-year-old Jersey City native, confessing to Jonathan that the chemistry that he "had thought he felt there in the beginning was maybe never even there at all." I tracked down a copy of what was to become Miss Lichtenstein's final column for the Jacobson Syndicate. Much of the advice she dispensed that day seems fairly innocuous. It was the final "confidential" that appears to have been the career-killer.

Confidential to Distressed in Detroit: The body behind the pool house and the other one beneath the gazebo are strong indicators that he may have buried carved-up corpses all over the bloomin' property! You'd do best to get a steam shovel to help you decide if this is the kind of man you want for a husband and future father of your children. And I'd keep the cutlery on a high shelf when next he comes a' callin'.

17. **This was followed by another death in the Dandy D family.** Reinhold, *The Story of Dandy-de-odor-o*, 245-47. Sadly, Arnold Haverty died before he could even begin his retirement. Addicus Andrew, while trying not to dishonor his father's venerable lieutenants by kicking them out the corporate door, nonetheless gave none-too-subtle nudgings here and there, sweetened by offers of enticing severance packages. Arnold took the bait, but never reached the fishing boat. As the company clown, he would be missed. His departure also signaled the commencement of a new era at Dandy D—one in which young turks would replace the old guard—a passing of the baton, as it were, that to many of the old-timers (most of them handpicked by Jonathan himself) seemed more like theft.

18. **He was waggish in life, impish in death.** Ibid. Arnold Haverty's unique funeral wishes were honored by his wife Constance to the letter. Not only did they include a burial at sea, but Jonathan's director of product planning had also requested that several hours prior to the ocean drop he be propped up in a deck chair, holding a good book. ("Give me something that'll have 'em all slapping their sides, like maybe something by Camus. I also thought, Connie, that this might be a nice way to remind you of that great cruise we took to the Bahamas. I sat in my deck chair and slept like ol' Van Winkle while you did the cha-cha-cha with that Caesar Romero look-alike from Tampa. You said you've

never been happier.") Constance kept her word, even whispering private comments to her Hawaiian-shirted exanimate husband as friends and family lined up to pay their respects, and only occasionally addressing mourners to say, "Please don't shake his hand. It's cold and stiff. You won't like it."

19. Sacco missed the funeral. A false alarm had sent the Sacco family underground for two weeks. Dandy-de-odoro's Vice President for Packaging had taken a television civil defense test for the real thing. Thinking the U.S. was under nuclear attack, he had hurried wife Elsie and their three children into the backyard bomb shelter he'd built from a kit only a few months before. Here the nuclear family remained for the next thirteen days. While underground, they were totally cut off from the rest of the world, due in large part to the fact that Sandron Sacco had forgotten to put batteries in the shelter's transistor radio. Neighbors, friends, and family debated over whether to inform them of their error. Except for one neighbor's unsuccessful renegade attempt to end the needless entombment, the Saccos were left to discover their mistake on their own. Embarrassment, it was thought, would be ameliorated somewhat if their emergence went unmonitored. Perhaps this way they could move more rapidly toward getting their lives back to normal and this humiliating chapter behind them. Which is exactly what Sandron, Elsie and their three children attempted to do. For all the years that followed, the couple never once mentioned their two weeks in the family bunker (although oldest daughter Lucy was finally able to laugh about it years later in her "My Turn" submission to *Newsweek*.) Therefore, I considered myself quite fortunate to discover not only that Sandron Sacco had kept a "log," but also that it was never destroyed. Lucy was happy to give me access. Here are some selected entries.

Day 2: A peaceful, uneventful night. I was first to rise this morning. I checked on the children for any signs of nuclear contamination. They seem fine. I have a rash but it does not appear to be related to fallout. The children are playing Candy Land. Spirits are fairly good considering what awaits us when we open that door. Elsie continues to believe that what I saw was a test pattern. I asked her, "Where was the Indian head, Elsie? Did you see an Indian head?" It will be a trial to make it through two weeks in the same room with this woman, although she is making a peace offering by preparing scrambled eggs. They are powdered but an egg is an egg. And I love eggs.

Day 5: I'm gagging. I can't get down another forkful of those powdered scrambled eggs. The children are in their corners after some misbehavior. They are obviously tired of Candy Land and Parcheesi. I don't blame them but look, I'm not the one who decided to drop bombs on the Tri-State Area, all right? Elsie and I are not speaking. She pushed me off the cot last night. She said that she was going stark-raving mad being cooped up this way and was thinking of taking her chances with the mutants out there.

Day 7: We had a real scare today. I was trying to teach the children how to play Seven Card Stud (Elsie and I have stopped speaking since I refuse to give up the Lucky Strikes and she is making a federal case out of the lack of ventilation. Look, lady, I, if anyone, should know if there isn't proper ventilation in here! I built this shelter! Built it with my own two hands, while you were lounging around eating Whitmans in your silk Capri pants!) when we hear a knock at the door. I'm thrown into a panic trying to remember how well I secured that door. I move quickly to it and find the crossbar still in place. There is another knock. Elsie's a basket case and the cards and poker chips are flying all over the place as the children scramble under the card table. "Who is it?" I ask. I hear a muffled voice. It could be human. I am not sure. I can't tell what is said. I yell, "WHO IS IT?" as loud as I am able, hoping that whatever mutant creature outside that heavy metal door will identify himself and state his purpose. I hear—or think I hear: "Come out. It's all right. Come out." Elsie relaxes. She seems to think this is a good thing. "Don't you see, woman?" I cry. "It's a trick. Someone out there wants our foodstuffs—or, or our precious medical supplies." Elsie laughs in that way that always makes me want to smack her: "*Supplies, Sandron?* Band-Aids, Rolaids, and Mercurochrome! Yeah, we're a regular Mayo Clinic in here. Open the Goddamned door." "Over my dead body, woman," I say. "We may need them to barter with on the outside. It's every man for himself in this post-apocalyptic world!"

Day 9: No one is speaking. We spend the whole day not speaking. I read a Mickey Spillane pocketbook. Elsie sews. The children stare at the walls. They all must think I'm the most heartless father on the planet. And yet don't they see that I do this because I love them? Because I want to protect their young lives?

Day 11: Lucy tried to get out of the shelter last night. I woke up and there she was fumbling with the crossbar. "Oh, no you don't! Two weeks, young lady! It takes two weeks for the fallout to settle. Go back to bed." I pull her away from the door and she goes back to her pallet and sits down. She gives me the eye. "*Better sleep lightly, old man,*" her eyes seem to be saying.

Day 12: Everybody hates me. I've never seen such animosity in one family. I'm going to open the door tomorrow. A day early. What can it hurt? A few blisters maybe? I'm going to open that door. A desolate, fetid, war-torn landscape is better than these narrow four walls and a family that doesn't appreciate you. I'll take the blisters.

20. **"The painting held me, riveted."** Jonathan's Diary, 2 July 1960. In fact, so taken was Jonathan with Wyeth's haunting *Christina's World* that later in the summer on a trip to Brookline, Massachusetts, to meet with inventors of a talking toaster, he made a special side trip to Cushing, Maine, to visit the Olson farm where Christina lived with her brother Alvaro.

It was the brother who met Jonathan at the door and who eagerly took him to the very spot behind the house where Wyeth painted the portrait of the backside of the indomitable Christina, disabled by a disease that no doctor could successfully diagnose. To Jonathan's surprise, a somewhat older Christina greeted him from that very spot, prone and looking much as she did in the painting except that she was now wearing a bikini and her skin was sunburned to the color of clown noses. Jonathan and Christina chatted for a while, Christina eventually becoming so comfortable with her new friend that she asked jokingly for one of his good legs. "I grow so tired of crawling about, as you can imagine." Although weary of this only form of mobility left to her, Christina Olson confessed to Jonathan a secret desire for world travel. "I want to see all the foreign capitals before I die. I intend to crawl and slide myself with a slow, methodical caterpillar-like inching along the entire length of the Great Wall of China!"

Later the three had tea. Refusing to be carried, Christina took a good thirty minutes to belly- and side-slither her way back up to the house. Jonathan and Alvaro waited on the porch. The three later discussed blast furnaces and various tropical fruits each had yet to taste.

21. **It was like taking hose to Hickory.** Hickory, North Carolina, has had a strong hosiery industry for years. In 1960, two years before Jonathan's death, the city inaugurated its hosiery expo, the only exposition and market devoted entirely to the hosiery business in the U.S. Simone Perry, *The History of Hickory* (Hickory, North Carolina: Hickory Chamber of Commerce Publications, 1999).

22. **Yet Jonathan refused to allow the gentleman to retire.** Uriah's nearly total blindness was evident to all but Jonathan, who apparently could not accept the prospect of losing the services of his faithful manservant. Tarara Masdick in her privately published society memoir *Feasting with the Famous,* comments on one of Jonathan's last dinner parties:

> It was a lovely evening, marred only by the bumbling of the bat-blind butler Uriah, who took my fox stole and deposited it in a place of oblivion, substituted shoe mitts for dinner napkins, and ladled terrapin soup directly from the tureen and onto my barter salad. I feigned inattention when the old man walked a serving platter of Duck Bourgeois *right into the kitchen door jamb.*

23. **He enjoyed his coterie of business associates cum friends.** Glover, *Three Legs, One Heart,* 256-59. Among others in the business community with whom Jonathan maintained close ties in his later years was McDonald's Hamburger mogul Ray Kroc. Jonathan had met Kroc several years prior to his formation of the partnership with Richard and Maurice McDonald that would eventually result in majority ownership of the McDonald's fast food enterprise. Over milk shakes whipped up in the five-spindled milk-shake "multimixer" which Kroc distributed early in his career, the two discussed Kroc's dream of corporate success in defiance of a host of medical problems including diabetes, arthritis, and conditions that ultimately resulted in

the removal of his gall bladder and most of his thyroid gland. Jonathan, commendatory of Kroc's pluck and drive, held some sway with his friend, later contending that he was the one who had talked Kroc out of renaming his sandwiches Krocburgers. "I told him," Jonathan wrote in his diary, "that nobody would buy a hamburger with that name. The entry continues:

> They would either associate it with crocks filled with Heaven knows what kind of unpalatable imaginings, or assume that the burgers were made from crocodile meat. After I left him, I recalled that in Britain the word has an even more negative denotation. Kroc didn't always take my advice, though. I recommended early on that he come up with some kind of advertising mascot. Remembering my days with the circus and this one fellow in particular —a Scots kid who made me laugh every time I saw him —I suggested a clown named Ronald. Ronald McDonald. Ray said, 'What does a clown have to do with hamburgers and French fries? What else you got?'

A year after Jonathan's death, Ray Kroc introduced the world to Ronald McDonald.

24. **"You're giving money to everyone you meet!"** Addicus Andrew Blashette to Jonathan Blashette, 13 August 1960. Young Addy Andy was clearly upset with his father, but there wasn't much that anyone, including A.A., could do to dissuade him. Incidentally, during those brief moments Jonathan's son allowed me to interview him, I asked if he might wish to address in more detail his feelings about his father's late-life benevolence-run-amuck. Blashette declined, stating that everything he wanted to say on the subject had already been told to Glover just moments before the author's painful gluteal encounter with Blashette's Tiffany desk-top fountain pen holder.

25. Jonathan's entrepreneurial spirit, coupled with a virtually nonexistent screening process, brought all manner of investor-hungry schemers to his doorstep.

Others included:

• Theatre impresario Darrell Platt, who sought $75,000 to mount a new Broadway production of *Streetcar Named Desire* featuring Don Knotts as Stanley Kowalski and Irene Ryan as Blanche DuBois.

• Environmental artist George Dellums, in negotiation with Buckminster Fuller to top the architect's famous geodesic domes with nipples. (The word "negotiation," Jonathan quickly learned, involved little more than pleading with Fuller's secretary to allow him into the architect's office.)

26. *The Epistle of Paul the Apostle to the Philadelphians*. The publication (Racine: Alternative Voices, 1960) created, as might have been expected, an ecumenical firestorm—one that singed Jonathan as well. Assuming that his financing of Umberger's trip to the Wadi Qumran would remain unpublicized, Jonathan was surprised and dismayed to find his name prominent upon the book's acknowledgments page. *The Epistle of Paul the Apostle to the Philadelphians*, allegedly translated from the "other" Dead Sea Scrolls, "*the ones they don't want you to know about*" was discredited by a multitude of Biblical scholars. Most regarded the book as a blasphemous hoax. Both Umberger and Jonathan were blasted in both the religious and mainstream press for attempting through this proposed addendum to the Bible to alter the "Holy Word of God." On the religious television program *Life Is Worth Living* Bishop Fulton Sheen became so exercised over the publication that his speech lost all coherence and the producer was forced to cut away to a rerun of *December Bride*.

The religious community was up in arms over the book for several reasons. Umberger contended that not only was it written by the Apostle Paul, but that it had every right to be added to the Pauline canon. More audaciously, Umberger defended the validity of its content, which, if accepted, upended 2,000 years of doctrine and tradition addressing the role of women in the Christian church. Anticipating this reaction, Umberger pushes his case full-throttle in his introduction, excerpted below:

> *The Apostle Paul was no dummy. He knew that his advice to the early Christian Church would not be regarded lightly. He took seriously this opportunity to guide and shepherd the growing Christian flock, even if it meant back-pedaling on some of his previous positions on important issues facing members of the Church. It was in this spirit that he wrote to the congregation at Philadelphia. Paul began by making passing references to his early pronouncements on hair braiding and the wearing of gold and pearls: "Perhaps I was a little too unyielding in my opinions proffered to good Timothy on this matter. Women have always braided their hair and they will continue to braid their hair and who am I to make them feel guilty about it? Say to the ladies, 'Braid if you must, but not excessively so.' As to the matter of accessories, perhaps I was a bit too severe here as well. Gold and pearls if worn with decorum and a certain modesty of presentation, should not impede one's ability to worship."*

> *More important was Paul's modification of his original position on the role of women in the family of Christ, a position which religious patriarchs (ignorant of the Philadelphia epistle which apparently never reached its intended recipients) would eventually set in stone, its contours etched deeper and deeper with each succeeding*

*generation, as male dominance of the Christian Church
solidified and then fossilized over two millennia. "But as
to this matter of the role of women, I know that I have said
on a number of occasions that women should keep silent.
(The Corinthians I especially singled out on this point.)
Yes, I was wrong and I admit it. Sometimes I simply do
not think things through. You will recall my directive to
the slaves at Ephesus to obey their masters. What was I
thinking? We are held in thrall—all of us—only to the
Lord our God! Slavery is wrong! wrong! wrong! So say I
about the women. Speak up and praise the Lord as loudly
and as heartily as the men around you! Shake off the
shackles of gender-slavery placed upon you. Preach and
teach the word of the Lord, and enrich and aggrandize the
family of believers! We are—all of us—master and slave,
man and woman, equal in God's eyes! Didn't Jesus tell us
this? I really should have paid closer attention."*

27. **The attack came out of the blue. It shook Jonathan to
the core.** Glover, et al.

28. **"This is not what I meant."** Andrew Bloor to Jonathan
Blashette, 2 September 1960. Bloor continues:

It serves you not a whit to give all your money to these
crazy people. It would be different if there were some
nobility or high purpose to their causes. There is not.
Nobody is approaching you with a proposal to find an
end to cancer, Jonathan. Or even to try to get that
godawful hour-long Lucy and Desi thing canceled. I've
always been supportive of your goals, your dreams, your
choice of female companions, all of your major life
decisions. But here I must draw the line. You are writing
the final chapter of your life in Crayola and I will not
have it! You were put here for a very important reason.
This is not it!

---

29. **Jonathan's reply was scathing.** Jonathan Blashette to Andrew Bloor, 6 September 1960. Responding to Bloor's last charge, Jonathan writes:

> You have been telling me this for years, Dr. Bloor, and I still do not to this day know what you mean. You are like the psychoanalyst who sits and nods while the patient fumbles and flounders and doesn't get a clue. You do not know what it is that will bring wonderful affirming purpose to my life any more than I do. All you've had is a feeling, old man. A feeling that betrayed you and betrayed me. I will hear no more of it. If these people want my money, so be it. I am doing nothing with it. My dream of making any kind of mark has melted away in the barren desert of my dried-out, dried-up, withered, broken-hipped, wife-bereft, freak-legged life. So why not let that money go to those who still have dreams with a pulse? What do you want from me? I am a man. That is all. A man who did some things. I didn't save the world. I did the best I could with what I was given. Let's end this discussion, once and for all. I've had enough of it.

30. **"Dear Mr. Blashette Stop Regret to tell you my brother Andrew Bloor passed away last night Stop."** Evetta Paton's telegram is preserved in Jonathan's papers. It is slightly crimped and discolored on the right edge where it had apparently met with some form of moisture.

31. **It was a deep depression lubricated by great quantities of alcohol.** Alvira Paine, *The Last Days of Pompous: Twelve Stories of the Famous and their Final Season* (Charleston, West Virginia: Royce Press, 1970), 190-222.

32. **"Uriah, my good man, there is something terribly wrong with these shoes."** Author's interview with Zachary Hensley. The very inebriated Jonathan simply hadn't the wherewithal to remove the shoe trees from within.

33. **The nightmares did not recede for several weeks.** Jonathan's sleep was often disturbed by images of Bloor's funeral in Omaha and attended by feelings of enormous guilt. No doubt, Jonathan was plagued by worry that the harsh words he delivered to his friend and mentor might have contributed to his death. During this period, perhaps for subconscious diversion, Jonathan also dreamed that he was being pursued by disembodied lobster chelae. In another dream he was called upon to address an annual stockholders meeting wearing only ruffled rumba pants. Jonathan's Diary, various entries.

34. **"You'll be Abishag to this David."** Alvira Paine, *The Last Days of Pompous*, 190-222. Wishes for comity between the two never materialized. Cloretta Connell withdrew her services to Jonathan three full weeks before Uriah was to return to resume his duties as Jonathan's manservant. Jonathan, who wasn't happy with even a temporary loss of his trusted man Uriah, went out of his way to make the young nurse and companion feel uncomfortable and unappreciated in her duties, putting to active use the ubiquitous drool cup, and on at least one occasion staging his drowning death in the koi pond. Such shenanigans were not at all in keeping with Jonathan's usual gentle and sensitive nature. Unfortunately, many of his last months were spent in broken spirits, often rising to heavy frustration and anger. God and fate were the usual objects of his bitterness and rage; but on occasion, a young nurse, pizza delivery boy, supermarket sacker, or his own son might find themselves inadvertent victims of Jonathan's contempt for youth and its taunting promise.

35. **And then, suddenly the clouds lifted.** The complete diary entry follows. This is the last time Jonathan would put down his thoughts here. Though he lived for another three months, he was never to pick up the book again.

May 2, 1962

Today I met a little boy named Robbie. He knocked on my door. Uriah was going to send him away, but I heard his wee voice and thought he was a little Brownie selling Girl Scout Thin Mints. Oh how I love Thin Mints. "It isn't a Brownie with Thin Mints, Mr. Blashette," said Uriah. "It's a boy. He says his name is Robbie. He would like to speak with you."

I asked Uriah to bring the boy into the living room. My legs were covered with a lap blanket. I was still fighting the cold that had arrived on Monday and I was, at the moment, slightly chilled. "Have a seat, young man. What can I do for you?"

Robbie sat down and immediately began to squirm as boys his age will do, especially when they set their eyes on bowls full of M & M's. I nodded for little Robbie to take a handful and he dug in. "I used to have a little boy like you," I said.

"What happened to him?" Robbie asked.

"He grew up to be a man. He now runs a very big company. Now, how can I be of service?"

"My teacher sent me here," Robbie answered, his mouth oozing the chocolate brown of the half-masticated candies. "She said you could help me with my composition. I have to have it finished by Friday."

"She thought I could help you? What is your theme about?"

"I had a funny idea. Are you a funny man? Maybe she thought you were funny and you could give me funny ideas I can put in it."

"I haven't been feeling all that funny lately, son. Uriah, do you think I've been very funny lately?"

"No, sir. Not for some time."

Robbie was eyeing those M&M's again. I picked up the bowl and set it in his lap. "So what's your idea?"

"I wanted to write a story about a boy who joins the circus. There is a very special thing about him. He has three legs."

I shooed Uriah away, afraid that he might divulge an important fact that I had no desire at that moment to convey to the boy. Then I leaned forward, feigning intense interest in this most amazing anatomical phenomenon. "Three legs! My, oh my. Now, young Robbie, why did you decide to give this boy three legs?"

Robbie shoveled another handful of M&M's into his chocolate-daubed mouth and replied, "My grandfather told me about a boy he knew who had three legs and he went to the circus and later he became a great man."

"A great man? Hmm. What did he do that made him so great?"

"He helped Granddaddy not be so afraid of squirrels. I think that my grandfather now knows more about squirrels that any man alive."

"And that makes this three-legged man a great man?"

"Granddaddy says he helped other people, too, this man. He spent his whole life helping people. My grandfather says that third leg—that's where his heart is."

Uriah dropped something in the dining room that made a loud crashing sound—a sound very near the door to the living *room. Uriah had apparently been eavesdropping. He'd rib me about this statement for the next month, I was sure of it.*

I looked the boy squarely in the eye and said, "And that's why you want to write about this man?"

Robbie nodded. "Do you think you can help me?"

"I just might be able to."

"Why do you think my teacher Miss Lyttle sent me here to see you?"

"Probably because I used to know that man, too. Used to know him very well, in fact."

Robbie set the M&M's aside. The thing about their not melting in the hands isn't entirely accurate. I called for Uriah to bring the boy a napkin.

"Did you know my grandfather, too?"

I nodded.

"What was he like—when he was young?"

"I'll make a deal with you, Robbie. I'll tell you everything you want to know about your grandfather as a young man. But do this for me: don't write a story about a three-legged man. Write one about your grandfather. He was a fascinating man. He was a good man. I've known a lot of wonderful people in my life—people whose stories hardly ever get told. His is the story you ought to tell."

I convinced Robbie. I also convinced myself of something: that there is no one great man. Only millions of men and women in possession of tiny pieces of greatness, which when put together, when assembled in the aggregate make the whole. I am a piece of a very large jigsaw puzzle. One of the corner pieces. The one you go for first—important for a time, different from most of the others. But then, in the end, in the big picture, just one of many. Maybe this is what had been percolating in the back of Bloor's mind all those years. All that wondering over how I was to fit in. How I was to contribute in a big way to that something bigger than myself. I wished that I could write to him and tell him what I now knew:

"Dear Professor Bloor,

It should interest you to know:

I am a corner piece."

I regret that I didn't have the chance to make things right with him before he died. He would have been proud that I'd finally figured it out.

36. **"Jonathan died as he lived—warm, funny, and generous."** *New York Clarion,* 3 August 1962. It seems only fair that, as the last person to see Jonathan Blashette alive, manservant Uriah should be entitled to such a poetic, tidy assessment of his employer's final minutes on earth (which, of course, made good copy for the morning dailies). When one reads Uriah's account of the conversation that comprised Jonathan's last words, one is struck by the fact that these words, while somewhat banal, were spoken by a man who had finally taken stock of his life, found it not so wanting after all, and could now relax and enjoy the remainder of his days in a way in which he'd never been able before. According to Uriah, Jonathan's spirits had greatly improved after the visit from Jiminy Crutch's young grandson. The cloud had lifted, and this fact offered Jonathan the chance to spend many happy moments in that final summer working jigsaw puzzles, watching old movies, and continuing to give

money to an odd assortment of petitioners, including a man who wanted to manufacture "word" soup:

> You see, Mr. Blashette, it would be like alphabet soup except the letters would actually be fixed together in words and by moving them about in the bowl, one could easily construct purposeful sentences, such as "Will you marry me?" and "There is a fly in here." I would not require much money. I will take preexisting alphabet noodles and link them together using some form of edible adhesive.

The final exchange between Jonathan and manservant Uriah Hensley follows.

JONATHAN (watching television): Uriah! Uriah, where are you?

URIAH: I'm coming, Mr. B.

JONATHAN: I want you to see this. That man is wearing a diaper.

URIAH: Will you look at that!

JONATHAN: Full-grown man wearing a big baby diaper. Say, do we have any more of that pea spread? I'd like to have some on a saltine or two. And make some for yourself.

URIAH: Would you like some Hi-C with that?

JONATHAN: Not tonight, Uriah. I'm in a Hawaiian Punch mood. Oh look at that! The man in the diaper is chasing a creature of some sort.

URIAH: It's a wild pig, Mr. B. See the tusks?

JONATHAN: That's a sight, isn't it Uriah? A diapered man in a baby bonnet chasing a wild boar. And in a glass shop, no less! Homph, homph, heh, hickle, heh, homph!

URIAH: It's something else, all right, heh, heh.

JONATHAN: My chest hurts.

URIAH: You're laughing too hard! Mr. B? Mr. B?

37. **Davison and Caldwell were both hit hard by Jonathan's death.** Both men lapsed into deep depressions. Although I do not discount the enormous loss that each must have been feeling from Jonathan's sudden absence from their lives, correspondence between the two men at the time also sheds light on other potential reasons for the depression: the possibility of global annihilation by a hydrogen bomb holocaust, thalidomide babies, a $300-billion-dollar national debt, and the inscrutable popularity of *The Beverly Hillbillies*. Reinhold, *The Story of Dandy-de-odor-o*, 299-309.

38. **He was buried in Pettiville.** A third memorial was held in Ottawaugus, New York, where Jonathan had served for two years as dog catcher (and related dog-adoption agent). The doors of the Ottawaugus United Methodist Church were opened to both friends of Jonathan and their pets. After a moving eulogy delivered by Jonathan's most treasured friend and supporter, Harlan Davison, Venetia House read from her organization's "Beatitudes for Bowsers." It was well received by most even given its potential for sacrilege.

Blessed are the sad and lonely pound pups for they shall find happy homes in the kingdom of heaven.

Blessed are they that moan at the door and whimper for need of an outdoor visit for they shall be released.

Blessed are the meek and small for they shall inherit serious lap-petting.

Blessed are they which hunger for dog chow and thirst for water on a hot summer's day for they shall be fed and watered, lapping the liquid with happy slaps of their slurpy tongues.

Blessed are those named Mercy, for it is a pretty name for a dog.

Blessed are all you precious pooches, for love and happy petting are sure to come your way.

After passing out glasses of grape juice to all in attendance, Venetia concluded with this observation:

If my friend Jonathan Blashette were a dog, I think he would have been a big, friendly Saint Bernard. He had a keen sense of smell, as all of his employees at Dandy D will attest—a gift for sniff that ended up making the world just a little more fragrant through his efforts in the marketplace. Like the Saint Bernard, Jonathan served as able guide over often treacherous trails—those daunting pathways of life, helping so many he knew gain a better foothold here and there. And in the snowstorms of travail that buried us, he was always there, Jonny-on-the-spot, to dig us out and offer something cockle-warming to drink. He drank with us all—famous and ordinary and everyone in between. So let us now raise our glasses to Jonathan Blashette. Cheers to the greatest three-legged man who ever lived.

Please join the family in fellowship and remembrance as they gather in the undercroft lounge. Beer nuts and figs will be provided for refreshment.

39. **Afterword.** This brief, seemingly irrelevant essay on the beauty, rich history and delicious municipal enchantment that is the city of Boston, while appearing to be the work of

the Boston Tourist and Visitor's Bureau (I have, in fact, quoted heavily, and with permission from that bureau's boosterish brochures) constitutes my humblest apology to a city which I have mischaracterized throughout this book. I hope that readers from that fair metropolis, the Cradle of Liberty, Hub of the Universe, and Athens of America will find it in their hearts to forgive me...and to buy my book.

ACKNOWLEDGMENTS

Thank you, David Poindexter and Pat Walsh at MacAdam/ Cage, for allowing this most recent, brazen attempt at redefining the American novel. I've always contended that there are a lot of ways to tell a story, and some that are rarely or never even tried. I appreciate this new opportunity to step wide of the narrative box.

Thank you to all my history teachers. You kept it fun and kept me reading and delving…and laughing.

Thank you, Woody Allen, who doesn't know me from Adam (Adam's slightly taller), but who is the master at mining history for all its comic worth. You have inspired me through the spirit of your *New Yorker* pieces and your films *Zelig* and *Radio Days* among others. And if you think this represents a bald attempt to suck up to you so that we might one day hang out at a Rangers game together,…you are right.

Thanks, Wayne Furman, for giving me access to the Allen Room for scholars at the New York Public Library where much of this book was researched. I also enjoyed our afternoon tea and M&M breaks.

And thank *you*, good readers, for giving me the chance to convince you that history can be more than dry facts and dates. And that naughty can be mighty fun. Wasn't it Mary Todd Lincoln who privately remarked, "I wonder how the play turned out."